Emotions

TIMMOTHY B. McCANN

Emotions

DAFINA BOOKS
Kensington Publishing Corp.
http://www.kensingtonbooks.com

CHAPTER

1

People live their entire lives wearing a mask. We go to the same church our parents go to. We live in the same physical and mental states in which our parents resided. We even find solace in pursuing the same careers as Mom and Dad. Is that who we are? A lost generation, indebted to a past generation?

—Ani Bella Ginsburg, 2002
Bronx, New York

Today Joi Weston must die.

The words throbbed in her memory. They spoke to her as she slept; they haunted her in the limo on the way to the studio; they whispered in her ear as she sat in makeup. She tried to ignore their presence; but never would they walk away, and as she walked onto the set, in her heart she succumbed to them.

Today Joi Weston must die.

* * *

In that amazing city of Technicolor dreams, the middle-aged woman stood on her marker and attempted to erase her fears, but knew that in twenty-four hours her life would change forever. She focused on the lines of dialogue and mentally watched herself exchange barbs with the legendary actor who played her husband.

"There is no way I'm not going to nail this scene," she whispered. "No way in the world."

In the old days she could sing or dance as well as anyone on the Great White Way, but after moving to L.A., she had focused on acting. She studied her craft and endured the rejection. She saw less qualified actors move from parking cars to Hollywood's "A" list. But Joi had come to terms with the artist inside and knew she would never experience a moment like this again.

Outside it was another hot day in July, but on the set the air was cooled with fans that were strategically placed to replicate rain. While actors and gofers, stand-ins and prop designers huddled in private conversation, Joi felt like a sprinter, muscles ridged, sweat pouring, heart racing, prepared for the sound of the gun that would bring finality to her doubts.

"Aye, eee, eye, owe, you."

She enunciated each syllable so the New England accent she had studied would sound authentic. Her lips were painted in smears of black, purple and blue, and her jaw accommodated the vowels; yet her tongue remained fixed, her neck elongated.

"Aye, eee, eye, owe, you." *I can do this. Dammit, I know I can do this.*

Joi was considered safe beautiful. Not pin-up model attractive, but more akin to the girl who lived next door that men could consider themselves dating. She had full, round lips, her complexion was smooth and due to man-made elements, her dyed black hair parted down the middle as if she had just resurfaced from under water and it tumbled carelessly over her shoulders. Her most valuable asset as an actress, one critic said, were eyes that glowed with a savage fire, yet there was also a tenderness in her demeanor. She was a taller woman than most, and due to her dedication to working out, her body was trim, with wide hips that tapered down to long, straight legs.

The rain from the wind machine pelted Joi's back. Above her the oversized circular lights intensified what was about to happen. After repeating her lines in a docile tone, she touched her fingertips to her forehead, the midst of her diaphragm, her left shoulder, her right shoulder and prepared to hit her mark. Her stomach rumbled from the missed meals; her ears burned with anticipation. This would be the role that would take her down the aisle and bring her the golden statue. And then she entered the moment of truth.

A distinct Scottish voice screeched from the P.A. system, "And action," and Joi felt the heat of the camera, which moved in for a close-up. In a tone so low her lips did not move, she repeated a ritual she had performed since she started acting. She whispered the word, "Purpose."

"So, Bobby, this is your decision?" Joi walked toward the red Mercedes soaking wet, ran her hand along the fender and leaned her hip against it like she had rehearsed numerous times before in dryer conditions. "You're just going to leave and not say anything to me or Bryan?"

Lance Fellows looked at Joi with one foot inside the car, the other on the pavement as the rain blew water into his face at full force. "It's always been like this. The only problem is you never knew, or dare I say, refused to know. This marriage has been over since Angela died. We—"

"Don't ever say that!" Joi's trepidation flowed unbridled.

The author of the novel the screenplay was adapted from never knew Joi had a child named Angie. The screenwriter never knew that like the Angela in the movie, Joi's child had been taken from her dramatically as well. So when Joi had read the role her first impulse had been to ask for a character name change, but then she had embraced her fear and denounced her weakness in hopes that it would propel her toward the delivery of a memorable performance. Unfortunately, hearing the name was more than she ever expected.

"Don't *ever* say her name again!"

"We just will not let it die in peace."

"Maybe," Joi said, and momentarily forgot she was acting. "Maybe we should just talk about it. Then we could—We've had seventeen years. Doesn't that count for something?"

"You wanna know what seventeen years count for? Almost two decades of nothing!"

"I know your feelings have changed. But you can't expect me to just love you one day and let you walk away the next."

"Damn, woman, can't you see it's over?" Lance screamed louder than he had ever screamed in rehearsal. His anthracite eyes were bits of stone. Skewed veins protruded from his temples and neck. "I don't love you anymore. When was the last time I even told you I loved you? When was the last time I acted as if I cared? It's as simple as—Look, you can have the other cars. You can have the house. You can have the other cars. I will not contest you having the investments and the savings. Just give me my freedom," he said, and then reached into his coat pocket and tossed their checkbook into a puddle on the ground. "That's all I want, Rachel, because right now, this marriage is killing me."

Joi watched in awe as Lance's body melted into the character. He was classically trained and a dark-skinned—a walking, talking Shakespearian midnight—that brought more to the role than any actor Joi had ever been paired with. His eyes dimmed to a whisper. His nostrils flared, and he started to breathe heavily.

"After seventeen years, have I asked you for one thing? Anything, Rachel? Just let me learn how to live again," he said as a bolt of light triggered behind Joi. "Just let . . . just let . . ." Then Lance looked stunned, as if he had mentally run dry.

"Just let us . . . enjoy . . . what's left of our lives," Joi whispered.

An amplified voice from the darkness shouted over the splattering buzz of the rain machine. "Lancy, don't stop, babe. Keep rolling."

"Cut, cut, cut," Lance said, stuffed his hands into the pockets of his overalls and walked off the set. Joi watched him head toward the producer as the hydraulic fans were cut off and ash-colored extras rushed to a stack of dry towels.

"What happened?" she asked anyone within ear range. The lights behind her were muted. Crew members wearing yellow raincoats started to mill as if they were on break, yet Joi held her spot. She could hear the voice of the producer bellow, "It's only the first day, Lance, for God sakes. Give her a fucking chance!"

Give her a chance? What was that supposed to mean?

Joi had signed on to do her first movie after being away from the bright lights of Hollywood for several years. She had been the star of a successful sitcom in which she was the mother to a "precocious" orphan girl named Potts McGee. The actress was a seven-year-old with red pigtails, large handmade freckles and green eyes that could cry on cue if the script called for it.

After the second season, the show that had been written and created for Joi Weston entitled "Still My House," was retitled "Potts McGee & Me." For the next five years Joi found herself the butt of the jokes in front of the camera and stereotyped amongst the movers and shakers in Hollywood.

When the actress who played the lead role reached puberty, her fame diminished, and Joi found herself out of work and severely typecast. At a crossroad, Joi and her husband Phillip Evans moved away from Los Angeles and returned to Florida.

After two years of trying to have a baby, the couple discovered that Phillip was sterile due to an accident. So in the midst of her thirties Joi reinvented herself. She was determined to be the dream wife and devoted hour upon hour to creating the perfect home. She took a class in feng shui, purchased books on the art of decoupage and even ran in marathons to maintain balance in her life. But soon the austere existence wore thin, and Joi found herself sitting in café-style bookstores, sipping triple latté mochas and scanning the pages of *Variety* until sunset.

One day as she sat in the corner of the café, a Hispanic lady walked up to her and asked for her autograph. Since such occurrences were rare, Joi gladly signed it. And then the woman told her how much she missed seeing her on television.

"You were so good. You are such a great actor."

The conversation, which lasted no longer than the time it takes for a light to turn from yellow to red, turned on the green light in Joi's mind, and to her surprise, a flame reignited in her heart. By the end of the day, Joi contacted her agent and told him she was interested in looking at scripts again. By the end of the week, she was flying to the left coast to audition against her husband's wishes. By the end of the month, she won the role of Rachel Wolvers, which was one of the most coveted roles in Hollywood, and seven months later, she stood on the sound stage alone wondering what had happened.

Joi's set assistant walked up to her with a warm towel and asked, "What's up his tail? I thought it was going to be great."

"I don't know. He umm," she said, still staring at Lance huddled with the studio heads, "he just walked off."

To Joi's surprise her agent, Cecil Toscana, walked from the darkness toward her. As she saw his smiling face of reassurance, Lance shouted, "Who approved these script changes? Mr. Step and Mrs. Fetch-it plus that bitch missed her mark. She was standing in the wrong fucking place. Damn! Can't anyone see what I'm talking about?"

"What!" Joi shouted back loud enough for everyone to hear on the set. "I didn't miss my damn mark. You forgot the line!"

"I fucked up the line because you were in the wrong place! I'm not going to deal with this *sitcom* shit for three months, Reeves! Let's open cast and get a credible actress in here while we still have a chance to save the film."

"I was not in the wrong place, you asshole, you were—"

Cecil grabbed his client by the wrist. "Calm down, Joi. Okay? Just calm down."

"You calm down! How dare he say I wasn't in the right place. Look at my marks Cecil. Hell, I'm still standing in the right spot. This is where I should have—"

In a pastoral tone, Cecil said, "Joi, calm down."

"Go to hell! He screwed up," she said, in a screeching voice, "and he's too unprofessional to admit he made a mistake?"

"What you want now, bitch, a laugh track? Take your non-acting black ass back to the squawk box," Lance yelled. "Let them find you another white kid to work with."

"Do not say another word, Joi!" Cecil instructed.

"But he——"

"If you still want to get work in this town, please do not say another word."

"What?"

"Let's have a Sulawesi Mocha Chocolate or something, and we can talk about it. A lot of things are going down now that you need to know about!"

Cecil tugged his client's wrist and repeated, "Come on. Let's talk."

Joi looked at the wind machine. Then, as the bright egg-shaped lights that had previously warmed her flesh faded to black, in her heart she knew she would never feel their heat again.

"Aye, eee, eye, owe, you," she said with her eyes closed for a reason unknown, and proceeded to leave the set.

CHAPTER

2

In that amazing city of eight million stories, a writer I paced outside a class longing for one. One story that would make him great on his own accord. Journal clutched to his chest. Copious doubts buried in his heart. Inside his pad were notes of numerous projects he wanted to complete, but he had yet to type the six letters that would give any of them closure.

Michael walked into the room with a commanding manner and assumed his desk in the last row against the wall. He was the first one to cross the threshold and found the professor bemused by what he was reading. Michael was tall, slender and athletically cut. He wore foot-long locks, a three-day beard, shades over his eyes and, like most NYU students, sandals on his feet. He was dressed in a form-fitting black silk shirt, loose blue jeans, silver buckles on his black sandals and a silver crucifix, which he held whenever he prayed.

Michael also wore an onyx ring in remembrance of his father. It was the only memory of his namesake he continued to hold on to. His father's papers had been auctioned. In Michael's mind, his voice had disappeared as well. But whenever he touched the ring, he felt his father's presence.

Dr. Anderson was a portly professor with rosy cheeks, salt-and-pepper hair and an untrimmed goatee. He wore his glasses on the edge of his nose, his pipe was always within arm's reach and his disposition was typically sarcastic.

Being the son of one of the first African-Americans to be selected as a finalist for the Pulitzer Prize for fiction was never a comfortable role for Michael. His father's best-selling novel entitled *One Witness* was referred to as the "Black" *Grapes of Wrath* and was used as a staple in many university English departments across the country.

One Witness was Michael Brockmier Sr.'s, singular tome. He had spoken of a novel he wanted to write that would expose the ills of living in America. A novel for which he would spend nights sleeping outside with hippies trying to understand their subculture, which he planned to entitle *God Turned Human.* But before his fingers could strike the first key on his Smith-Corona, he snuffed out his candle. His wife found him slumped over his typewriter with his wrists slashed and clumps of blood caked between the keys. He was pronounced dead on his thirty-third birthday and the country was robbed of one of the most unique literary voices ever produced.

Like a blaze of glory or the soft quell of the sun, he was gone. I never heard my father addressed by the word "sir." Never heard him call a woman anything but "madam." And like that blaze and like the quell he left us, and we were never as good as we were when he was here.

As he sat in the creative writing course, Michael reread the first paragraph of *One Witness*. Words he had read more times than he had made love and they still held his attention like the outline of a woman's breasts. While he read the words on the page, they were akin to dummy cards to a skilled thespian. Just there. Just in the way.

His fingers slid across the paper so he could feel the texture of the words. As Professor Anderson smirked at the test scores, a few more students trickled into class. Michael closed his eyes as his fingers attempted to unravel mysteries his eyes and heart could not. The words felt smooth, fleshy and harmonious, yet he knew in his heart he would never replicate or touch them. No matter how many classes he took. No matter how hard he tried.

"You know something," Professor Anderson said to no one in particular, yet to all of the students. His eyes still reviewed an inch-thick stack of papers, smoke dribbling from his lips like a chimney. "Some people shouldn't be allowed to *own* a book, so why should they attempt to write one? Just because you have spell check doesn't mean you should write a novel." A few students snickered; Michael continued his one-way communication with his father.

A flood of students poured into the class as the long hand found its place over the twelve. Dr. Anderson stood, scratched his bushy eyebrows, pushed his glasses up on his nose with his index finger and paced in front of the class as if he were part stand-up comedian, part caged tiger.

"I gave you a scenario in your examination. A very *simple*, I might add, writing exam. And this is what I get back?" he said, retrieving the papers from his desk as if he were handling toxic waste without gloves.

"Some of these papers——" Professor Anderson paused in mid-sentence as if disgusted by the thought of what he had read. "Kendra, did you feel as if the assignment I gave you was unfair? I simply requested that you give a comparative analysis of the work of Richard Wright and Ernest Hemingway. Please tell me, for an English Comparative course, was that unfair?"

Kendra sat erect. "No, sir."

"Thank you, Kendra. I was starting to wonder."

Since he was a decade older than most of the students in the class and he wore his father's name, Michael resented being called upon. But like clockwork, Professor Anderson looked at him from across the room.

"Sir?"

"Your father studied under Misters Ellison and Baldwin. Am I not correct, Mr. Brockmier?"

"For a brief period of time. Yes, sir."

"Do *you* think it was an unfair assignment?"

"No."

Professor Anderson gazed at Michael before returning to the front of the class and leaned against the chalkboard. "There will not be a curve in this class. Like I've told you before, there are no grade curves in life, so get used to it. If any of you failed this test—and many of you did, I might add—you will just have to dig yourself out of the hole. Maybe *next* time you will take the lectures more seriously."

Professor Anderson looked at the name on the first paper. "Oscar McCray." Seeing the student, the professor walked over to him and returned his paper facedown on his desk.

"Someone," Professor Anderson continued, "received a forty-eight, and yes, I did say a forty-eight, on this examination." Then he looked over his glasses again and said, "Jean Norman?" The student raised her hand as the professor continued to dole out papers and insulting words.

"To have gotten a forty-eight on my test you would have to study failure. Just being inept would not give you such a low score. Now to this soul, who I surely assume has grandiose intentions of passing this course, I have a bit of advice I would like to openly share with the rest of the class. I am not doing this, to use your jargon, to call him *or* her out. But to point them in the direction they should *consider* proceeding in their collegiate career. This student had no idea what made either of these literary giants great, and this saddens me." He distributed another paper and another. Each time he handed one out, he placed it facedown on the desk. The student would either read the score through the paper or slowly dog-ear it over to read the verdict. "For the soul who achieved a forty-eight on this most basic of exams, I have a bit of advice for you. Carlos Edmonds?"

The student, with consternation in his eyes, raised his hand. Professor Anderson gave him his graded paper, which made the student sigh audibly.

"As soon as this class is over, I would immediately leave this campus, go to the Greyhound bus terminal and *call* your roommate. Have them *send* your clothes to the Port Authority. And if I were you, I would make haste and leave this city immediately. Because let's face it, you should not be in New York." The professor paused for dramatic effect and said, "Actually, if you made a forty-eight on my test, you should not be in college unless it's Nail College, if that's what they call it. In actuality, there should be legislation enacted to prohibit you from being in *any* city where any institution of higher learning exists."

Students with graded papers said, "Owww." Others remained silent.

Professor Anderson passed Michael's desk and laid his paper facedown. Then he said, "Sharon Pilling?"

Michael didn't need to turn his paper over. The forty-eight bled through the fibers. He folded it crisply, tucked it into his notebook, stood up and walked toward the door.

"Brockmier? You might not want to miss the next portion of the class," Michael did not reply. "I'm preparing to lecture on existentialism in literature, and it would be to your advantage not to miss it."

Michael stopped before opening the door and turned around.

"Damn. He failed a test on his daddy's friends?" an anonymous male voice said, but Michael continued to gaze at Dr. Anderson. He wanted to leave the class saying something dramatic. Maybe even shouting a profanity. But he didn't. As the two men stared at each other, in Michael's mind the professor's animus for him was never greater.

"Brockmier, what are you going to do?"

Michael turned, walked away and allowed the door to close behind him.

As he sat outside the guidance office, Michael thought about his immediate future. He was born the week after his father was notified he was a finalist for the Pulitzer. His first baby picture was taken with him lying in his father's arms and his mother holding a copy of *One Witness*. The picture was enlarged and hung in the foyer of their home for years, and Michael despised it because his mother would say it was a picture of her two children. Since one of the children was known all over the world, he felt he would never be able to compete with the success of the novel in his parents' eyes.

During school he went by the name Brock because he got tired of the "Guess what his name is" comments and the inevitable comparisons. Then one day he ran home because he was awarded with the Crest Smile Award and was rewarded with three tubes of toothpaste and a new toothbrush.

When he arrived home, Michael snatched open the door, yelled, "Daddy, Daddy," and then ran up to his father's study atop their Strivers Row apartment.

"Momma, Daddy, look what I won," he yelled, and saw his mother holding the lifeless body of his father in her arms. For forty-five months Michael would not say another word. For months his mother thought he was mute, or worse yet, mildly retarded as a result of what he had seen. He spoke to no one but himself and God and rarely showed emotions. But when he spoke again, he reclaimed his smile and his name and felt obligated to do something that would make his father proud.

Michael enrolled in college after graduating from high school, but dropped out to follow his true passion. Music. But eleven years later he had found himself back in school attempting to learn the art of fiction. With the ridiculing sounds of Professor Anderson in his ear, he sat and waited, but in his heart he felt he waited in vain.

CHAPTER

3

L ife radiated from the blond actor who spoke to a woman with knitting needles in her hair. "I can't believe I got the role. Are you serious? Did he say it just like that?"

Cecil walked past the actor sitting in front of Starbucks nursing a cup of coffee and a script.

"Where are we going and slow down," Joi said to the thirty-something agent who pulled her wrist as if it were a leash.

"I'm going to use the temple. I have a key," he blurted out, and led his client toward the double-wide trailer at the end of the road used by the movie's producer.

Reeves Breidenbaugh was the number one movie executive in Hollywood. Before starting Whisper Films, he bankrolled over a billion dollars for other studios and was known for his uncommon knack of keeping his finger on the pulse of moviegoers.

In a highly publicized auction, he won the rights to the novel *Purchased Tickets* and immediately tagged Lance Fellows as the lead. After auditioning twenty B-list actresses for the female lead, he had chosen Joi for the one-hundred-million-dollar bio-pic.

Still upset and unsure, Joi pulled her wrist away from the agent as they walked up the steps to Breidenbaugh's trailer. "Listen," Cecil said, "I've been there from day one. I'm watching your back just like you've watched mine."

"I'm glad you remember that."

"I don't forget, Joi. You know that. That's why I demanded that they audition you as soon as I got the call. That's why," he said, then looked around as he opened the door to the trailer. "Let's go inside. I hate talking in the open."

Upon entering the temporary home/office of the producer, Joi noticed the elaborate furnishings. She noticed the fully stocked bar, the freshly cut floral arrangements, the four televisions built in the wall and the big screen projection monitor. Joi also noticed on the mantel behind his desk stood the Oscar. It was the fruit garnered from winning Best Picture for the blockbuster entitled *Watching Men.*

"Listen, do you want something to drink?" he said as he sat at the conference table.

Joi gave him a blank expression. "Cecil, what's going on? I don't want a drink. I don't want to sit in this office. I want to be out there shooting this movie. I spent three hours getting into character this morning, and I'm ready for this. Now, what in the——"

"Hey, Magda? Would you fix me a Tom Collins? Heavy on the Tom, light on the Collins?"

Joi crossed her arms over her waist without smiling and stared at her own face in the blank TV screen.

"Anything for you, ma'am?" Magda asked as she placed a coaster with the Whisper Films crest on it in front of the actress. Joi did not reply and gazed elsewhere.

"Okay," Cecil said as Magda retrieved the coaster from in front of Joi. "I came out to the set today because there were some rumblings last night. Reeves called me around three this morning actually and asked me to come over."

He turned squarely in front of Joi and said, "It's Lance."

"Hell, Cecil, I know that."

"What I mean is . . . He missed that damn *People* magazine fifty most beautiful people thing, again, and his people were campaigning hard for him this year. Now they're telling him it's an age thing."

"His age? That doesn't make any sense. When has a man in this town had a problem because he was getting older?"

"That's true for . . . That is true for *white* actors, Joi," the Greek agent said. "I hate to be so blunt, but it's true. Some of the black male leads in this town are feeling the heat as much as white women or Hispanics."

"You've *got* to be kidding me. And if he's getting old, what's that got to do with this role?"

After Magda brought him the drink, Cecil ogled at it as if it were a tea leaf. "It has nothing to do with you, yet everything to do with you. In this town, youth rules no matter what they tell you. To be young and good-looking in this city is to have a blank check signed by Bill Gates. But if you're Lancy and you want to stay young——"

"You get a younger costar," Joi said, finishing his sentence.

"Correct."

"That son of a bitch is at least ten years older than his own mother, Cecil. Is that what's going on?"

"Exactly."

"Well, I have a contract. They can't just kick me to the curb like a bag of garbage. What are we going to——"

"That's not correct."

"What's not correct?"

"They have a contract with you, but Lance has final approval on any and all casting decisions. I'm told it's a condition he held out for during negotiations."

Joi's shoulders withered under the weight of her career crashing to the floor. "For weeks we rehearsed, and nothing was said. He even told the press I was his first choice to play—"

"I know. But all of a sudden he's not feeling like the stud he was in this town a few years ago. All of a sudden everyone is worrying about that sixteen- to twenty-four-year-old dollar. Everyone's job in L.A. is based on the whims of people who think break dancing is something you do in a Jeep. On top of that," he said, rubbing his hands together as if deep in thought, "all the Lance roles of three years ago are going to Omar and Lorenz, and that's not helping us—him either. If this was a fall release—maybe early spring—we could get around it. But it's demographics, Joi. They want *Titanic* numbers, and that's hard to do with ethnic flicks."

"What about the quality?" she said, and formed quotation marks in the air. "I worked on this role for months. Every day. I worked with that sadistic dialect coach. I stayed in Maine. I worked on the fishing boat. I even—"

"Girl Scout, you're forgetting. This is no Swiss picnic for me either. I'm on your side, okay? I owe you, sweets, and this is a simple problem with a simple solution."

"Cecil"—Joi stood and walked around to the back of the chair—"I *need* this role. This has nothing to do with the money or the fame or—God forbid I should say the word—*box office*." Joi held a gasp of air in her chest before continuing. "This is a quality role that a black actress, hell, any actress, would kill for. I can play Rachel. I know this woman. There's no way I won't be recognized in this role. I can feel that in my bones. When I die," she said, "they'll say actress Joi Weston, who acted in several TV shows and movies, but was best known for her role in the movie *Purchased Tickets*, died today." After saying the words, her heart stumbled as she thought of the sentence that started her day. "That's what I want, Cecil. It may sound pompous, but I want immortality. I don't want to be remembered as a faded sitcom star. That's not why I came to this town. I want to be remembered for a role with substance. Something I can watch years from now with pride."

Cecil hesitated and appeared to gather his thoughts. "The first time I met you, and I called you Joy, you corrected me and said 'It's Joi. It rhymes with star.' I knew at that moment you were special. I also remember when I was down to my last dime, you were there for me. You and Phillip put me up in your guest house. I know I was not supposed to, but I was snorting in the bed you gave me to get back on my feet. And then one morning," Cecil said, "I was up all night cranking, and it must have been around five. I watched you in your backyard with your sweats on. You'd just come back from jogging, and you were going through acting drills." He shook his head as he appeared to replay the scene in his mind. "You were walking around your pool, and it occurred to me how fortunate I was to have someone like you who even believed in me. Who would even give me a chance," he said, looking up at his client. "That was the last day I got high." Cecil sipped from the drink in front of him and said, "You saved a lot more than my marriage and career, so this you can be assured of. We will get through this shit to—"

Reeves Breidenbaugh opened the door with a burst of energy, and the rush of wind could be felt throughout the trailer. He was an extravagant man who stood over six feet seven inches in his bare feet and would often make multimillion-dollar deals while he sat on the toilet and called executives in the "can" to join him.

As Reeves walked into his trailer's office, Cecil immediately stood.

"Sit your heb ass down. This ain't the military. Magda, bring me three fingers of Jack and my Italian phone directory!" Breidenbaugh walked across the trailer toward his desk. Every step caused the floor to give a creaking sound as if the double-wide was about to split into halves.

Joi remained standing near the wall. She knew he knew she was there, although he never looked at her after sitting behind his desk.

"God damn that fucking cocksucker. I swear"—he looked at Joi and said—"Dear, I'm sorry for what just happened out there. I'm in this business forty years and I've never—You know," he said, and looked at Cecil, "I have half a mind to purchase his fucking ticket. How dare he pull a stunt like that on the—Well, anyway, Joe, I know it's the first time—"

"Joi," she corrected.

There was an air of tension, as Breidenbaugh seemed to be put off by her correction. "Anyway, I know it's the first time you and I've worked together. I've produced Lancy's top three films, and he has never done anything as idiotic as this."

"You think it's because of his divorce?" Joi asked. "Maybe he just needs some time to—"

"Divorce, shemorse. Shit, people get divorces in this town faster than sunburns. It's not about the divorce, and we don't have time to piss around with another shrink. This fucking dinosaur is costing me over—well, anyway," he said, and looked at Cecil. "You can rest assured I'll get Joe something. Now, when can you get Mendez in here? Can you fly her out today?"

"I spoke to her on the phone, and she—"

"Mendez? That Dan'ela Mendez girl? You're replacing me," she said, looking at Cecil with her hands squeezing her hips, and then looked at Breidenbaugh. "You're replacing me with a twenty-five-year-old Hispanic bitch?"

"Miss Mendez," Breidenbaugh said while scrolling for a number in his directory, "is twenty-nine and—"

"Rachel is a forty-three-year-old black woman for Christ sakes!"

"Cecil, would you mind?" Breidenbaugh said as he picked up the receiver to his phone and pointed it at Joi before placing a phone call.

"Cecil, you sold me out. You gave him that Puerto Rican rapper, and you knew all along I was out the door. What happened to that 'I will fight for you' shit!"

With his nose only a few inches from Joi's, Cecil whispered, "Are you finished?"

"Fuck no! I've worked too hard for this role to let it get—"

"I'll have my wife write something else for you. Don't worry. We'll get—"

"Write something else for me like the Potts McGee show? I don't need any more favors from Ashley."

"Listen. Might I remind you that Potts made you a multimillionaire before thirty," Cecil replied. "How many women in this town can say that? Just a handful. And last time I checked, you were still cashing the syndication checks. A lot of things are going down now, and you are still a bankable commodity in this town. You can still pull box. But you have to—"

Like a ray of sunshine, the first smile of the day came to Joi's face. "You fucking sold me out, you prick."

"Remember that book you wanted to option a while back?"

"*One Witness?*"

"Yes, that's the one. I hear it's going to be auctioned in a few, and that would be the perfect vehicle for you."

Joi's face darkened as she said, "It sold last year, Cecil. Damn, I knew that living in Florida."

"Oh. Well, there are a lot of—"

"Go to hell. Listen," she said, raising her voice as she walked toward the producer's desk. "What happens now, Reeves?" Breidenbaugh was still on the phone speaking to someone in broken Italian. "Reeves, I need to talk and I need to talk now." The producer raised a finger and spun away from her.

"Not acceptable, Reeves. I need to talk right now. You owe me a role goddammit, and I am not leaving here until I get some form of satisfaction."

"*Sto benissimo, grazie. Addio.*" Hanging up the phone, Reeves Breidenbaugh looked at Cecil, who stood silently in the corner, and again at Joi as he counted off on his fingertips. "I have investors I have to show a mid ten-figure return on this thing or I am shit in this town. It's a big summer release. I'm taking a huge gamble. I have to make damn near every nickel domestically 'cause over-seas for films like this is for shit. I'm coming up against Cruise, Harrison and fucking DeNiro. Plus I have to have Lancy in this role, and he's starting to smell his shit. He and I don't agree at times; but guess what, beautiful, neither do my mother and me, and I dropped out of her fucking pussy. So if you have problems, you have to deal with them 'cause my plate is full."

"Why did you give me the role if you didn't think I was the one to—"

"I had no idea this asshole would go ape shit crazy over this. Talk to her, Cecil!" he shouted, and started to dial another number.

"I can play this role, Reeves. I know I'm not a twenty-million-dollar actress, but I can play this role."

"There will be other projects. In fact—"

"This *is* my project."

"Not anymore, Joe."

"My name is Joi! It rhymes with—"

"Go to hell, cunt, and get the fuck out my office be-fore I call security!"

CHAPTER 4

Life radiated from the teenager who wore a weave in hair that extended to her lower back. Her counselor had just advised her of her MCAT score and given her the Maharry College brochure. As she walked up to the pay phone, she appeared to be overcome by joy, and a tear tumbled down her cheek. She took the receiver, dialed the number in an unhurried manner and said, "Mommy, I made it."

Michael watched her as he continued to clutch his leather-bound journal. He noticed that the more she would smile, the more she would tuck her chin and allow her forehead to bounce off the silver covering of the wall-mounted phone. With her back turned to him, he could see the profile of her face. Michael noticed the triangular shape of heels that were run over and how she would playfully thump the return coin receptacle with manicured nails as she intently listened to her mother's voice. She then repeated the words with tears rolling to the tip of her chin. "Mommy I'm in. I made it."

With pen in hand, Michael opened his journal to paint

the moment with words. He wanted to describe her clothing without using words like baggy or ill-fitting. He wanted to raise her from the clichéd and give her depth. *Maybe,* he thought, *she could meet Julius who is in that novel about that fire.* He had begun writing the novel *Speaking in Tongues,* but the more he worked on it, the only thing he liked was the title.

Michael's counselor came out of her office, and as soon as the door opened, a coed immediately walked in.

"Excuse me, Mrs. Stephens?"

"Yes," the statuesque sister replied as she looked at Michael.

"I was wondering if I could—"

"Brockmier. Michael Price Brockmier II, right?"

"Yes."

"I remember you from a few months ago. You know," she said, shifting a stack of folders from the bend of her right elbow to the left, "my book club just picked your daddy's book to read next month. A few of the ladies were bragging about how much the book moved them, and I just had to tell them that you were attending NYU."

"Thank you. But listen, I need to talk to you about a class I am having a little trouble with."

"No problem. Let me take these documents down to registration, and I have one student in my office. After that we can talk. How are you doing for time?"

"I'm fine."

The counselor took several steps toward the administration office, when she stopped, turned and scratched the area above her diamond nose ring. "You know what would be cool? If you were to come to my book club the weekend we discuss your father's work."

Michael hoped she was joking, but she stared at him

as if she was serious. "I don't know. To be honest, I haven't read that novel in about five or six years myself. I'm sure," he said with a smile that showed his dimples at their fullest, "the ladies in your club would have more insight than me."

"I'm sure you just coming would be more than enough. That's if you don't have any reservations. I know they would just like to hear whatever you say. Besides, aren't you working on a novel or something?"

Michael bit the soft fold of pink skin on the inside of his jaw, then said, "Where do you guys meet and what time should I be there?"

After the counselor went to the elevator shaft, Michael remembered he wanted to capture the essence of the ebony Doctor-in-Waiting with his pen. While she was still speaking to her mother, the words to describe her did not flow from Michael's heart to his head and through his pen.

"Her clothes were droopy," he wrote and drew a line through it as he looked upward and to the right for a suggestion. He looked at the student again and wrote: "Her clothes fit loose, yet her face expressed a puffy glow."

Damn, he thought. *What in the hell is a puffy glow?* Michael x'd out the sentence and wrote another, then another, then a fifth and a sixth. Each time he would cross it out of his journal and look at his subject as if he were a visual artist spying a nude subject. The words were inside him, but he did not know how to slide them down his arm. The young lady turned in his direction for the first time, and he felt a rush of excitement and wrote:

Her face was a magnificent black pearl. A ghetto child trapped within a woman's body, and she had a ticket to ride. She had a gold tooth, complete with all the attitude it brought with it. A woman-child headed for a promised land.

Michael's eyes scanned the paragraph, and he added,

In a land of promises.

"Why is it so hard?" he asked himself after drawing a line through yet another literary creation. Michael continued to ogle the woman for the spark that would set his creative juices afire.

After saying good-bye to her mother, she hung up the phone and walked in Michael's direction. Michael looked away, but noticed her reach into her mouth, take out her gum and flick it into the trash can beside him like Sheryl Swoops. Then she walked away. He watched her step through the crowded hallway and wondered if he would ever feel what she felt now. If he would ever feel he was on the right path in life.

Michael looked at his watch and thought of a call he had received a year earlier from a former high school girlfriend. At the time he was playing in a piano bar called The Past-Time Paradise ten to twelve hours a day. But one night when he returned home after 3:00 A.M. the green LCD message light on his answering machine was blinking, and there was a message marked urgent for him to call the woman from his past.

When Michael dialed the number later that day, the receptionist answered, "Charisma Books. May I help you?"

Michael's first instinct was to hang up the phone, but he was intrigued as to why she would be calling him after nine years. Did she want to interview him as the only heir to a literary giant? Maybe she wanted to invite him on a cruise with the descendants of Zora Neale Hurston and Alex Hailey so he could discuss his father's work with the attendees for a weekend. Maybe she was yet another editor calling to find out if the rumor for years was true. If his father left an unfinished manuscript behind or if he kept a journal or other notes that could be collected to assist in forming a critical perspective of his work. Then he heard her voice.

"Janessa Harvey's office, this is Pamela, may I help you?"

"Pam Wilson? This is Michael."

With her voice barely above a whisper, she said, "I was hoping it was you. How are you doing?"

"Long time no hear from," Michael replied. "What's going on?"

"There are a lot of shake-ups here at Charisma. I've been here for three years, and I was sitting in a board meeting last weekend for my editor, and they were discussing hot new black authors. Someone asked if there was any way we could find an heir to James Baldwin who might be able to write. Well, I immediately thought of you. I remember you used to dabble in a little in high school, and I was wondering—"

"Pam, if memories serve, you were the writer. I did more of the reading of your writing than anything else."

"Yeah, that's right, now that I think about it," Pam said in her rock salt voice. "But there's this new wave of interest in African-American titles, especially fiction, and what would be better than a book by someone like you?"

"What do you mean, someone like me?"

"A book by you. With your name on it. Let's face it, there's a market out there that would buy anything with the name Michael Brockmier on it. Your name alone would sell fifty thousand copies, I'm sure."

"You're talking non-fiction? Like a living-in-the-shadows type book? I floated that idea to an agent a few years ago, and she stopped returning my calls."

"Those books work every now and then, but for the most part, they're dogs. But a novel by you would be a home run out the box. I just *know* it. Look at the brothers and sisters out there writing today. With your name recognition, Michael, you could zoom to the top of the best-seller list, and I'm sure we could get more than our share of national publicity out of it. I'm talking *Time, USA Today,* "The Today Show," "The Early Show," "Dateline," "20/20," all that."

The words spun in Michael's mind for a moment as he could see success he would never achieve playing in The Past-Time Paradise. But reality fell heavy on his heart. "To be honest, Pam, I don't write fiction. I tried a few years ago, but those days are behind me. I'm a pianist. Now, if you want a book on say the history of jazz or blues pianists, then I think I could contribute to something along those lines."

"That's dead," she said, her voice no longer a whisper. "It's an interesting small book, but I'm looking for fiction. I am looking for a slam. Something that can bring people in stores, not just catch them in stores. Something that will sell at least two hundred and fifty thousand hard- and softcovers, and a piano book won't cut it."

"Thank you for the call, but I don't think I could give you the type of book you're looking for."

"Michael? Who's looking for a novel? I am looking for an idea. Just pitch me an idea, and I'll take it to my senior editor who owes me a favor. And we'll get the approval board to give us the thumbs-up. Then you'll get up to a year to write the darn thing."

"Thanks, but no thanks."

Twelve months after the call, Michael was hard at work trying to sharpen his skills as a novelist. He did not want to be considered until he knew he was being awarded the opportunity based on his potential and not on the remembrance of his father's genius. He knew whatever his fingers produced would be scrutinized and held up beside *One Witness*, so it was important that he get it right. Whatever he wrote had to have a resonance to it that would allow Michael the opportunity to walk out of his father's shadows.

Within the year Michael started five novels, but not one piqued his interest enough to complete it. So he decided to take a creative writing course by day and continued to tickle the ivories by night.

Michael looked at the clock. The counselor had been in the registrar's office for fifteen minutes. *Maybe I should just go back to class,* he thought. *Maybe I should let Anderson know he can't do anything to me that hasn't been done already.* Michael picked at a patch of peeling skin in his hand and decided he would face his trepidation. Then he stood and stretched his body. As he did, his silk shirt came out of his pants, and a teaching assistant sitting across the hall gathered an eyeful of the top edge of his pubic hair at the bottom of his rippled stomach. After tucking in his shirt, Michael said aloud, "That old man can't break me."

Michael reached down for his backpack and noticed in the garbage can beside him a large manila envelope addressed to Rock, Pebble, and Stone Books. *It has to be a manuscript,* he thought as he looked down at it. *And it has to be a reject or it wouldn't be in the trash.*

"At least, I'm not the only writer catching hell," he said as he hoisted his backpack on his shoulder and prepared himself for Dr. Anderson. Michael headed toward double doors, which were plastered with neon signs bearing the word PARTY in bold print. The counselor walked past him at a brisk pace. "Give me another moment. I need to put a fire out in my office, and I'll be right with you."

Another moment? Michael stood in the middle of the hallway as students streamed past him. With his arms folded high on his chest, he watched a janitor walk toward the trash can he had been sitting by, and before he knew it, Michael called for his attention.

"Excuse me?"

"Yeah, let me grab something out of there before you empty it."

The custodian stepped aside as Michael retrieved the sand-tone envelope and returned to the place he had sat previously. He had no idea why he was rummaging through the trash to look at an obviously rejected manuscript. Maybe his misery needed companionship. Possibly someone had abandoned an idea that he could develop. All he needed was one halfway decent thought, a seed, and he could approach Pam. He looked at the thick ream of paper and pulled out the top sheet, which was a letter to the author.

. . . but I think you have a wonderful idea for a novel, and your execution is very effective as well. I utterly fell in love with Paula. I think she harbors feelings that most children feel but have no way to voice to the world. This is a story that will be relatable on numerous levels. However, I did have a problem with the ending, which I believe would be a little didactic in today's marketplace.

Overall, I think you are a quality writer who will no doubt, in my mind, be published. Unfortunately, I do not possess enough enthusiasm in regard to this project to assist you in creating its full potential.

If you should write another novel, I would welcome the opportunity of reading it. Good luck in placing this work elsewhere."

Michael reread the letter as he attempted to read behind the lines. Then he tossed the rejection notice in the empty trash receptacle and read the first page of the manuscript.

Seasons of Regret

A novel

by Ani Bella Ginsburg

Nice title, he thought, and he read the first page of the story about a Jewish girl named Paula Anielewicz who was the butt of all the jokes in her class. She was the child deemed to have "cooties" by the rest of the children as the teachers gave them permission to taunt her, by their omission to stop them.

As he read, Michael was enveloped by her poetic verses. Enthralled by the fact that he could see the little girl with the shoes that were three sizes too big walking into school with newspaper in them. He could feel her trying to stretch her toes so they would not fall off. Trying to spread her toes so the other kids would not laugh at her again. Michael could feel how Paula felt in the opening scene when she stood in the breakfast line and someone noticed a dead roach in her hair. She immediately shook her head, and the deceased insect fell to the floor. The other children exploded into a shower of laughter in the center of the cafeteria. Michael felt her pain as she stood alone, and as she turned, every face she saw laughed at her. Laughed at her clothes. Laughed at her nose. Laughed at the place she lived. Laughed at her mother. Laughed at the roach.

Before he knew it, he heard the counselor say, "Michael?"

"Oh, yeah," he said as he shook his head in order to return from the place he had traveled within the pages.

"I called you three times," she said, poking her head out her office door. "Right this way."

Michael looked down at the manuscript. Before he knew it, he had read the first thirty-one pages. He pulled off a half-inch stack of sheets, stuffed the rest of it in his backpack and went into the office. As he entered, she was busily at work on another chore.

"I hate this time of year," she muttered. "I have to fill in for Dean Archer, who is out recruiting, and I have to—" She looked down and noticed a pink return call note. "Fuck me! One second, okay?"

As the counselor dialed the digits, Michael set his backpack in the chair beside him and then started to read *Season of Regret* again.

"Don't tell me," the counselor said as she waited for the party on the other end of the phone to pick up. "You're here because of Dr. Anderson. Correct? I pulled up your course load."

Michael nodded once and returned his eyes to the manuscript.

"So, what are you complaining about? The sarcasm or the smokers' breath?"

Michael continued to read without replying.

"I wish this man would answer his damn phone. You know," she said, gazing at the top of Michael's head, "of all the fictional characters I have read, I loved—Well, let's say I was intrigued the most by Ralph Stallings in *One Witness*. He was a little like Bigger Thomas in *Native Son*, but I think I hated Ralph even more." Her words went seemingly unnoticed by Michael.

Behind Mrs. Stephens was row after row of books. All fiction. All African-American titles. All organized by author's last name. There were so many books that many of them were stuffed into the shelf horizontally just so they could fit in the allotted wall space. As she began her conversation on the phone by saying, "Listen, Kenny, this'll be quick because I have a student in my office . . . ," Michael reentered the fictional world.

He read about Paula Anielewicz's home and saw how her mother would demean her by calling her names. He felt her angst from being forced to sleep in the bathtub because she would wet the bed. He felt how she felt to fall in love from afar. How she tried to come to terms with how to tell him or what to do with the sentiments that kept her awake at night.

"What are you reading?" Mrs. Stephens asked, and extended her hand with rings on each finger as well as her thumb.

"Just something I found."

"Right, something you found. Let me read it?"

"Why'd you say it like that?" Michael asked with a smile and skimmed off the first few pages for the counselor.

"I've talked to a few of your teachers. Carolyn Jefferson for one? You had her for comp last semester? She and I are best friends. She told me she thinks you have talent, but you are afraid to share it because of your fear of"—and then the party came back to the phone—"one second," Mrs. Stephens said as she looked at the manuscript while talking on the phone.

Michael leaned to one side in the chair as he replayed

in his mind what she had just said. He was flattered that Mrs. Jefferson thought enough of his writing to suggest he had talent, and then he watched Mrs. Stephens's eyebrows draw downward, like two stab wounds. Her lips parted as she said to the party on the phone, "Listen. Can I call you back in a quick second?" Mrs. Stephens looked at Michael like a deer watching an oncoming truck on a country road. "Did you write this?"

"No. I found it in the hallway. Actually, someone had thrown it in the trash bin, and I knew it was a reject because—"

"Are you sure you didn't write this? I know you might be concerned about showing your work for obvious reasons, but this shit is tight. I read a lot of books, Michael, and I like what I see."

And then Michael had an epiphany. He started to give Mrs. Stephens the cover sheet with the author's information on it, but changed his mind. The solution he had sought for so many years was at his fingertips.

"Are you absolutely sure this is not yours?" she asked again. Mrs. Stephens slid her glasses to the top of her head and said, "I've read the first page, and I want to cry for Paula. And that's not like me at all."

"No, ma'am. I didn't write it," Michael stood and said, "But to be honest, I have to go."

"Go where," she asked as he tugged the sheets of paper from her grasp.

"Something I just remembered. I'll try to get here tomorrow. Bye."

In the exact same spot he watched the previous student share her joy with her mother, Michael listened to the phone ring in hopes that he, too, may have found his course in life. And then a masculine voice answered.

"Hello, is this 555-8016?"

Like an awakened bear, the voice growled, "Depends on who this is."

"Is this the residence of an Ani Bella Ginsburg?"

With excitement in his voice, he said, "Umm, no, I mean yeah, this is where she live. This one of them publisher people?"

"Well, did you recently send a manuscript to Rock, Pebble, and Stone Books?"

"Yes," the man shouted in exuberance. "I mean no, I mean, I mean yes, I sent it, but no, I ain't the one who wrote it. My wife wrote it. Well, she ain't really my wife, but anyway, I just sent it 'cause I live, I mean work by the post office so I—Wait a minute, maybe you should talk to her!" he said before Michael could cut into his ramblings. "Ani! It's one of them publishers! Pick up the phone."

"How you know?" a female voice asked in the distance.

"He asked for Ginsburg. Get on the phone."

"Sir?" Michael shouted into the receiver to get the man's attention. "Sir, I am not a publisher." But he could hear her say in a faint voice, "Which one?"

"Hell, I don't know, wait a minute. I think he said it was that Rock, Scissors, Paper, Stone Company."

"Oh my God, oh my God, oh my God," he heard Ani pant in the background. Although the name implied that she was Jewish, she sounded like a black woman as she thanked Jesus Christ in the distance. And then she picked up the phone and attempted to squelch her excitement. "Umm, hello?"

There was a pause as Michael tried to decide how to get out of the situation he had created. He could just hang up, but then he could not call her about the manuscript again. Or he could tell her the truth, to which she would more than likely hang up on him. "Hello, Ani, this is . . ." and then he did not want to say his name since it would more than likely add to the drama.

"I'm a student at New York University, and I was sitting in the counselor's office where I found your manuscript. I was thinking you may have left it there or something by mistake 'cause I found it tossed in the trash."

There was a hesitation, and then she said, "I thought you said you were from R.P.S.?"

"No, I said the manuscript was sent to——"

"Johnny," she shouted, "did he tell you he was from Rock, Pebble, and Stone?"

"Yeah! He said he was calling from that Rock, Paper Company. He not?"

"Listen, ma'am," Michael said, "I'm sorry for the confusion. I just wanted to say that I read a few pages of your manuscript, and to be honest, Ani, it's one of the best stories I have read in a long time. I started reading it, and before I knew it, I was almost fifty pages into the thing and wishing it was longer than five hundred pages." Silence revisited the phone line again. "I read a lot, and I have connections at——" He could hear the lady whimpering on the other end. "I have a connection, and I would just like to show her what you have. I think you are enormously talented."

In the background Michael could hear the man's voice get closer to the phone, and then she said, "So your connection is with what publication? That NYU newspaper? Maybe I should let them run an excerpt next to the tutor ads in the classifieds."

"Ani, my name is Michael Brock——"

Before he could finish the sentence, the masculine voice returned to the phone and said, "I don't know what kinda game you're playing, but——"

"I'm not playing a game. I saw the manuscript in the trash and—"

"Dammit, nigga, I put it in the trash. She and I talked about it when I picked it up from the post office, and she told me to throw it away. Now you call here and get her all upset. Let me tell you something. This shit ain't funny, and if I knew where you were, I'd come and kick your ass myself."

"Wait, wait, wait a minute. The reason I called is—" The line went dead. Michael swallowed and looked at the cover page of the manuscript. He then walked across the hall, sat beside the half-full trash receptacle again and, as his fingers slid across the page, plotted his next move. He knew in his heart he was too close to great-ness to walk away.

The following day, since he did not have classes, Michael found himself outside of Ani's apartment. She lived in Tracy Towers, an apartment building in the north Bronx near Yonkers at the end of the Number 4 train. With the manuscript in his backpack, Michael wondered if he could be making a mistake. But in his heart he knew he had to, at a bare minimum, meet the woman who created Paula.

Stepping past security, he looked for apartment 18-K, saw the name Freeman and then checked the coffee-stained cover sheet on the manuscript to make sure he was buzzing the right apartment. *Unless this is a typo, this is the place,* he thought to himself. Michael rang the buzzer.

There was silence.

But maybe the dude who was on the phone is named Free-man. He buzzed again.

Silence.

A group of Catholic schoolgirls walked past him and opened the door with their key. Michael started to walk in with them, but decided that if she was there, this was not the way he wanted to meet her after the earlier misconstrued phone call. He buzzed again.

"Hello," a woman's voice said out of breath. *Damn. Now I caught her in the midst of fucking.* "Hello," the breathy voice repeated.

"Umm arrha yeah, this is . . . This is the person you spoke to earlier about your manuscript, and before you cut me off, ma'am, let me say that my name is Michael Price Brockmier, II and I just want to talk to you."

There was a wave of silence.

"Since I spoke to you, I've read most of your manuscript, and I think you're a true wordsmith. I love where it's going. I'm feeling the parallelisms, the subplots and the thematic devices. There was a line you used on page forty-eight that I still remember. The rabbi tells Paula that people feed pigeons yet shoot at eagles. That was right on time."

"Would you," she said, and caught her breath, "leave me the hell alone? Whoever you are. I don't know what you want. I don't need a book doctor. I don't want an agent. I don't want to do subsidy publishing; I just want you to leave me alone. Is that asking too much?"

"Ani? All I have to do is make one phone call. That's all. One call and I can—"

"Excuse me," a deep voice behind Michael said.

"All I need to do is call my friend who is a junior editor over at Charisma, because I know she's looking. She and I talk about once a month, and I am trying to get my stuff up to par to submit to her. In fact, I—"

"Excuse me," the voice said with added bass.

"You're excused, nigger, damn!" Michael said as he moved out of the way.

Looking at Michael's finger pressing the 18-K button, the man said, "Didn't I tell your punk ass not to bother my woman again?"

Michael turned quickly and noticed the size of the man wearing the brown NYU custodial shirt. He was well over six feet tall, at least four feet wide and smelled of ammonia, bleach and sweat.

"I was just—"

"I told you earlier if you bothered her, I'd dig my foot up your ass sideways. Now you gonna come to my apartment . . . fucking with my lady," he said, and walked to within a few inches of Michael's chest. So close Michael could feel the heat from his nostrils. "Wussup with that?"

The two large men were broken up quickly by security, but not before Michael sustained a mouse under his eye. After calling the club and asking for the night off, Michael sat in his home alone with a cold compress on his face and watching "Jeopardy." It was the same apartment he had lived in his entire life and had been left to him in his mother's will. There were no pictures of his parents or copies of his father's work displayed. Shelves of books and videotapes covered the walls of the living room where Michael sat. There was an expensive sound system he had splurged on after receiving one of his father's royalty checks and rack upon rack of CDs.

"Who is Hitler," he said as he watched the game show with his swollen eye covered by an ice pack. *I can't believe he tried me like that. I ought to go back down there and—*"Oliver Wendell Holmes. Who is Oliver Wendell Holmes?"

Michael shouted as if he were a contestant on the game show.

"Try to do someone a favor and this is what happens. Next time I'll think twice." Michael reached for the box of raisins on the end table beside him and noticed it was on top of a few pages from *Season of Regret.* "Who is J. Edgar Hoover." He looked at the pages once again. This time, not reading the words, simply scanning their lay-out on the page. *If she's getting rejected and I think she is great, then maybe I have no idea what it takes to get published.*

There was a faint staggered knock at the door.

What the fuck? He thought. No one knew he was not working, so why would anyone be knocking at his door. Still sitting in front of the television, he shouted, "Who?"

There was no answer. Just another knock.

Michael removed the cold compress from his eye, tossed his hair from his face, stood and walked toward the door. He could see the trace of a woman's hair through the glass in the door. There was yet another knock. Michael looked through the window and saw it was her. His ex-wife.

After he opened the door, Michael's eyes met hers, and then they immediately met the eyes of his son. "Hey, Blair, how are you?" Michael said, and squatted down to speak to the seven-year-old.

Blair did not answer.

"So, what am I? A pile of garbage? I don't even get a hello?" Robyn asked.

Michael continued to look at Blair, who drew closer to his mother. "I thought you were living down in Alabama with Grandma?" he asked his son.

Silence.

"What's that?" Michael asked, unfazed, looking at

the cryptic scribble on the back of his son's hand. "A happy face?"

"Boy has a thing for tattoos. He likes watching the NBA, so he's always trying to draw on himself with magic markers, although I've *told* him to stop doing it."

Michael looked up at his ex-wife.

"Listen, Momma is taking care of Samantha's children now, so I brought him back up north. What happened to your eye?"

Standing, Michael said, "I've been sending checks there every month. Why couldn't she afford him?"

"I know, I know, but it's still too much. They don't have room in the house, and she has to keep Sam's children. They don't have nowhere else to live."

"So where are you living?"

"I still work in D.C. I'm working for the federal government, and you don't let jobs like that get away."

"So why you never let me speak to my son?"

"You could have—Listen, can we come inside?"

Michael moved to the side as Robyn and Blair walked through the door, and he noticed a yellow taxicab in front of his apartment with the motor running.

Robyn walked inside the apartment they had shared at one time and immediately looked at the empty spot on the wall where their wedding picture once hung over the fireplace. She looked at Michael and said, "You could have called."

"Listen, Blair," Michael said, and squatted so he could look in his son's eyes. "If you like, you can turn to something good on television. Me and your mom need to talk for a moment, okay?"

Blair walked over to the chair Michael sat in previously and picked up the remote as his parents went into the kitchen.

"I called. I used to call him every weekend, and then she would always tell me he was at the neighbor's house or he was asleep. Then I would call at least once a month; then I stopped calling altogether."

"He's your son. You should have never stopped calling."

"That's easy for you to say. When you sign checks every month for a child you can't talk to, we'll talk. Anyway," Michael said in disgust. "I bet you get to talk to him, but when she wanted to send him to summer camp, who did she call? For school clothes who did—"

"Listen, I didn't come here for you to disrespect my momma again. Like I said, she has a houseful and so—"

"And so what?"

"And so Blair doesn't have a decent place to sleep. He was sharing a mattress on the floor with his cousins."

Michael was silent for a moment and then said, "Are you suggesting that—"

"Are you going to say no to your son? You have this big ole apartment, and no one stays here but you. I have a small, overpriced piece-of-shit apartment in Georgetown, and besides, I would have to pay sitters and everything else. You could have neighbors here watch him."

"Are you suggesting that I—"

"It will only be temporarily. Just let me get in a position where I am able to get a bigger place, and then I will come get him."

Michael shook his head. "No. I mean, I don't mind taking him, Robyn, but I am not going to have him bounced from Alabama to Harlem back down to D.C. That's ridiculous. Now, if you like, I'll see what I can do to help you get a bigger place, and I'll pay for the day care but . . ." Michael paused as he saw Robyn's eyes look beyond him.

"Blair, I need you to watch television for a little while longer."

"I—I don't know how to work the TV," he said with his lips curling downward.

As she walked past Michael toward their son, Robyn said, "One second."

Standing in the kitchen alone, Michael felt the vessels under his swollen eye pulsate. "There's no way I can raise a seven-year-old. No way in the world," he whispered. Since he was an only child, the only child he had ever lived with was Blair, and he had not been a part of the boy's life since he was two. "There is *no way*."

Robyn walked back into the kitchen and said with her eyes stretched, "Listen, one way or the other this is going to be an adjustment. In a perfect world, it would not be like this; but she can't keep him, I don't have the room and you are the only other alternative. Now what we can—"

"I'll—If *he* wants to stay with me," Michael paused, "I'll keep him. But dig this; this is not temporary. This is not a children's rest haven. Okay? I mean it. This child has lived in five different places that I know of in seven years. He needs some stability in his life. Now, I don't know much about raising kids and shit, but I'll learn." Michael looked at his ex, who was on the verge of crying, and said, "So if you leave, Robyn, *sayonara*."

After Robyn left, Michael ordered take-out, walked with his son to the store to rent videos and felt he had made a big mistake. Although he tried to talk to him, Blair was unresponsive. He showed him the playground as well as the school he would possibly attend the next day.

"That's the school I went to when I was your age."

Blair remained silent.

"I think some of the same teachers might be there. And if this is the right school and they serve you that puke green Jell-O . . . don't eat it. Okay?" He glanced at his son with a smile and noticed that Blair looked at the school once and then looked away. Even though he had felt like a real father again for only an hour, Michael saw the pain in his son's eyes. Most of his life Blair had lived in a small southern town. As he held his son's hand, Michael felt him jump every time he heard a siren. Every time a car sped by blowing its horn, Blair would squeeze his father's fingers tighter. As they passed a homeless man asleep on the street between two cars, Michael led his son to the bus stop and sat on the bench.

"Listen, Blair, I know this is different than Alabama. I've been to Grandma Ester's house, and I know it's nothing like this. But trust me, there are a lot of things to do in New York that you can't do in Alabama."

Blair looked into his father's eyes.

"For instance—umm." It occurred to Michael that he had not viewed New York from a child's perspective in years. "I know what we could do. We could go see the Knicks play at the Garden. You can't do that in Alabama."

"Can I get a tattoodal?" Blair asked with his lips quivering with emotion.

"A tattoodal? Oh, you mean a tattoo. Sure. When you get eighteen or you develop a killer crossover to get you in the NBA sooner," Michael laughed.

"I want my mommy."

"I know, man. But dig, right now your mom's going through some changes and has—I should say she's headed back to Washington. You know where Washington D.C. is on the map?"

"I want my mommy."

"I understand, but she'll call you as soon as she gets home. She should be there tonight around—"

"I want my mommy."

"Listen, Blair, I'm doing the best I can, man. I—just give me a chance. You might just like it here, and you might not. If you don't—well . . . dig, what I'll do is take tomorrow off from work, and we can go buy you some new gear. Some Knicks gear if you like. You know, new clothes and stuff. Have you ever heard of F.A.O. Schwarz? You still play with toys, right?"

Tears appeared for the first time in his son's glassy eyes as he repeated once again. "I just want my mommy."

Michael leaned back on the bench as New York's Finest zoomed past them, which caused his son to bring his wrist up to his eyes and cry even more. "Now what am I going to do," he whispered as the sound of Blair's crying increased from a whimper to a sob.

CHAPTER
5

Morning splashed the honeyed skies over Atlanta, and Joi watched another plane disappear into the heavens. Since he lived minutes away from Heartsfield International, Joe told his sister he would keep her company during her three-hour layover. So she waited in the airport restaurant, gathered her thoughts in regard to the past weekend and watched planes take off and land.

When she had received the call from her former agent, Joi initially did not want to participate in the cast reunion. There were too many unanswered questions in her mind concerning Hollywood, and she preferred keeping the better part of a continent between her and the city of lost hopes. But Cecil told her how many of her former cast mates were looking forward to seeing her again, so on a sound stage in Burbank, Joi reunited with her past.

It had been two years since the debacle with Lance Fellows. Two years since she picked up a script of any kind. The press was there asking each and every cast mate the same questions.

"Did you think people would fall in love with this show when you filmed the pilot years ago?" "What's your lasting memory from the 'Potts McGee' days?" "So what are you working on now?"

The crew was there, many of whom talked about what they had gone on to do since the close of productions, but the first person Joi saw when she walked onto set 38-B was Alicia Morrison. The actress who had played Potts McGee.

Although the two women never spoke during the time of separation, Joi had followed the post-career drama of the child star via reports on "Entertainment Tonight" and E! Television.

When Alicia graduated from high school, Joi was stopped at the drugstore for a comment. After Alicia's car accident, Joi was contacted on vacation for her thoughts. Joi was interviewed when Alicia was busted for smuggling marijuana into Miami as well as when she graduated from college with a degree in adolescent psychiatry.

When Alicia saw Joi she walked up to her without saying a word. The two women met on a mock design of the kitchen of their old set and simply hugged.

Joi took a sip of coffee in the airport restaurant and glimpsed at her watch. As she looked up, she noticed a woman gaze at her, then walk away. Such stares had been common in the past, but were more and more infrequent as she slipped from the fame pages to the where-are-they-now column.

While the red-eye from L.A. to Atlanta went uneventful, to Joi's surprise the in-flight movie was the Academy Award–nominated *Purchased Tickets*. She had purposely avoided watching the film that had garnered the Best

Supporting Actress nomination for Dan'ela Mendez and cheered from her home when the Hispanic actress lost the prestigious honor.

As Joi traveled east, she watched the actors in the opening scene without putting on her headphones. Although she could have watched a "Frazier" rerun, she could not turn away from the movie.

She watched Lance slam the Mercedes door and walk down the street soaked to the bone by the rain. She watched Dan'ela run into the house and retrieve the revolver. The actress fumbled all five bullets just as called for by the script and then promised to teach him a lesson as she scrambled to shove them into the chamber. Joi watched her storm outside, the gun tucked in the waistband of her skirt. Then the actress put her finger on the trigger, and at that moment the director moved in for a close-up of Lance's face. Although she hated to admit it, there was something in his eyes, Joi thought, which made him perfect for the role. The two actors walked toward each other in the rain, then kissed, and for the first time, Joi put on the headphones and allowed herself to enjoy the rest of *Purchased Tickets*.

For the first hour she watched the movie, Joi found herself taking the movie apart as if she were a paid critic. But then she fell into the experience just like any other moviegoer. Her heart raced, although she knew what to expect. She felt sad when Dan'ela was forced to take her first victim's life and smiled when she escaped the law. Then she watched the other individuals in first class watching the movie. She observed them laugh on cue and get quiet or say "Shhh" to their travel companions during pivotal scenes. And when the movie ended, Joi watched the lady sitting next to her grab the armrest and squeeze it while smiling.

Joi wished she could have been a part of the epic, but

for the first time, she felt closure in regard to the role. When she was in her twenties, acting was perfect for her. When she and Phillip were married, it was fun to be a part of the party scene. But at this point in her life she did not think Tinseltown had a place for her, and she realized she no longer allowed Hollywood's description to create the perception she had of herself.

"There you are," Joe said as he walked up behind his sister, dressed in a black pinstriped suit and cream-colored tie. "I was at the restaurant in Terminal B." With his phone pressed to his ear, he said, "Okay, I found her. Want to talk to her?"

Joi stood and hugged her brother and asked softly, "Who is it?"

Before he answered, Joe handed the phone to his younger sister.

"Hello?"

"I had no idea you were flying out of LAX so early," Joi's father, Jonathan, said. "Your mom and I thought you were flying out later this afternoon."

Joi sat on the stool at the unstable circular table as her brother got the waitress's attention to take his order. "I wanted to get back earlier than I planned. I was supposed to be home around six tonight, but I didn't want to lose a day when I could be home working on the campaign or doing something at the office."

"So is it official official? Is he actually going to run for the state house?"

"He has not filed with the state as of yet, but yes, he decided to run last week. We're sure as soon as he does, since it's an open seat, a few more Republicans and Democrats will get in the race."

"I can't believe I raised a Republican," Jonathan said over a smile in his voice.

"You can't believe it? I'm still getting used to the idea

myself. You know how active I was in the Democratic party in Orange County, and now I find myself going to things like the Republican Wives' Caucus. It's enough to make you sick," she said, looking at Joe, who simply shook his head as the waitress brought him a drink.

"So when are you coming back to P.G. County? It's been about a year now, you know."

"I will, Daddy. So much is going on now, but you know I'll be home as soon as I get a moment to breathe. Is Momma there?"

"She's out walking. She was worried about you last night, you know. You need to call her and let her know you're all right from time to time."

Joi noticed a tall, brown-skinned gentleman with dreads in his hair walking through the crowd toward the restroom. For a moment she forgot what she was going to say, and then she replied, "Well, tell her everything is fine, okay?"

"Take care, and tell Phillip to call me when he gets five minutes."

"Love you, too, Daddy."

Hanging up the phone, Joi looked at her brother and said, "You smell good. Check you out."

"Hey, I have to show them young bloods how to advance in life. You never get a second chance, you know."

"How long have you been with Morris Brown?" Joi asked as the woman who had been watching her before stood in the middle of the passageway gawking at her again as if she was afraid to ask for an autograph. Then the woman walked away.

"I've been at Mo B for fourteen years, believe it or not."

"Listen at you trying to sound like a teenager."

"Do I look like I am forty something? Baby, you're as young," Joe said, "as you think."

"Whatever." Joi took a half sip of her drink and then said, "But it must be rewarding to do what you do."

"Rewarding? Yes, I get a lot of satisfaction out of my job. I keep a list of students I've helped get jobs with Fortune 500 companies, and the list fills up a couple of spiral notebooks now."

"See," Joi said, "you can't beat that. Daddy always wanted you to follow his footsteps."

"Yeah, I know. I used to go to the school with him, but I don't know how much of what I am doing now is because of my belief in the art of teaching or because the women at Morgan State were so damn fine. Don't get me wrong, I wanted to be a professor even when I was in high school."

"Don't I remember," Joi said.

"But I admit, there is a part of me, even now, that wonders 'what if.' I know analytical theories behind business, but I wonder if I'd have what it takes to actually generate wealth instead of talking about it."

"Wondering is as much a part of life as breathing. We all do it, and it's funny you would mention that, because on the plane this morning I was wondering what would have happened had I not met Phillip. Then I would not have met Cecil, and I would not have gotten that sitcom. But I also would not have been put in this box as an actress, and who knows, maybe I would have had a more rewarding film career or maybe I would have been a dishwasher."

"That's what you've always wanted, isn't it?"

"I don't know. I guess I just wanted creative freedom, but in all honesty, when I watched *Purchased Tickets* on the flight here, I let it go. All the anger I had built up inside. All the animosity in regard to L.A. I just released it. To be honest, I am very happy in Florida. I don't have the pressure of casting and kissing ass and worrying about getting older. In the real world I'm still considered a moderately young woman. In Hollywood I am a grandmother-in-waiting, and I decided *that* was a battle I'd rather not fight."

"You don't see yourself ever going back?"

"I'm content. I made a couple of decent films, had my own TV show, and as long as there's Nick At Night and TV Land, I'll have a nice residual check coming in."

Joe stared at his sister.

"What?"

"But who are you?" he said, staring deeply into her eyes. "Are you transforming into Mrs. Phillip Evans?"

"I don't mind being Mrs. Evans. In fact, I'm thinking about taking his name legally. I guess I was the one out front for so many years, and he never complained, so I look forward to being in the background and pushing him awhile."

"But beyond that," Joe said as he stirred his drink in his hand, "how's the marriage?"

"Why do you ask like that?"

"Sorry, I asked the wrong way." Joi's brother smiled at her and said, "Let me put it another way. Howst art thoest marriage!"

Joi laughed. "My marriage has never been better. I think getting away from the industry helped us in a number of ways. We were both reaching burnout. His prospects of being a producer were going nowhere, and of course, we didn't have the constant reminders."

"Reminders of what—oh," Joe said, looking in his sister's eyes. "*Those* reminders."

"The psychiatrist said by staying there, we'd face our fears; thus we'd be able to heal faster. But I don't think she knew what the hell she was talking about.

When you see other people at graduation ceremonies with their kids, or you see kids speeding down the highway, it hurts like hell." Joi could feel sorrows rise in her chest like molten lava. "Especially when it's two girls in the car."

Joe paused before speaking to seemingly reflect on what was said. "Going through that must have been the closest thing to death. How old would Angie have been now? Nineteen?"

"Twenty-three as of the third of next month," Joi replied. "And that ass that hit her is up for parole next year. I pray to God they don't want us to appear, because I don't want to be in the same—Anyway, if there is anything that the accident did, it brought Phillip and I closer together. I always worried about him sleeping around, but he came out of this a changed man. I saw him humbled by it all. The old Phillip would have never run for office, and if he would have run, it would have been for all the wrong reasons. This Phillip has a plan for a better after school program and making the work environment safer for people in the state. I love that about him."

"It's good to see that someone has a good marriage today."

"Meaning?"

"It's just that when you get our age, it seems everyone you know is either divorced or talking about the possibility, and I am glad you're happy."

"Are you happy?"

"I'm happy," Joe said, and sipped his drink. "We're . . . we're . . ."

Then Joi saw the lady watching her in the passageway talking into a cell phone so loud it seemed she was trying to talk over a jackhammer. "Listen," the woman said, "you will not believe who I am here looking at in the airport. Unh unh, not her. Nope, not him either. Nope, keep trying."

"We have done better, I guess," Joe lamented.

"Don't tell me, you slipped up again."

"Slipped, tumbled and rolled but this time I couldn't help it. This new intern came in to help in the department, and she was about thirty. Used to be a stripper, believe it or not, and is pursuing a postgraduate degree. I didn't mean to, but I found myself alone with her and—"

"I don't want to hear about it, Joe."

"I wasn't going to give you details. It's just that G.G. found out about it."

"How?"

"This punk-ass student who was failing my class saw her at the Underground and told her. I wanted to kick his ass, but instead I just gave him an *F*."

"You are wrong. You know that."

"His ass earned that *F*. He never turned in—"

"I'm not talking about that. You're almost forty-five years old. When are you going to stop acting like a child?"

He paused, looked at his sister and said, "I don't know. I really don't. I will tell you no lie. I love G.G. like there's no tomorrow. If she were to leave me now, I don't know what in the world I would ever do. But there is also this part of me that craves the . . . the escapism, you might say, of an affair. I've never felt anything for the women I've been with. But it's the hunt—the sport—you might say."

"See, you sound just like—"

"Daddy never said that. He always said, 'It's not what I do in the streets; it's what I do at home that counts.' "

"That worked until the streets followed him home, and that lady showed up with the ice pick," Joi said.

"I remember the look on Momma's face. How embarrassed she felt that the neighbors heard it."

"Momma is a hell of a woman to have taken that," Joi whispered as another plane parted the heavens in the distance. "She never complained or talked about leaving him. When that woman left the house that night, I just knew they were going to have a knock-down-drag-out, but Momma went back in the kitchen, told me to dry the dishes, and she finished cooking."

Joe leaned against the wall recollecting the moment and said, "I remember I was playing with my G.I. Joe, and she just stepped over me like I was a box of shit or something. She was wearing that long laced apron and went into the kitchen as if nothing had happened."

"Joyce never got outwardly upset about anything, though. Never developed high blood pressure keeping it bottled up inside," Joi said. "She just took his affairs for years and years, and all she would do is take us with her to church, come back home, go on her walks, clean up after him and cook. The woman was June Cleaver with afro puffs."

"That's why it's so hard for me to believe you'll be a housewife all of a sudden after running from Joyce's shadow all of these years."

"Ahh no, we're talking apples and biscuits now. I worked outside the home for years, the only reason I'm back is because I need some me time. Don't get me wrong, when Phillip screwed up, I thought about that look on Momma's face, and I wondered if I had turned into that woman; but then we did have a knock-down-drag-out. Right in his office. Right in front of the secretary he was screwing. And I think he understood that was the last straw.

"I'm not Joyce, and I'll never be Joyce," she continued. "I love my momma to death, but I can't see that woman in my reflection. I don't know how she was able to do it. Never drinking. Never cursing him out. Just 'yes, Jonathan' this and 'yes, Jonathan' that. She's a better woman than I can ever aspire to be."

"Better woman? Or weaker woman?"

"Momma is not weak. It would have been easy to leave him. But she stayed, and I have always loved that about her. I want to believe she stayed for her, but in my heart I know she stayed for us. But you know what I hate?" she said, looking at Joe.

"What? Wait a minute. Don't say it."

"You know what I am going to say, don't you?"

"I did *not* turn into Pops."

"Let's see. You are a tenured professor. You teach in the college of business. You have affair after affair. You—"

"Okay, stop it. That's not called for. I love my wife and—"

"And are you saying Daddy didn't love Momma?"

"That's not what I'm saying. All I am saying is this . . . "

As he spoke, Joi noticed the lady from before had returned—this time with another woman—and they both stood pointing at her. Joi smiled at her and redirected her attention to her brother. Then from the corner of her eye, she saw a green balloon. The child with the balloon walked toward the ladies, and he held the hand of the gentleman Joi had seen for a split second before. He was well over six-three. He wore shoulder-length dreads in his hair and wore a gray suit and tie, although he looked as if he would be more comfortable in jeans and a tee shirt.

And then he looked down at the child's sneakers, and although people ran to catch planes all around him, he kneeled down and tied the child's shoelaces as if nothing else in the world was as important. Joi watched him look at the child as he tied his laces and smiled at him in a way only a father could smile at his son. He kissed the little boy on the nose, then stood, and the two of them walked toward the baggage pickup.

". . . so I know that I love her, and I know this time will be the last time. My hand before God."

"What?"

"You didn't hear a word I just said, did you?"

"I heard enough," Joi said, and leaned forward toward her brother on her elbows. "I'd suggest you do something radical. In times like these, what you should do is go out on a limb and talk to her. Tell her—"

"No. Why don't you talk to her?"

"Me?"

"Yeah. Tell her how much I love her. How much I care. You know, just tell her the truth."

"Now, you of all people know me and G.G. don't have that type of relationship."

"That's why it will work. If you call her and tell her, then she'll see how sincere I am."

"When was the last time you slept with this woman?"

"The other woman?" There was a pause, and then he said, "Last night."

Joi's mouth opened. "How?"

"The boys were staying with the neighbors; G.G. went shopping with her sister to buy clothes for the game tonight. The calls forward to my cell phone. Simple."

"And this is the part you like. The getting away with it. Don't you feel funny having sex with this *tramp*—and yes, I called her a tramp—and then having sex with your wife?"

"Damn. Since you put it like that, I do now."

"No you don't."

"Well, there was a time I didn't, but I do now."

"No you don't, Joe, 'cause if you did, you wouldn't do it. Like you said, you like the game. The conquest. The fact that you can keep them both in the dark."

"Baby girl, you don't know me as well as you think you do. G.G. and I will be together for the rest of our lives. But I have this weakness inside of me, and I am trying to fight it. For the first few years of our marriage, I would never even look at another woman. Then about six or seven years ago . . ."

Joi's attention was diverted once again by the green balloon, but this time the child stood alone. She looked left and right to see if she saw the child's guardian, but did not see him. As Joe continued to speak, she started to go to the child's aid, until Joe called for her attention.

"Excuse me?" she asked.

"Am I boring you?"

"Sorry. It's just this little kid is walking around by himself, and the guy who was with him apparently left him."

Joe turned around, and as soon as he did, Joi stood to retrieve the little boy. But before she could take a step in his direction, she saw the dread-wearing Adonis returning to the child with a bag of popcorn. "Oh, there he is," she said, and sat down. "That's the guy who was with him."

Joe gave the gentleman a double take and said, "You know something? That looks just like . . . Well, I'll be damned. That is him."

"Who? You know him?"

"Yeah, I know him alright, and I'll bet you Cynthia doesn't know he's in town either." Joe stood up and shouted, "Mike!"

Joe and G.G. were introduced to him several months

earlier when his sister-in-law, Cynthia, and Michael were dating seriously. At the time Michael would fly down once a month with gifts in hand, spend the weekend in a suit and leave Cynthia with a smile. Since Cynthia lived in the basement of Joe and G.G.'s home she would often speak to Michael on the cordless while in the common living areas of the house. But Joe had noticed that the phone calls had become infrequent and Cynthia rarely mentioned the Harlem author.

The gentleman, who was wearing dark shades, looked both ways, and then at Joe as he heard his name called again. "What's up with him sneaking in town," Joe said in a mumbled tone without moving his lips as Michael Brockmier II headed toward the restaurant with the child in tow.

"I had no idea who that was calling me," Michael said, and he and Joe gave each other a masculine bear hug and a pound to the back. "What's up? You headed out of town?"

"No, actually my first class is not until two today, and my sister has a layover; so I was up here chilling with her."

As he looked at Joi, Michael took off his shades. "Hello, how are you? I remember Cindy telling me that Joe's sister was an actress, but I didn't know it was you. I was just watching you in that movie, *Lately*."

"You mean that thing is still coming on TV?" Joi said with a smile as the kid looked up at her with large doe eyes.

"No, I bought the DVD. Guys, I am being rude. This is my son, Blair. Blair," Michael said as he sat down and hoisted his son onto his lap, "this is Mr. Joe and Miss Joi Weston." Michael stared at Joi as if he was waiting for her to correct the salutation. She did not.

"So what are you doing in town?" Joe asked.

"I'm in for only the day to do a signing at Medu Books, and then I am headed back home tonight."

"Oh, Joi, I should tell you. This is Michael Brockmier. He wrote that novel *Season of Regret.*"

"I saw the book in the store the other day. I'm a big fan of your father's work. I loved *One Witness.* When I was more active in Hollywood, I wanted to buy the rights to it."

"Well, I am happy to hear that," he said as his eyes roved from her eyes to her ring finger, then back up to her face. "The rights were sold a few years ago, but who knows if the project will ever get the green light. It's such a difficult novel to bring to the big screen, but then, you must know that better than me."

"So," Joe said, pulling Michael's attention away from his sister. "Does Cindy know you're in town?"

"No. I spoke to her a few nights ago, but I didn't tell her about this 'cause I knew I'd only be in town for a few hours and she'd be teaching. I'll call her when I think she's home."

"It seems the book is doing pretty well," Joe said. "I saw it in *USA Today* a few weeks ago."

"Have you read it?" Joi asked her brother with her head tilted down.

"I won't even fake it, 'cause you know I ain't *trying* to read no fiction," Joe replied. "But G.G. loved it, and so did the women who read it in my department. But who knows, I may read it in the future. What you should do is put the book on CD. Then a brother could listen to it on the ride into work in the morning."

Michael looked at Joe and said, "Don't worry, *my brother,* there is still hope for you yet." Then he looked at his watch and said, "Listen, guys, the store is sending a car, so we need to get to the lower level. He looked at

Joi and said, "It was nice to finally meet you." Then he turned to Joe as he stood up and gave him another hug. "I'll be back in a few weeks, I'm sure; then maybe we can hit the links or something, okay?"

As they hugged, Joi caught one last whiff of his cologne and felt something stir in her stomach she had not felt for some time, and for a moment she could understand why Joe had taken a chance on the previous night.

With his son's hand in his, Michael walked away, and as soon as he did, Joe said, "I wonder if that's really why he's in town. And on top of that, Cindy never told us he had a child. I wonder why?"

"I don't know. Maybe knowing you all she thought it was none of your business. He seems like a nice guy."

"He's cool, but then again she's been dating someone else for a while also. She's wanted Mike to ask her to marry him, but he hasn't popped the question, so I guess she is moving on."

"Really?"

"Cynthia wants to pick out china patterns, and Mike isn't there yet. I've talked to him man to man, and I personally don't think he is anywhere close to being in love with her. I think he enjoys her company, but he's just in that get-the-milk-for-free mode."

"You think that's all he's interested in? He seems like a nice guy."

"You said that 'cause he was looking you up and down." Happy that her brother had noticed, Joi replied, "No, he was not. He was just making conversation."

"Please. His eyes were sliding between your navel and neck like I don't know what. I thought his tongue was going to roll out his mouth. I didn't know you were into younger men."

"And you're right. He's at least five or six years younger than me." She looked at her brother and said, "Right?"

"At least," Joe said, smiling.

"See, you're just nasty, and you think everybody's nasty just like you. He was a gentleman. Plus, the fact that he is taking care of his son on a trip like this tells me a lot about him as well."

"Like what? Like he's a certified player 'cause he knows women will fall for that?"

"Just the opposite, actually."

"Whatever."

"Well, let me just say," Joi said as her lips flattened and a serious nature came to her voice. "I'd *never* have an affair. You cheat because you get excited and you need the conquest. It's not about that with me. If I were to cheat, trust me, the marriage would be completely over in my heart and in the courts. There would be no washing up in the basin; no hotels on the other side of town. If I were to leave Phillip, I'd never come back. With me there are no shades of gray in that area." Joe listened intently to his sister, and then she said, "Look, I better be getting down to that gate. Are you going to come down to Florida with the kids this summer?"

"No, I was thinking of spending a few weeks in Prince George. Why don't you come up? You know Daddy's going to get on you for not visiting more often."

"I wish I could, but I can't. We'll be in the midst of the campaign around that time. The primaries will be in March, but this is the time people start declaring."

"I never knew so much went into running for the state house."

"It's very time consuming and——"

"Excuse me."

Joi turned around to see the woman who had watched her from the passageway.

Smelling like a Big Mac, she said, "I hate to bother you, ma'am. I just couldn't believe it was you."

"No problem," Joi said. "How are you?"

"You're that lady, on that show, with that little girl; right?"

"Yes, that was me," Joi said, waiting for the woman to hand her a pen to sign an autograph.

"I watch you almost every night. You come on at six and I watch you and then I start cooking. I remember when that show came on, 'cause in those days I couldn't watch it. My momma made us go to church, so we couldn't watch your show or "Family Ties" or "The Cosby Show" or what's the other one?"

Joi was silent.

"You know, the one in the bar. Sam Malone? "Cheers." We couldn't watch any of them shows. Matter of fact, I saw you on the "Tonight Show" with Johnny Carson. You were on there with George Michaels. You remember doing that show?"

Joi continued to listen to the woman ramble.

"There was one show when you—"

Then she heard his distinctive voice. It sounded rich yet very New York. "Excuse me," he said to Joi with his son's hand clasped to his side and a paperback copy of his novel in the other hand. "I hate to cut your conversation, but I was headed downstairs when it occurred to me that I had an extra copy of *Season* in my bag."

"Who he," the woman asked indignantly.

"Sorry, ma'am," Michael said, and then directed his attention back to ignoring her presence. "You don't read, Joe," he said, and looked at Joi with a smile. "I was wondering if you would like it. That way you can read it and tell me what you think. My Web site is in the book."

"Thank you," Joi said, with the woman still staring at her only twelve inches away. "I'll read it on the plane ride home."

"Great." Then he looked at Joe and said, "Tell Cindy I'll call her, and I'll see you in a few weeks, okay?"

"It's a date."

As he walked away, Joi wanted to look elsewhere, but his stride demanded her attention. His shoulders were broad, and for a split second she could imagine his body, covered head to heels in—

"Excuse me?" Joi asked the fan.

"I was saying if I could ask you to wait here while I called my momma on the phone so she could talk to you. She watches your show also."

Appearing to have heard enough, Joe stood up and said, "Madam, I'm Ms. Weston's bodyguard, and I am going to have to ask you to keep moving so she can catch her plane."

"Bodyguard?" she said in disbelief. "Excuse me, but what she need a bodyguard fo'? Ain't nobody here but me."

Joi picked up her purse, left a tip for the waitress and put on her shades.

"She ain't all that anyway." The woman shouted as Joi opened the book to look at the inscription and walked toward the security gate.

I love your smile and the way you made us all smile every Wednesday night for years. I hope you will enjoy this journey through the Season of Regret.

M. P. Brockmier, II
Summer 2001

Joe and Joi walked away from the angry woman, whom they could still hear mumbling in the background, "Tramp ought to be *glad* somebody want to talk to her has-been ass in the first place."

Seeing her brother's brown eyes claw at the woman

like talons, Joi said, "Do not say a word. That'll only encourage her."

Joe looked back at his sister, cleared his throat loudly and said, "So, what did Mr. Nice Gentleman write? Did he give you his phone number?"

"No, he did not. There are still *some* gentlemen left," she said, and then she thumbed through the pages to find his card. On the back he wrote:

The wedding band tells me you're married, and I am with someone as well. But I would love to talk to you about the entertainment business. 212-555-8071.

"What's on the card," Joe asked as Joi thought about his eyes, the V shape of his muscular torso and scent of his cologne. And then she tore the card up and placed it in her brother's hand. "Okay, I was wrong. He's a dog, too."

Joe laughed aloud. "He tried to mack a married woman in *front* of his woman's brother-in-law? Now that takes balls. I'll have to give him credit for that next time I see him."

As they walked toward the security checkpoint, Joi said, "Just when you think there are some decent men left—"

"There are decent men left. I'm decent. I am not perfect, but I'm decent."

Moving closer to the front of the line, she said, "Yeah, but I forget. Where were you again last night?"

"See you throwing old stuff in my face," Joe replied with a smile.

As Joi prepared to walk through the metal detector, she asked the attendant, "Do you read fiction?"

"Sometimes," the young girl answered.

"Here's a gift for you." Joi handed her the freshly

signed copy of *Season of Regret*. Then she looked back at her brother and said, "I'm just tired of the games, I guess."

A layer of sadness veiled his eyes as he said, "I can tell. Do me a favor? I want you to talk to G.G. I think if you called and talked to her, it would let her know that I am sincere."

"I will, but before I call her," Joi said, walking backward, "you talk to her. Don't ever lose the communication in your marriage. Don't be like——"

"I'm not like Daddy," he said to his sister, who was walking away. "I know who I am."

CHAPTER

6

The afternoon sun splashed orange over the gold-domed Georgia state house. In an African-American cultural arts store, Michael read a passage from *Season of Regret* to the attendees, but as he read, his thoughts took flight.

After receiving a substantial book deal for a book he never wrote, Michael kept most women at arm's length, except for Cynthia, whom he had met years before his newfound fame. He depended on her insight as a school-teacher to assist him in smoothing the transition into parenthood. She advised him not to stifle his son's angst concerning his mother or his adjustment to life in the big city. To allow him to heal at his own pace would be healthier for both of them.

The first year in Gotham was the toughest for Blair. He did not do well in school and had run-ins with several bullies in Harlem. One day he even got on the A train, rode into Manhattan, and hours later Michael got a call from his son who was lost in Little Italy.

Blair complained about the food, about the weather and about the parochial uniform he had to wear to school. After his mother moved from D.C. to find work elsewhere, she and Blair rarely spoke on the phone, and whenever he returned from his visit with his grandmother in Alabama, there were tears in his eyes.

The second year in New York was a little easier for Blair, who grew to enjoy playing in the snow and catching an occasional game at Yankee Stadium with his father in the spring. Eventually he stopped crying at night. Eventually he stopped calling Alabama. Eventually he no longer asked for Robyn.

As he now stood before the large gathering of women, Michael read the words he knew by heart and thought about Joi. He had never been attracted to women his age and could tell she was a few years older, but there was something about her that haunted him even hours after saying good-bye. Her eyes were soft and dark, and when she smiled, they squinted in a way he could not forget. There were streaks of gray in her hair, which she wore pulled back into a bun, and not a wrinkle to be found on her face. Her complexion was dark brown, her lips a sensuous red tone, and her perfume had an airy scent to it as if she had spent time at the ocean.

Reading the last paragraph to the attendees, Michael wondered if Joi would call him. He had no idea what he would say to her since there were three degrees of separation between she and Cynthia. Michael also knew there was a distinct possibility that Cynthia would find out about the enclosed business card, but he had to take the chance.

A force pulled him toward Joi that was larger than lust, and Michael could not put his finger on it. She was attractive, but Cynthia had once been a *Fashion Fair* model. Joi was successful, but successful women had surrounded Michael for as long as he could remember. While he did not understand her magnetism, he knew he could not walk away. He had to know about the woman who was at one time the biggest star on prime-time television.

The attendees clapped as Michael closed the book and took a sip of water from his glass. A few of the women had tears in their eyes after hearing of the jagged pitfalls of the little girl who found out she had a terminal illness. "Any questions?" he asked, and several hands rose immediately.

"Are you married?" a striking woman with tears in her eyes asked.

The women in the room giggled as Michael blushed and said, "No," as he pointed to the next reader for her question.

"Has anyone told you how much you look like that guy?"

"Lenny Kravitz, girl!" another woman shouted loudly.

Michael smiled and pointed to the next woman raising her hand as the other women chuckled like school-girls.

"Personally," the woman said loudly to bring a note of decorum back to the room, "I was amazed by the fact that you were able to get inside this little girl's head." As soon as the rotund lady wearing kente cloth and an African headdress said the words, a number of the other attendees voiced their agreement. "I kept looking at the picture on the back of the book and saying to myself, 'A *brother* could never have written this.' How were you able to understand Paula on this level? Didn't I read that you were an only child?"

"I still am," Michael said, which caused the readers in the room to laugh. As he pulled one of his dreads from his face and tucked it behind his ear, he said, "Believe it or not, when I initially wrote the character, she was a lit-tle Jewish girl."

"Really?" a voice said from the back of the room.

"But the more I wrote, the more I understood her motivation. Often," he said as he took off his jacket, which caused a number of the women to sigh quietly, "when you write, you throw words on the paper like an abstract painter. Then you shape the words and even brush them like a sculptor to find the art in what you've written. So the more I carved this story out of the pages, the more it appeared that the thoughts and themes I wanted to convey would be clearer if the character came from the African-American experience."

"And what did you want to convey?" a lady asked before Michael pointed to her for her question.

"Six months of joy. In the chapter,"—Michael walked through the crowd—"entitled Six Months of Joy, Paula looks at the people around her. This is a little girl who came from nothing. Who was molested, who was homeless, who at one time had used drugs. After cleaning herself up, she watched the old people and noticed that they were constantly looking back to the good ole days, and she looked at the young people and noticed they couldn't wait to grow up. And as she says, 'in between darkness and nothingness there's light.' In this novel, Paula finds light, and the light is a metaphor for more than bliss or happiness. And instead of her being content in life for about six months, she makes it her goal, since she had such a horrible childhood, to enjoy every moment of the rest of her life. And that was the message we—I wanted to leave the reader with in this novel. I wanted them to find their light, whatever it may be, and to hold on to it."

There was the staggered sound of a woman clapping in the front row, and then others soon joined her. Michael smiled at his son sitting in the first row as the readers voiced their approval for the pearls of insight he had shared with them.

Michael answered the readers' questions and signed their books for well over an hour, after which he gave a radio interview and taped an interview at CNN. Before he knew it, he and Blair were in a car and being whisked toward Hartsfield International Airport.

"So tell me," he asked his son, who laid his head on his father's lap on the backseat of the limo. "You always wanted to come to Atlanta. How was it?"

"Boer-ring," the nine-year-old said as he buried his face in the warmth of Michael's thigh. "We didn't even get to see the Braves play."

"Good point," Michael smiled, and then retrieved the car phone to call Ani. "Next time maybe we will hit Turner Field. How about that?"

"The Braves *suck!*"

Since everything about the South was always superior to things he found in the North, Michael was shocked as he laughed aloud with his son. "Okay . . . no Braves."

Ani's boyfriend, Johnny, answered after the first ring. "Yeah!"

"Man, you really need to learn some phone etiquette."

"Wussup, nigga," Johnny said, laughing. "I thought you were on the road this weekend?"

"Actually, I'm calling you from down south. I just had to pop in and do a signing and this thing on TV and then fly back. I didn't want to stay overnight this time because I brought Blair."

"Well, watch out for them crackers. Don't come back here hung!" he said, laughing as if he was intoxicated. "Let me get her for you."

As Johnny called for Ani, Michael's fingers touched the inch-long scar Johnny had left on his forehead after their encounter. The two men had scuffled in the entrance of the hallway until security broke them up by threatening to call NYPD. Michael went to the hospital to get patched up, and a week later he called Ani again. Once more she hung up on him. Then taking a chance and returning to the Bronx when he knew Johnny was at work, he buzzed her intercom. After speaking to her through the intercom for five minutes, Ani told him he could not come up, but he could call her to discuss the manuscript later that night.

During their one-hour conversation, Michael told Ani that he carried her novel with him everywhere he went and told her about his publishing connection. He then asked for her permission to share *Season of Regret* with a friend.

Immediately Ani told him, "No." She said she had changed her mind about the possibility of being published. After speaking with her a little longer, Michael found out the real meaning as to why she did not want to be published.

"You read my novel, so you'll understand when I say I'm afraid of the light," she said, and made a noise that sounded like she was sucking air through a straw. "Just like my character, I guess."

"Why?"

"I have a health problem. I have severe asthma," Ani said with a heavy breath, "and if I get published, it would put a lot of stress on my condition."

"I'm sure my friend could work it out so you would rarely have to travel. For someone with your skills that shouldn't be a problem."

"I'm not interested. Thank you for calling me, though.

I am just glad"—her voice weakened—"that you can see something in my work." She hung up the phone.

A month later Michael once again called Ani when he felt confident Johnny would be at NYU. This time he told her he had dropped out of the creative writing course and wondered if she would tutor him. He offered her the money he was paying for tuition for her services and agreed to pay her in advance.

Admiring his tenacity, Ani agreed to do so; but only if he could e-mail her passages from his novel, and she would correct them by way of e-mail and return them to him.

"I don't mind coming over," Michael said. "It's a straight shot on the four and—"

"Let me tell you something. You must never come by here. Okay? You can mail the check to my apartment, but if you come over, the agreement is off. Understand?"

The plan worked, and after five months of tutoring Michael proudly submitted his novel to Pamela Wilson, but was summarily turned down. Sitting in her office, she told Michael that her initial idea might not have been a wise decision. She asked him to outline his thoughts for the piano book, and she would see if she could generate some interest with one of the editors specializing in nonfiction.

Faced with the possibility of never being able to pitch her another novel, Michael reached into his backpack and pulled out the first ten pages of *Season of Regret*. He would carry portions of Ani's work with him and study how she would turn phrases, in the hopes that it would influence his writing style.

"Let me show you something else I've been working on," he said, and swallowed his chagrin as if it were a dusty lump of coal.

Looking at the disheveled pages extended toward her, Pam took them and said, "I got more shit on my desk than in a horse barn. Leave it and let me get back to you on this in a couple of—"

"Now or never, Pam," Michael said, regretting the words as soon as they passed his lips. "This is the best thing—I've ever written, and all you need to do," he said, and then paused, in search of the courage to stop himself before doing the wrong thing. "All you need to do is to read the first page. If you don't like it, I'll leave, and we can still be friends."

Pam leaned back in her chair and stared at Michael as if she saw a different side to his personality. She said in a flat tone, "Then, I'll take a pass. But thank you very much."

Biting his lip, Michael reached for the pages. Then Pamela said, "One second." Pulling the pages from his grasp, she read the opening, and just as they had done to Michael and his counselor earlier, the words stole her breath.

Intrigued by what she saw, Pamela asked him if she could take whatever he had of the manuscript home with her to read. "I'll call you tomorrow and let you know if this is what we're looking for. Deal?"

The next morning before eight she called. Michael was half asleep, having played in The Past-Time Paradise until 3:00 A.M.

"Michael, wake your butt up!"

"I'm up, I'm up," he said, wondering who would be calling him so early.

Then he looked at the clock and heard her say, "I

need to see the entire manuscript, yesterday. Do what you have to do to get it here!"

Within a week he was offered a two-book deal, and *Season* was scheduled to be on shelves the following year.

After the meeting, Michael walked into the plush lower Manhattan offices of Charisma publishing with the mindset that if he could not level with anyone else, he had to level with Pam. She was the first girl he had ever kissed. The first person who had ever seemed to notice a special quality about him. Michael and Pam had a history, and if he was to go through with this, if anything was ever made public, it would affect her as well.

"Well, Mr. Brockmier," Pam said as she met him in the reception area. "You are, indeed, the buzz here this morning."

"Glad to, umm—Glad to be here."

"I would imagine. I'm just glad that my old playground friend," she said as she looked at the receptionist, "is going to be a best-selling author. Vivian, let's take his hat size now, 'cause in a few months, he won't be able to talk to peons like you and me."

The ladies laughed, but Michael wanted to put an end to the indecision in his heart. "Listen," he said softly. "Can we go back to your office for a second?"

"Yeah, sure," she replied, and cleared her throat. "Oh, yeah, Miss Vivian, if I have any calls, *please* hold them for me. I'm—"her voice went up an octave and she rolled her *rs*—"meeting with an author!" The ladies laughed, and Michael smiled with the knowledge that every word she said made what he was about to do more difficult.

After walking into a cubicle with framed pictures of white children at play on the desk, she said, "So, what's up?"

"Why can't we use your office to talk for a second?" Michael remained standing as Pam sat down.

"No, the office we used before was not my office. That was one of the senior editors' offices. You wanna know where my office is? Look down the hallway. See that desk with the ficus plant on it? That's where I take your calls. I wish that other office was mine."

"Damn. They got you sitting in the hallway? By the Pepsi machine?"

"It's temporary. Trust me—" Then they were interrupted by a woman in what appeared to be an expertly tailored brown suit.

"I am so sorry to drop in like this, but I was headed to lunch and wondered if you had made it in yet," she said, extending her hand toward Michael. "I'm Janessa Harvey. I have heard so many wonderful things about you, and in fact, a friend of mine at your father's old publishing house had the opportunity to actually work on *One Witness*. So to finally meet you is an honor. We're so glad to have you on board."

Michael shook the large, rawboned woman's hand as Pam said, "Michael, Janessa is the senior editor I was telling you about."

"They give me credit for acquiring this book, but to be honest, this will be Pam's baby."

Michael looked at Pam's beaming face.

"She found it and she went after you, and for years I would ask her, 'Are we going to *ever* get anything to read from you.' And when she walked into my office with that manuscript, we were all taken aback. No offense, but a lot of people like you—with fathers or mothers who were great writers—are not necessarily in their parents' league. I really think you will break that trend."

"Thank you. I guess—I owe it all," Michael said as he

looked back toward his friend once again and then directed his attention to the editor. "I owe it all to Pam."

"Pam, would you all like to join me for lunch. I'm meeting with an agent for about five minutes to pick up a proposal, but then we can grab a bite."

"Sure. I would, but I don't know what Michael's plans are."

"Ahh, no. I'm still playing in the Village almost every night, plus my son gets out around two; so I need to get out of here in a few."

"Okay, that's fine. I've talked to your agent already and told her we would like to sit down and discuss something a little longer termed in the future because we would like for you to one day be one of our cornerstone authors. To be honest, I truly believe you have the makings to do just that."

After she left, Pam pinched her elbows to her waist, thoughtfully picked at the balls of lint on her pants and looked up at Michael. "I cannot believe," she whispered, "that you turned down lunch with Janessa L. Harvey. That woman is one of the most powerful women in publishing in this city. Three publishing houses are begging her to join them. How many sisters are that powerful in publishing? People are trying to get on her schedule three months from now for lunch, and you turned her down? 'Cause you have to play in the Village tonight?"

"I turned her down 'cause I have to pick up my son. I'm sorry."

"Anyway, Michael. The publishing business," she said in an even quieter tone, "is very cutthroat. Just like any business. But for some reason in publishing and music the—"

"I didn't write the book." Pam's lips froze mid-sentence as Michael blurted out the words. This was his window of opportunity to redeem himself. "That's what I have been trying to tell you from day one. I didn't write the book."

"What you mean is you had someone edit it for you?"

"No. This is—What I mean to say is I found—"

"You found a book doctor?" More silence. "If that's what you are saying," she whispered in a quieter tone, "it's fine. You wrote part of this book, and someone else helped you with the writing of the rest of it. It happens in this business. Especially with celebrities or whatever. Let me tell you something." As Michael sat down, Pam rolled her chair closer to him. "I have been with Charisma since I was nineteen years old. It's the first job I ever had. So what if I started in the mailroom. It felt good to say I was in publishing. When I started here, there were about three of us on this floor. Publicity, art, editorial were all white, white, white. Then things started happening about seven years ago when they brought Janessa in and moved me to the glorified title of editorial assistant. What that means here is that I read unsolicited manuscripts for the most part, get doughnuts and drive authors around when they are in town. I'm a gofer. I've been a gofer for too many years. I could have left. I could make more, I guess, with a few of the other houses, but this is personal. I refuse to allow them to break me. I am going to make senior editor with *this* company. And that office you and I sat in before, that will be my office. You can believe that."

Michael inhaled quietly. He had to tell her before they both got any deeper in the situation.

"This is my shot. You hear me," she continued, pointing toward the copy of *Season of Regret* on the desk. "This is my book, my ticket out of the hallway. This is my opportunity to have two-hundred-dollar lunches at the Russian Tea Room. This is my chance to realize a dream

I had since I was in grade school. So what if we are going to profit on the name your father left you. So what if you used a book doctor to *help you* fine-tune the book. This is our shot, and in life, trust me, you don't get many opportunities like this."

Pam leaned back and allowed her fingers to intertwine over her midriff. Janessa Harvey walked by the cubicle one last time before heading out the door, and Michael looked at his high school friend and said, "Pam?"

After a hesitation, she replied, "Yes?"

"I just wanted to tell you that—I came here today to tell you—" Michael watched the disappointment of a lost dream settle on his friend's face and heard his window of opportunity close before he said a word. "I came to say that I'm excited to be a part of the Charisma family."

Pam's smile appeared more so in her eyes than on her lips as she said, "And we are glad you're here."

After the meeting Michael called Ani to tell her what happened. As he waited for her to answer the phone, he hoped that she would not expose him as a fraud to the publisher. Choosing his words with care, he told her about the events of the day and added that if she had a problem with him using her work, he would immediately call and cancel the deal with the publisher.

After a moment whereby she appeared to ingest everything that was said, Ani replied, "This is wrong. This is *so* fucking wrong."

"I know, I know. I was sitting there and she shot me down and I could tell by her face that she was looking for this profound, overwhelming piece of literature. So before I knew it, I reached into the bag and—"

"But no. This is sooooo fucking wrong, though."

He sighed. "I'm not making any excuses. I should have known better."

"Years ago, my father would tell me that to every advantage, there's a distinct disadvantage. The beauty queen sits at home at night because everyone thinks she has a date. The muscle-bound guy can't buy a shirt 'cause his neck is too big. The smartest kid in the class is alienated. But my father also added that to every disadvantage, there was an advantage."

"So?"

"What I am saying is this. No, this is not ethical. Hell, it may even be illegal. But there is an advantage to your situation."

"And that would be what?"

"I love to write. If I could, I'd lie in my bed and write on my yellow pad from sunup to sundown, I would. I love creating fictitious worlds that people enter and forget how to leave. I even love coming up with the perfect eye-catching title. But the thought of standing in front of a crowd and reading to them gives me the shakes. Makes me almost nauseous. Going to a radio station and having people hear your voice all over town? Having people ask you for your autograph? To me that's a hard concept to wrap my thoughts around. It's a part of this business I always knew I could never do."

"Listen, Ani, are you suggesting that—"

"Michael, to *every* disadvantage, there is an advantage. I'm strong in the one area you are a little weak, for now. And you are definitely strong where I am sure I will forever be weak. Yes, this is unethical. Yes, it could be embarrassing if anything came out, which I don't see how it could. But you know something? It's a chance I am willing to take to have people enter this world I've created."

"Ani, you are aware that—"

"All I want to do is write. Not promote. Not even make millions of dollars. I don't want my face on the back cover of a book, and I don't want people going to the store and asking for my work. None of that is important to me. All I want to do is tell stories, and in my heart I know you are my advantage."

After a few modifications, *Season of Regret* was resubmitted to Charisma Books, and Michael and Ani's literary odyssey had begun.

"Hello?"

"How are you feeling today?" Michael asked. "Didn't sound like you were doing too good last night."

Almost out of breath, she said, "Better. I'm doing . . . I'm doing much better. How was Hot-lanta?"

"Atlanta was amazing. Had a great turnout at the store, but then I always get mad love down here."

"That's good. I wish I could come with you sometime."

"So do I. I would love for you to just see these women's reactions. It makes it all worthwhile."

"What questions did they ask?"

"Same ones," Michael said, rolling one of his son's tender locks around his finger. As Blair peacefully slept on his lap, he continued, "How could a man write a story like this, where do you get your ideas for stories, how do I get into the publishing business—"

"Same old, same old, it—"

"It never changes. But the reason I called is to tell you about the bonus check."

"What bonus check?"

"In my—our contract with Charisma, there's a clause that says if we sell a certain number of books, we get a fifty-thousand-dollar bonus, and I found out we hit it last week."

"That's great!"

"But this time, I can't give you fifty percent of it."

Ani took a sip of air and said, "In all fairness, we only agreed to do fifty-fifty on the advance. I wasn't expect-ing any of the—"

"I'm giving it all to you."

"What?"

"Everything," Michael said. "I don't want it."

"But you're entitled to the bonus. You're out there on the road almost every weekend, and it's because of that the book is doing so well."

"The book is doing so well because you are an incred-ible author." There was a heavy silence as Michael lis-tened to the sound of his conscience. The sounds that would keep him up at night had made a return visit. "I feel a little sick doing this anyway, although I know it's helping both of us."

"No. Put that money in a trust fund for Blair. I can't accept it. You worked hard to earn that."

"The money is yours, Ani, and that's the end of the conversation. You also helped me with my novel as well. By the way, how did you like the rewrites?"

Michael could hear her staggered breathing on the phone. "To be honest, Michael," and then Ani hesitated before saying, "I don't like it, and I hate to be so blunt."

"What do you mean? I did everything you told me. I put the imagery in there, I tried to write it so it would feel lyrical, I—"

"You tried too hard, and it shows. It looks . . . It reads like you're pushing the narrative and not allowing it to come to you. Several of your plot points are contrived to say the least, and in a number of places you slip into telling the story again instead of showing the story. We've talked about that. You can't force art. I think we can"—heavy breath—"rewrite this and get it up to standards, but it's going to take a while. At least two or three months."

"I don't have three months. They're ready to shoot the cover, and I've been stalling them. Everyone wants to see it," he said, running his fingers through his locks. "And you don't think I have anything to work with? Not even something we can fix in the next couple of days?"

"The plot is antiquated, Michael. The premise is okay, but not what the readers today will expect. It's just not fast paced enough. Ask Pam for an extension."

"I already did, but she doesn't want to lose the momentum. Since *Season* is doing so well, they promoted her to senior editor, and she has a lot riding on the next novel."

"Well, do this. Take your manuscript to her and see what she says. And just like before, if you don't think she likes it, use mine. I have another novel that I think is even better than *Season*."

In a pained whisper, he asked, "What's the title?"

"Don't laugh," Ani said. "It's entitled *Mule-Drawn Wagon*. Can you believe a woman who has never been as far south as Virginia is writing a novel entitled *Mule-Drawn Wagon*? And you know what the topper is? It's literary, and it's head and shoulders above *Season*."

Reluctantly Michael said, "I'll think about it. I just see myself falling into this trap I can't get out of."

"Meaning?"

"I tried to come clean with Pam once again when I was at Charisma. A part of me thinks she knows something is up but doesn't want me to tell her. But then I found out she was made a senior editor based on the success of the book, and I just couldn't burst her bubble. Besides, I think it's best to insulate her at this point in the event something comes out. Pam has her issues, but I don't want to take her down with me."

Ani was silent as Michael continued. "I'm a fraud. That's the bottom line. I'm fake. Mom used to tell me that my father would work on a *sentence* for over an hour." He shook his head in amazement of his father's dedication to his craft. "One sentence, Ani. While other people read fiction for entertainment, this man would read the thesaurus. I made more on the advance for *Season* than he received in his entire life from this business, and I go to signings and answer questions like, 'Boxers or briefs?' It can't be just me. Isn't something terribly wrong with this situation?"

"I see your point. Believe me, I do. But we've made our bed, and we must come to peace with it. No one will ever find out unless you tell them. You know we won't tell anyone because I need you as much, if not more, than you need me. We're in this thing together. And if it works, they will release your novel next year, and no one will be the wiser."

"It's not even about people finding out, though."

"At the risk of sounding like an enabler, is what you are doing all that bad? Yes, we are misrepresenting the truth. You will get no argument from me about that, and right after I told you it was okay to use my words, I felt sullied. I swear that first night I picked up the phone to call you and tell you not to do it ten times if I picked it up once. But is it the crime of the century?"

"Don't go there, Ani. Yeah, I'm—We're published, but at what price? We have a story that has touched a lot of people's lives. I'm touched when women tell me they know a Paula, or like the sister in San Diego who told me she *was* Paula, but no matter what spin we put on it, it's wrong.

"Remember back in the seventies and eighties when

a lot of blacks were never even given the opportunity to get their books published because the powers that be decided that blacks didn't read? How many *Native Sons* or *Bluest Eyes* do you think are in attics or closets today because people gave up hope of them ever being published? How many *The Color Purple* or *Invisible Men* are in graves because they were never seriously considered? Because they came after my father and before Terry McMillan. Ani, we lost an entire generation of writers telling our stories. So if anything blows up in regard to *Season*, how will it affect the next generation of black writers? We have to be mindful of that."

Above a whisper, Ani answered, "Good point."

"I tried to look at the greater good; but I feel I'm sinking in quicksand, and every time I do a signing, every time I speak on the radio, I get deeper and deeper in something I can't get out of."

"Books, words can heal." Ani paused and then added, "All my life, Michael, I knew there was a reason I was catching so much hell. It was to help others. I know this as sure as I know I'm black. The end justifies the means. And I know that's one of the world's oldest clichés, but it's true.

"You always tell me that women ask you how could you understand Paula, and the reason they are asking that question, whether they know it or not, is because to write her well, you have to know about the papier-maché-covered shoe box. You have to know what it feels like to sit next to it at the front door of the prom. To write Paula, you must see girls pass by you dressed in pastel chiffons and boys in tuxedos wearing butterfly bow ties. You must ask them for their ticket and see them mock you with their eyes; that's if they see you at all. To write this child, you must leave the prom before it's half over and sit in your room, listen to your mother sexing a stranger 'cause she did not expect you back so soon, watch the evening news and cry. You must make up lie"—she paused—"after lie, after lie about this boy who was in love with you but lived in Nevis. How he wanted to marry you after high school, which is why you could not stay at the prom because he was so jealous. That's the place you must come from to write this girl.

"My best friend, Lisa, was a cheerleader. She was part of the 'in' crowd, but she always had time for me. We'd talk on the phone for hours, and sometimes I would help her with her homework. But while she was out partying and allowing me to live vicariously through what she was doing, know what I was doing? Studying. My mission in life was to show her—show my friends in high school—that in ten years, I'd be a lawyer, a doctor . . . maybe even a novelist. I would return to the reunion and show them all where to stick it.

"When it came time for the reunion . . . Lisa married a prominent doctor, has three children, works for Paramount Pictures and lives on Sutton Place. I could not leave my apartment here in the Bronx to even attend the get-together, which was ironically two miles from where I live.

"So you can back out if you like, because I don't want you to do anything that makes you lose sleep. But I told you a long time ago; it has to be about something bigger than the fame. Bigger than the fortune. Having that woman come up to you and thank you in San Diego is bigger than anything Charisma can do for you. She knew about the shoe box, Michael. She has her own Lisa, and as long as I know that, I have no problem closing my eyes at night."

Silence.

"Thank you," he sighed. "I needed to hear that."

"Michael, Lincoln signed the Emancipation Proclamation. Do you really think he did it *only* to free the slaves? He weighed how many people he would help versus how many he would hurt and made a decision. We entered World War II. Do you think we did it only because of the Holocaust? Some things are black and white. Most things are found somewhere in the middle. Tonight, somewhere, there's a Paula out there, and if she has not read it already, she will read *Season of Regret* and find solace in what you and I have done. Next time you're ready to tell Pam, ask yourself how many people we *may* hurt by what we're doing? Then ask yourself how many people we're helping every day."

"Oh, well," Michael sighed, as the limo got closer to the Delta Airlines terminal, "enough of talking about that. Tell me this. Why won't you ever let me come over to the Bronx and meet you? It's been what, two years, and all we ever do is talk on the——"

"I've told you a thousand times. This is a dangerous neighborhood, and to be honest, because of my condition, I just don't like taking company. Half the time I'm on oxygen; half the time I'm medicated. There's just not a good time to come by."

"You know I'm going to have to meet you one day. You can't keep avoiding me."

Breathing heavier than before, Ani said, "One day. Just not any day soon. Okay?"

"Okay."

"Oh, yeah, one other thing. How's Blair doing?"

"He enjoyed returning to the South, although we were only here for a few hours. I took him to this soul food place in the West End area, and he ate grits and crawdads or whatever people eat down here. You know, the first year was tough. Waking up at night and sometimes crying for hours it seemed for Robyn. But now that a few new kids have moved into the neighborhood, it's working out. It's not perfect, but it's doable."

"I can see the contentment in your words."

"You think?"

"Definitely," Ani replied. "When you talk about him, your tone changes. I can see that change also in your prose. It's not as—It's not as spirited, you might say, and that's a good thing."

"Once again, the end justifies," he said, "the means. I'll call when I get back in the city."

As the driver gave Michael's overnight bag to the sky-cap and then opened the door for him, Blair lifted his head and looked around sleepily.

"We're here," Michael said.

Blair yawned, wiped his mouth and then looked at his father and asked, "Daddy? Why don't you write books by yourself?"

CHAPTER

7

Some days are just born ugly. They awake and cast their willowy shadows across fields and depress everything and everyone unfortunate enough to be under their presence.

On such a fall afternoon, two months removed from her Hollywood reunion, Joi looked outside her window and searched the rain for answers. Nothing about it seemed beautiful. Nothing romantic, poetic or remotely calming. Sitting in front of the television, Joi watched a Cary Grant movie, but in her mind she revisited the last conversation she had with her daughter.

"Angie, will you be back for dinner?"

"I'm going out."

"With who?"

"Friends. Just hanging. Why?"

"Because I was cooking dinner for—"

"No can do tonight, Joi, see ya." Angie walked out the door into the garage, and before the door closed, Joi could hear her daughter deactivate her car alarm.

Angie was the president of her junior class, a member of the debate team, and although Cecil had spoken to her about the possibility of auditioning for a feature film, she wanted a career far from the spotlight—in dentistry.

Joi dropped the dish towel she held in her hands to the floor and ran toward the door. "Since when are you going out on a school night?"

"Since you said I could come in at midnight when I turn seventeen."

"And?"

"I'll be seventeen next week, Joi. Geez, I know you're not going to rag me about coming home an hour later." And then Angie paused dramatically. "Besides, I'll be home around nine anyway. I'm going to pick up some shoes, and then I'll come home to get dressed."

"Where's the party?"

Angie looked at her mother as she opened the door to her car, smiled and then returned to her. "Listen. I'm growing up. I'll be all right. I know it's hard for you to see that, but just think, a year from now I'll be enrolling in UCLA."

Joi looked at her daughter, not impressed by what she had said.

The sarcasm left Angie's face as she put her arms around her mother and kissed her on the cheek. "If you must know, I'm going out with Cassie, and we're going to shop for shoes to match these outfits she bought for us." Then Angie held her mother closely as if she wanted to say more.

Joi stood still, her arms lethargic, the words lodged in her throat.

Angie backed away and asked, "Is that okay?"

Joi stood in the doorway as her daughter sat behind the wheel of the current year sports car and backed out of the driveway. And then she waved at her mother for the last time and drove away.

As the garage door returned to the concrete, Joi thought

about the last time the three of them had eaten dinner together. It had been months. With her hectic shooting schedule and Phillip spending much of his time working on television projects, it was rare they met at home before ten at night. But since she was not shooting, and Phillip's meeting was cancelled, Joi had prepared a special Italian dinner. Unfortunately, it would be an intimate dinner for two.

Phillip arrived home a little before eight, and he and Joi had dinner as she watched "Hollywood Homes" on TV and he read Variety.

"You know they're casting for that big budget cow Con Artist," he said without looking at his wife. "It's not public knowledge as of yet, but I had a meeting, and it was mentioned. Someone connected to the film asked me to ask you if you would consider it."

"Not interested," Joi said, and looked at the phone.

"You haven't heard the offer. What I suggest you do is run it by Cecil to see what he thinks."

Joi looked at the clock, and it was half past eight. She could taste cotton in her mouth, and she had no idea why. She pushed her plate away from her with her thumbs.

"Not hungry?" And before she could answer, Phillip noisily turned the page and said, "I hear Universal is putting one-fifty just into advertising for that new Murphy movie. Can you imagine? But," he said, and turned the page again, "they'll easily make one hundred back in merchandising, so it's a wash."

Joi looked at the wall for the cordless, and it was not there. She then noticed it was beside Phillip's plate. As she reached for it, he said, "I'm expecting an important call from D.C., so please click over." He turned the page again and mumbled, "I might get to work with ABC on a project dealing with AIDS in prisons. They're going to call me tonight to get my thoughts on a few things. Besides, who're you calling?"

"Angie. She went to the store, and I need her to pick something up for me."

After dialing the number, Joi heard a voice with a pronounced Asian accent say, "Hello? Hello? Is anyone there?"

"I'm sorry, wrong number."

Hitting the red button on the phone, Joi looked at the ceiling as she tried to remember Angie's cellular phone number. "Phil?"

"Yeah," he said, putting the paper on the floor beside his chair. Then he said, "I cannot believe that Spike Lee and John Singleton are going to—"

"Listen, what's Angie's number. Yours is 0191 and hers is 0719, right?"

"Yeah. I can't believe they are going to produce a—"

"I just called that. At least I thought I called that number," she said, and redialed the digits. "Must have dialed too fast."

Joi put the phone back to her ear and heard the voice again. "Hello?"

As soon as she heard the man's voice, she panicked, yet showed calm. But deep inside she knew her life would never be the same.

Joi and Phillip ran through red lights, on top of street curbs and on the median to get to the emergency room. As Phillip drove with his horn blaring and blinkers flashing, Joi pressed the floorboard on her side of the car as if she were in the driver's seat.

As soon as they arrived, reporters and TV news crews surrounded their vehicle. Burley hospital security personnel ran to their red SUV and told Phillip to drive to a special discreet entrance, but Joi could not wait and flung open the door, pushed her way through the crowd and ran into the hospital. As she ran, miscellaneous voices from the media shouted, "How does it feel!" and "Joi, do they expect your daughter to live!"

Once in the emergency room, Joi was taken to Angie's bedside. A yellowish solution mixed with blood was caked to the sheets. She looked at her mother and incoherently spoke words Joi couldn't understand.

"Boo'da," she said, calling her daughter by her childhood nickname, "it's going to be all right. Okay? Just relax."

"I just . . . wanted to say . . . I was not drinking." She tried to lick her badly swollen lips, but could not will her tongue out of her mouth.

"Honey," Joi said, too bold to show a tear, "you don't have to explain anything. Just relax."

"Cassie wanted—Cassie wanted drive. I . . . let her 'cause I didn't know . . . how to find—" Then her words froze like a piece of ice.

"Boo'da, Angelina, don't even try to talk."

Angie's eyes expressed sentiments the rest of her body could not. "I had—soda. That's all, Mommy. Honest."

"Baby, I love you, and I just want you to relax. I'll see you through this." Joi reached down to hold her hand and noticed it was in a temporary cast. "I'm going to see you through this. I swear to you. I'll be here for you until—

"Where . . . Daddy?"

"Parking the car. He'll be up shortly."

"I want Daddy," Angie said as a tear slid past the stitches under her eye. There was a collar around her neck, a blood-stained bandage on her forehead, and Joi was told before going in that Angie's body had sustained at least ten fractures.

"Shhh, be quiet, Boo'da. I just want you to calm yourself."

"I want . . . my daddy."

Joi ran her fingers on the outside of her face, just as she would when she would read Angie bedtime stories. She traced her daughter's eyebrows and lips slowly and felt the warmth of what would be her last breath on the tips of her fingers.

The code blue alarm went off violently to alert the staff, and immediately the hospital personnel rushed into the room.

Joi was elbowed against the wall by a man twice her size

who checked Angie's vitals, looked at her pupils and snatched the paddles from the wall before yelling, "Give me one-fifty! Twenty CCs of lydocaine and **clear!**"

Joi was escorted out of the room by a nurse's aide and reluctantly walked down the hall. *The woman said something to her, but she never heard a word. To Joi, everything was quiet, almost surreal. People ran back and forth in slow motion as the woman sat her down, but Joi could not feel the lady's presence. And then she saw a bright yellow light leave the hallway in a flash. Joi closed her eyes and reopened them to find her husband's face.*

"Where is she? Have you gone in to see her yet?"

Joi stared at her husband and said, "Phillip? She's gone. *You just missed her. She's gone bye-bye.*"

As Joi reflected on the sorrowful night she looked down at her hands and clasped her fingers together and could feel her daughter's life slip through them once again.

Years had passed since her season of regret, which had no ending, had begun. Joi sat on a lounger on the patio of their home crocheting yet another afghan with her cordless phone just beyond her sun tea. From her viewpoint she could see the crystallized waters of St. Petersburg complete with ships decorated with colorful mastheads and families enjoying each other's company on the shore.

"You love lounging out there, don't you?" Phillip asked as he stood in the doorway buttoning his shirt.

"To be honest, I love just doing nothing," she said with her eyes fixated on the triple stitch she had just learned.

"I can understand that. Hey, are you sure you don't want to ride to that council meeting with me? It might be a little boring, but we could go to Vito's afterward."

"Naw," she said as the phone rang. "I have a standing date on Thursday night to watch television. But you have a nice time and do what you can to save the state. Maybe I'll help you next week."

"Funny," Phillip said as he walked back inside the house.

With the receiver pinched to her ear and eyes focused on the stitch, Joi answered, "Hello?"

"Yes, is this Joi?"

"Speaking."

"Cool. Well, I won't go into the who-do-you-think-this-is-calling routine. This is Michael Price Brockmier, II."

Joi's eyes rose from the yarn as she looked down at the waters in the distance.

"How are you?"

"I'm, umm—fine. I'm fine."

"I was talking to Joe, and he mentioned your husband's name to me. And since I'm coming down to Florida in a few weeks for a signing and to get some writing done, I thought I'd check and see if he was listed in directory assistance, and that's how I got this number. I hope it's okay."

"Honey," Phillip said, walking onto the patio adjusting his tie. Then his voice lowered as he noticed she was on the phone. "How does this tie look?"

"Fine," she replied. "This—This is just a friend of mine from New York." Since Michael had heard her lie, she knew she had sent the wrong message and immediately regretted doing so.

"Wonderful. Well, if you need me, hit me on the cell. I'm headed out." Phillip gave his wife a tight-lipped smile and returned into their home.

"Was that your husband?"

"Yeah. He's real active in the local political machine, and he's—We're making a run for state office."

"That's very admirable. Maybe he can come to the signing with you. The more the merrier."

"Maybe he will."

After a hesitation, Michael said, "So, how are you adjusting to life in Florida?"

"It's okay. It's slow down here, but relaxing. I'm originally from New York City. Grew up in Brooklyn and spent a lot of time in the rat race of L.A."

"I've never lived outside the city, and my son moved back up here with me a couple of years ago from the South. I thought it was going to be a rough adjustment for him, but after the first year he's enjoying it, for the most part."

"For the most part?"

"I think he misses the wide-open spaces of the South and being able to play on grass instead of asphalts, which is really all we have where we live. And while I hate to admit it, there is no substitute for—for a mother. But she hasn't called him in months, and I don't know where she's living now."

"I'm sorry to hear that."

"She was in D.C. Then she moved to Ohio and then New Orleans and God only knows where now."

"It's good you have him. That type of instability is not good for a child."

"I agree," Michael whispered. "So do you have any children? I don't think Joe mentioned you having any—"

"No."

"Oh." Pause. "Never had the time, huh? I know a lot of people caught up in the industry sometimes put off having children until—"

"My daughter—Our daughter was killed by a drunk driver."

Joi could not hear Michael on the other end of the phone. Then he said, "Must have been painful."

"Painful?" she replied as she rested the crochet needle on her lap.

"To lose a child. I have been a father for a while, but I just became a dad a few years ago. And to have to go through that I can only imagine."

"Painful," she repeated, and focused on a ship with a tall purple masthead. "I read something on you in *Ebony* that mentioned after your father's passing you stopped talking for years. Even before I met you, I wondered about that level of pain. And then I lost my child, and I understood. You stopped talking; some stop eating. I am sure others find it difficult to trust again. I just could not stop crying. I—listen to me rambling. Yes, it was very painful."

"No, please . . . continue."

"No. We've hardly said hello and here I am telling you about all of this—"

"Go ahead. I understand you." Silence. "You know, after my dad killed himself, it was months before anyone would ask me to share what I felt. It's a dark place, and people don't want to go into it with you. And I appreciate that. But how else are we supposed to heal. So for months—hell, even years—I sat and let the thing fester. I wanted to talk, but there was no one to speak to. I blamed my mother, I blamed the publishing industry and of course I blamed myself. Did you guys talk to a professional?"

"Yes. Unfortunately it didn't do us alot of good."

"I never really talked to anyone about my father's death. My ex-wife, Robyn, when we first met, would always change the subject. I had this girlfriend, Joe's sister-in-law, who would allow me to open up a little, but eventually she, too, wanted me to move on."

"Yeah. How many times have I heard those words?"

"People love you," Michael said, "and they are trying to help; but sometimes they do not know how."

"What do you miss most about your father? Or should I say having him in your life for such a short period of time?"

"The things he could have taught me. How to change spark plugs. How to put on a condom," he said with a smile in his voice. "How to shave and not get razor bumps. How to love a woman. Simple things."

"You know what losing my daughter robbed me of more than anything else?"

"What?"

"It stole my joy. I don't know if I've had a truly happy day since she left. And the saddest thing is I don't know if I'm ready, even now, to have one."

"I would imagine something that traumatic would almost most have to pull you apart. Have you thought about possibly having another child?"

"Please. That's not a possibility."

"Why not?"

"I am too close to the change to put my body through that."

"I'm shocked that you would tell me you were close to the change."

"Most people are when I mention that. Everyone knows my age after being in Hollywood so long. I have zero vanity, I guess. But for some reason when you lose a child, you feel as if you are putting another child in their space, and that's not what I want to do. God gave her to us—for a season, you might say. God brought her home for a reason, I believe, so I just try to celebrate the dash."

"The dash?"

"At her funeral, the reverend spoke of the dates that are etched on tombstones and said that we're often defined by the number on either side of the dash, but never the dash itself. The dash is the life, and she gave us so much life in her few years here."

"I never looked at it that way."

"I look at a lot of things in different ways. But going back to your question," Joi said as the sun started its descent into the bay. "One of the things it took from us is the closeness. The tragedy helped our marriage in some ways, because we were tested but you know, I used to enjoy lying in bed with him as much as sex. Damn," she said with laughter in her tone, "I'm letting you get all up *in* my business now."

"No, please continue."

"I love my husband."

"We've established that."

"Love him to death. But I used to enjoy lying in bed with Phillip and just holding hands. Just playing footsy. Just looking deeply into his eyes. That to me was even better than sex at times."

"And you lost that after Angie's passing?"

"That's at the top of the list of things that were lost. And of all the things that we no longer have, it's the one that matters the most."

"I wish I could have had someone to talk to myself. But we are all given a hand to play, and we do the best with what we have."

"I love Phillip like crazy."

"I know you do," Michael said. "I know you do."

Two weeks after the conversation with the author, Joi returned home exhausted from a jog through her subdivision. She had beat her personal best time and could feel her body getting stronger. Muscles were in places where soft skin resided before, and it felt good to her emotionally. She sat in their family room and gazed up at her two People's Choice Awards on either side of her Emmy. She had worked so hard for each one of them and after they were presented, she never took the time to appreciate what she had received. But as she took off her sweaty clothes and walked toward the bathroom, in her heart she knew those moments were as good as it would ever be for her professionally.

With the water running in the tub, Joi poured in two cups of Epson salt and a dash of rubbing alcohol to relieve her sore muscles. There was a time when Phillip would join her for her three-mile journey through their neighborhood; but since he had thrown his heart into the political arena, his waistline was expanding due to the number of rubber chicken dinners, and yet one more activity they had shared had gone by the wayside.

In spite of all they had gone through, she had never been seriously tempted to stray from her marital vows. Especially there had been numerous opportunities. Especially the week after he had punched her and she had to go on location to shoot an episode of the TV show in Hawaii. She lay in bed with one of the supporting actors with her hand on his chest, and she could feel his excitement rise on her leg. Every time she moved, the director requested she move back so the continuity would match the previous shots. As soon as the director shouted, "Cut," she walked off the set without speaking to the apologetic actor, returned to her trailer and took a cold shower.

Often she asked herself why she never cheated on Phillip. The excuse he had used for hitting her was because he feared she was cheating on him, when in actuality she had just been talking to a male friend in the parking lot after a cast party. A part of her knew that if she ever cheated, she would then be the type of person that for years she tried to prove to him that she was not. She would be on his level, and she knew she was better than that as a person. But since she had been with only four men in her life, she also wondered how it would feel to be held in the arms of a man who did not bring all the baggage Phillip brought into the bedroom.

As soon as Joi turned off the lights and sat in the tub, the phone rang, but since she had planned for such an occurrence, she had placed the cordless on top of her towel on the floor beside the tub.

"Hello?"

"Hey, lady," Phillip said, "I was just wondering if a FedEx came for me this morning. I'm expecting some documents from Tallahassee."

"I just got back, but there wasn't a note on the door. But then again, sometimes they leave packages——"

"Where were you?"

Joi slumped in the tub and allowed the massaging waters to slide over her shoulders. "Excuse me?"

"Where were you?"

She paused. "Sometimes he leaves packages around to the back of the house if no one is here. I'll see if it's back there when I finish taking my——"

"So you're avoiding my question?"

"Phillip, for Christ sakes, stop acting silly. You've known where I was twenty-four hours a day since the day we were married. Why are you doing this?"

"Doing what?"

"For the last few weeks you've acted suspicious. Have I ever given you a reason to think I was doing anything outside the marriage?"

"What in the hell are you talking about?" he asked. "I just asked where you were. Is that acting suspicious? I thought you might have gone shopping earlier."

Joi closed her eyes and heard the call-waiting click

on the phone. "One—one second, okay? I have a call coming through." She pressed the flash button on the phone and said, "Hello?"

"Hey—yes, Joi?"

"This is Joi."

"Michael Brockmier. Did I catch you at a bad time?"

She closed her eyes and said, "Actually, you did."

"Sorry. I know it's early, but I could call you later, if it's okay."

"No, I mean I can talk. One second please." Joi pressed the flash button again and could hear Phillip speaking to someone in the background. "Phillip?"

"Yes?"

"I have a call coming through. It's my friend from New York if you must know."

"Joi what's going on with you?"

"Nothing. I just feel you want to know everything I am doing, so I am telling you."

"Listen, we'll talk about this when I get home."

"As you wish, Phillip. We'll talk about whatever you want to talk about whenever you want to talk about it. Okay?"

"I have to go." The line went dead.

I can't believe that son of a bitch hung up on me without saying good-bye. "Hello? Michael?"

"Yes? Hey, sorry to call you at a bad time. I just realized it's eleven o'clock. But I found out this morning that the signing in Tampa will be moved up an hour. There's a conflict in the schedule, and they had to change the time. But listen to me assuming you were coming. You never even told me you were coming for sure."

"I'll try. It's in Tampa, and to be honest, I don't cross the bay that often nowadays."

"Why not?" he asked, and there was a sound in the

tone of his voice that seemed to be sincerely interested in her answer.

"I just don't. For years you work hard to be noticed. Then you get to a level of notoriety. Then you get the bodyguard or whatever just to go to the mall, and then you get to my level where no one notices you anymore."

"And you have a problem with that."

"Not so much not being recognized, because I know, as my acting coach used to say, 'fame is a vapor, popularity is an accident and money takes wings,' so I was ready for this phase of life years ago. I just gave so much of myself to the public when I was in the game, you might say, and it feels good to just be to myself now. To just sit," Joi said, "and do nothing for hours." She reached for the sponge in the water, squeezed it between her breasts and allowed the warm water to cascade over her torso.

"It can be exhausting. This year has been a blur for me. I've always enjoyed the interaction with the public, but—but—excuse me," Michael said. "Is that water I hear splashing?"

"Yeah. You kinda caught me taking a bath."

"Oh. I'm sorry. Listen, I can talk to you later if—"

"No. No, that's okay, go ahead. I'm just sitting here marinating."

"You do that, too?"

"As often as I can."

"Have you ever taken a bath with frankincense?"

"The stuff they brought baby Jesus?"

Michael laughed aloud, and there was something in his tone that was deeply erotic. Sensuous, yet infectious and happy. He laughed almost like a teenager. "No, no, what I mean is—Well, yes, I suppose it's the same stuff. But you take a little frankincense, a little basil and a whisper of juniper and it will turn the water red. It's very," he said as his voice rumbled like an engine, "relaxing."

"I'd imagine. I usually just toss in a little Epson salt and I'm done."

"You're kidding me."

"Yep. That's what I did just before you called, actually."

"That's almost like saying—and I hope I am not out of place saying this."

"No, go ahead."

"It's almost like saying you just cook with a little bit of salt. It's a'ight but if you really want to do something special for yourself . . . and your husband, here is what you do. Up here we have a store called the Bath Warehouse where you can get this stuff, but you may have a similar place in your town. You need some chamomile, some yarrow, some stuff called ylang-ylang and a little bit of palmarosa. Put all of that in the bathwater, and it will turn the water Carribean blue. It's erotic. It gives off this aroma that is guaranteed to drive your man out of his mind."

Joi rubbed her fingers over the back of her neck and imagined herself immersed in a hot, sudsy bath with the novelist with the alluring eyes. After clearing her throat, she said, "Did you say yling-a-ling? Where in the hell am I suppose to find yling-a-ling? In the frozen food section at Food Giant?"

"See, you're being silly," Michael said with a smile. "Tell you what, I'll send you a package with everything I just mentioned, and you can try it out—with your husband—and tell me what you think."

"No. I—No, it would not be a good idea."

"I'm sorry. I know you're married, but sometimes I forget how husbands can react to another man calling—"

"No, it's not about that as much as it's about me."

"Meaning?"

"Just don't send it. Besides, if you are creating all these romantic baths, are you taking them alone? I know there must be someone special."

"Cynthia was special for a while, but like I told you, that's over. And for now I'm just ready to be to myself for a while. You know how it is after you've been in a relationship forever and you try to—I'm sorry, I forgot. You've been married for a while, I bet, huh?"

"Well, actually, we'll be married five-ever in March." Michael laughed again. "High school sweethearts, I'd imagine."

"No, but close to it. He was always there for me. I got pregnant early and we knew we'd always be together, so when I decided to move to L.A., he moved with me, and we got married."

"How do you keep the music playing after all these years?"

"It's hard. But to be honest, Michael, we've grown apart," she confessed as her fingertips created a rippling wave in the water. "He's doing his thing and I'm doing mine, but that's okay, because we're still growing together. I don't think we have to be joined at the hip to make our marriage work. We just have to be joined some place deeper inside."

"I like that," he whispered. "I like that a lot."

"I—I love my husband."

"I know."

The night of the signing, Joi was still undecided as to if she should attend. Since she had purchased and read his novel, a part of her wanted to attend so she could ask a few questions in regard to the main character. But even though she had made it clear she was married, she thought attending would send the wrong message.

Joi sat in front of her makeup mirror and looked at the first signs of crow's feet around her eyes. With the back of her hand she tapped the flesh beneath her jaw, which showed the early signs of sagging. *Who am I kidding,* she thought to herself. *This brother more than likely has women half my age chasing him. I can't see him going after me like that. Besides, I made it very clear I was married.* Joi picked up the book with the stark white, textured cover and bold blue print on the front. She turned it over and looked at his picture. For a moment she allowed herself to indulge in the what ifs. After all, Phillip had broken the bonds of their marriage before, and although she told herself she was over it, every time he called in late, she knew he was cheating. Every time a stray hair found itself on his jacket, she considered it evidence.

"You going out?" Phillip asked as he walked into their room wearing only a tee shirt and boxers.

"I'm thinking about it. Just don't know if I should."

"Why?"

"I just don't—Well, you know, it's a book signing. And whenever I go to things like this, authors pitch movie ideas, and sometimes it gets a little old."

"But you haven't been to a signing down here, have you? It might be different."

"Possibly."

"Is it for that Brockmier guy?"

Joi looked at her husband looking at her in the mirror. "How did you know?"

Phillip walked out of the room and said, "Because that's all you were reading for the last few weeks. See, contrary to what you might think, I do pay attention."

Joi found herself wondering, if she had an affair, would

he notice the change in her? Or was his awareness limited to the physical?

"Maybe I should go with you," he added as he returned to their room with a bath towel draped over his shoulder. "I might just get back into reading. I think the last book I read was . . . was . . . ," he said as he opened his dresser drawer.

"You don't even remember. Now that's sad. But anyway, you can come with me if you'd like. It'll be like a date."

"Naw, not tonight. I'm watching the game and most likely falling asleep on the couch. By the way, it looks like we'll be announcing around the first of December."

Unwilling to discuss politics with him, Joi said, "Well, I think I'll just have to go alone."

"Okay." Phillip went to their closet and slid his feet into his house slippers. "What time will this thing be over?"

"I have no idea. But listen, I may go out to L.A. for a few days next month."

"For what?"

Joi paused before answering the question, hoping he would remember why. Then she said in a low tone, "Eight years?"

"Eight years for what?"

Swallowing, she repeated, "Phillip, it's been *eight* years."

"Eight years for what. Besides, if I announce in December, you'll have to—oh," he said as the realization as to why she would want to travel west fell on him. "That's right. It has been eight years."

With her eyes piercing with anger, Joi stood and walked into her walk-in closet.

"I'm sorry. I've got so much on my mind," she heard him say. "Do you—Do you want me to go with you?"

* * *

Joi arrived at the signing late, and in spite of the rain, the store was filled with readers and fans of the author's work. After signing the guest book at the store employee's request, she sat in the back row and watched Michael work magic. His locks were gathered in a red scrunchy, and he was dressed in a black silk shirt, black satin slacks and wore a silver watch and medallion.

"By the time the train stopped," Michael said, holding the book with one hand and moving the other dramatically as he read, "our troubles were over. Or so we thought. I walked toward the caboose of the rambling locomotive, past the bald man with the sad comb-over, and she was sitting there. She started to yell at me, and I was trying to apologize; but she wouldn't listen.

"She never listened.

"Miss Big Girl was more of a screamer. I could see sweat rolling between her breasts and forming on her upper lip. And then from nowhere she smiled at me, and from that moment on my life changed forever."

The women in the room laughed. Joi heard a lady in front of her say to another, "If he want to see some sweat rolling between breasts, he can call me."

"Girl," the lady next to her said in a staggered whisper, "don't you know I would *hurt* something like that? And you can tell by the way he walk, it's big."

"You are *too* through."

"Please. I bet that brother could get friction on a mayonnaise jar."

"Leave me alone," the woman replied as she laughed so loudly other women's heads turned in their direction.

When Michael finished reading the passage, there was applause. The bookstore owner took the microphone and said, "Okay, ladies, if you have any questions, feel free to raise your hands."

All over the room hands sprung upward, but Joi noticed that Michael did not turn to look at them, opting to keep his back to the attendees and speak to another woman who appeared to accompany him. She was a tall lady, well over six feet, professionally dressed in a black suit and pearls.

The owner of the store whispered in Michael's ear and then turned to the attendees and pointed toward a woman who stood and asked, "Well, I have several questions," she said and sucked her teeth. "But I'll just ask two of them now. Who is the brother on the cover, and where do your sex scenes come from?" A cavalcade of giggles saturated the room as Michael kept his back turned, speaking to the tall woman who appeared to be his escort. "Don't be shy now. Are you that fine ass'd Jamal from Tennessee who met Paula? I bet that's you, isn't it!" Smiling broadly, the woman gave the lady next to her a feminine high five and shouted, "Come on, tell the truth and shame the devil!"

Michael reached for his jacket and walked through the rear exit, and the laughter died. The escort spoke to the store owner with her hand cupped over her mouth to ensure every word was heard.

"Why you asked that question, Gloria," a lady shouted at the woman still standing, arms crossed, weight on one foot.

"'Cause I wanna know. When you get the mic, you ask what you wanna ask! I know he didn't leave because I asked a simple question."

"Excuse me, ladies," the store owner said.

"It was just not appropriate to ask something like that!" A miscellaneous voice said.

Clearing her throat, the owner repeated, "Excuse me."

"If I wanted to know," Gloria said, "then it's appropriate."

"Ladies," the owner repeated, this time looking directly at the lady in the middle of the room. "If I could have your attention for a moment? Mr. Brockmier unfortunately has a bad case of food poisoning, and he'll not be able to take your questions, but—"

"Will he be signing these books? I bought five."

"He'll reschedule with us for another time. More than likely the beginning of the year."

"The beginning of the what? Unh-unh, you mean he ain't going to sign *none* of these books tonight?"

"Unfortunately, ma'am, the escort will be taking him to the *hospital* shortly. I apologize, and what I'll do if you buy the books tonight, I'll give you an additional ten percent off."

As the buzz in the room heightened, Joi wondered what hospital he would be going to. For a split second she thought of sending him flowers, but washed away the thought and instead she gathered her purse, tucked her book under her arm and headed for the door.

"Excuse me," Joi heard someone say to the escort, who had followed him out the exit but had returned. "Is he going to be all right?"

"He's fine, ma'am. We went to a steakhouse before coming here, and he has been cramping all night long. I gave him," she said as the other women started to gather around her, "some club soda, but unfortunately that has not helped a lot. What we think he needs is just some bed rest to allow whatever it is to clear his system."

"Oh, I got a vibrating bed and a jar fulla quarters for his fine ass," a woman said as the other women laughed.

Michael's escort smiled and then walked toward Joi. As soon as she approached her, someone said, "Hey, that's the woman who played with that little girl. Potts McGee!"

"Sorry about that," the escort said in a hushed tone to Joi, and then said, "Can you follow me for a second?"

"Sure."

As she followed the woman through the double doors of the room into the hallway, the woman never said a word to her. Then she took out a key, opened an office and, after Joi followed her inside, closed the door behind her. As soon as she walked in, she asked the woman, "What's going on?"

"Right this way, ma'am."

The escort led Joi down a much smaller passageway into another room, and the first face she saw was Michael's. As soon as their eyes met, the woman said to Michael, "I am going to go back out there and try to help them with crowd control. That's if you don't need anything else from me."

"Thanks," Michael said without taking his eyes off of Joi. After the door closed, he said, "So, Miss Weston, have a seat." Michael sat behind a large oak desk with his feet on a small ottoman. "I was so glad you came out. You had me worried for a while."

"I never knew you noticed me."

"Do you think I'm hard of seeing? Why do you think I stopped reading as soon as you walked in. Of course I saw you. This is my fourth appearance in the bay area today, and I was looking for you at every event."

"To be honest, I had no intention of coming here when I woke up this morning."

"So what happened?"

"I've been cooped up in the house for so long, I guess. I just needed some air."

"You know I asked your brother if you were enjoying the book and he mentioned that you were raving about it."

"And he told you and never told me?" she said, leaning back and crossing her arms over nipples that were in the act of embarrassing her. Although she had been physically attracted to Michael before sitting near him in the office, she had not expected the reaction to his body, his smell, his exotic looks, to be so pronounced.

"Sorry. But I didn't ask him as if I was trying to make a move on you," Michael said as he secured his locks. His eyes were clear, but to Joi there was something in them that looked old. That looked as if he had been here for years. "I also asked him if you were still acting, since I have not seen you on anything for a while, and he said you were not considering anything to his knowledge and had moved with your husband, and he emphasized *husband*, to St. Petersburg."

Joi laughed. "That's my Joe."

As she laughed, Michael smiled at her. "I love the sound of your laughter." Joi immediately subdued the sound. "It sounds like rain on a tin roof."

"Listen. I'm trying to get this book," Michael continued as he picked up a copy of *Season*, "made into a movie. I've been turned down more times than I want to admit by the major players. I have several people who would like to act in the film, but I can't seem to attach a big name producer. You know, someone like Spielberg or Breidenbaugh or Opie Taylor. To make this thing work, I need someone with juice. How would you recommend I go about doing it?"

Instantaneously, Joi could feel a cold wind blow over the flicker of desire and wash it away. Previously she had thought he was attracted to her, but as he sat holding his novel, he sounded like a thousand other people she had met in her life. Uncrossing her arms, she said, "Well, I guess the first thing you need is a tightly written screenplay. If you don't know of a screenwriter, I may have a few names at home I could give you."

"No, I know a woman in the Bronx who could do it."

"Then next I would secure a top screenwriters' agent, if you haven't already."

"Cool," he said as if he were taking notes mentally.

Joi tried to guess Michael's age by looking deep in his eyes as an unwelcome thought slid through her mind: *Why does he have to be so damn young?* "And if you have time, there's a big gathering of movie producers," she added, "and people in the industry that meet every year in Acapulco. I think I'd go down there with the spec script and express to them that you have a few top names attached to the project and would like to——"

"Wait a minute," he said, leaning back. "This is too much. I need to write this down." Michael pulled open the top desk drawer and looked for a pencil. "I want to get a few names. I want addresses, everything from you. Thanks so much," he said, and opened another drawer, "for giving me a little time."

"So, your stomach feeling much better?"

"Oh. Yeah, I guess that was kinda shady, huh? I had to get out of there," he said, and closed the desk drawer. "Today I've visited four stores, done three radio interviews, I did something for the BBC from one of the studios here and now this; so I'm beat."

Standing, Joi said, "Well, can you sign my book for me?"

Michael opened the book to the title page and before signing it said, "Wait a minute. I signed this book before I gave it to you at the airport? You bought an extra one?"

"Oh, umm, well I kinda sorta gave the other one to a friend."

"You gave a signed first edition to a friend?"

"Call me generous. But after you called me, I decided to pick up another copy."

"Cool."

Michael signed his name only and said, "If you could give me a few minutes, I'd love to ask you a few more questions about the business. That's if you have time."

Joi looked down at her watch. "I may have a few minutes," she said, and sat down again.

"Can we possibly sit in the car and talk? Charisma is paying by the hour for the limo, so we can relax a little more." He paused as if he were reading her eyes. "I mean, if that's not a problem with you."

Joi continued to stare at him. Her life was bland. For the first time in her life there was time, but she had nothing to do with it. The fire had long since died in her marriage, and they rarely took trips or spoke of their shared loss. There was something inside of Joi ticking and was about to explode. Nothing in life tasted right. But, it was the life she chose. She was financially secure, had a home that was free and clear, and she had achieved everything in television she wanted to achieve. Although Phillip was driven in another direction, she knew his love for her was sincere. So why should she get into a limo with a man she barely knew? "I'll get my jacket and meet you in five minutes."

"It's funny you should ask about Blair," Michael said. "I was just talking to him on the phone before you came into the office at the store. He's fine. The lady who helps me with him when I am on the road told me he found a magic marker and was drawing tattoos on himself *again*, but otherwise he's fine."

"So he wants to be a rapper or something? Have tattoos on his arms like Tupac?"

"Naw, he's an Iverson fan. Wants to have tattoos on his arms, legs and neck, I might add," Michael said with a smile. "He's a trip."

"I give you credit for even trying to do the whole single father thing. It's very admirable."

"Admirable . . . I'll accept that. But he's my child. Women have been doing it for years, so I don't expect a parade down Main Street for doing the right thing."

"Good point."

"It's by far the toughest job I've ever had. But it's also the most rewarding. It defines you. Gives you purpose, you might say."

"I, umm—I understand completely."

"New subject," Michael said, and sipped from his wineglass. "I was thinking about this earlier. I like Tampa and all, but do you miss L.A.?"

"The smog, the crime and congestion? Umm, let me think for a moment."

"Okay, let me ask you this? Do you regret leaving Hollywood? Do you regret not being in *Purchased Tickets*?"

"Man, I have not thought about that in years," Joi said as she leaned into the white leather seats of the limo and listened to Anita Baker playing in the background. The previous smile left her face. "I was upset, but I must say Dan'ela pulled it off. It was a tough role to play, and she got the call and was on the set in less than a week. For a movie of that magnitude, that's no small feat."

"But I think you would have been perfect. I personally always thought—and this is saying nothing against television—but I always thought you were better suited for the big screen. I'm no Gene Siskel or whatever, but I know what I like."

"Thanks. But television is a tough medium to conquer as well. I don't see it as a step down. I see it as—"

"No, that's not what I am saying. I just think you would have been *better* suited for more dramatic roles. Something that could show your range as an actress."

"Thank you."

"Is that why you left Hollywood?"

"Yes, and no. I was disappointed in a lot of ways. I will not lie. Hollywood can be very cruel to women over thirty-five, so I walked away after the show and just did a few plays before coming back for the *Purchased Tickets* role. When I lost that, I lost the fire, you might say."

"No way."

"Excuse me?" Joi asked.

"If it's something inside of you, be it poetry, writing, music or even acting, if it's your calling—your passion—how can you lose the fire?"

"Point taken. I will not say the fire has burned out, but it has been reduced to a tiny flame. I was disenchanted with the business aspects of the industry—like a lot of artists, I guess. So I walked away on my own terms."

"Can I ask you a personal question, and then I'll back off."

Joi looked into his large brown eyes. They were extremely expressive, and she found an honest, sincere quality in them. "Go ahead," she whispered.

"Does the phone ring?"

"It used to. The first year I would get a script or a phone call at least once a month. But then it died down, and now I can't tell you the last time someone"—

she broke away from his stare and looked out the window of the car—"showed interest. But I'm happy. I don't want this to sound like I am sitting home doing nothing and letting life——"

"What do you do?"

"I am very active in the Republican party. I do charity work for the United Negro College Fund, and I take a class at the community college once a week. It may sound boring, but I was busting my hump for years to achieve the level of success I achieved, and I am kinda glad it's over."

"I can definitely understand that. Sometimes I wish I could take a break from it all, sit in my music room and just listen to old Sade CDs for about a week."

"So," she said as she looked at Michael once again, "let's shine the light on you for a moment. Since this has all happened relatively fast, what has been the biggest surprise?"

"The biggest surprise?" Michael asked as the car came to a traffic light stop. "The biggest surprise," he mumbled again.

"Yeah," Joi said, and then sipped a little more of the brandy that had a warmth she could trace through her body. "I know when I became quote-unquote famous, it wasn't what I expected. I thought it would be nothing but riding around in these things, no-limit credit cards, and life would be perfect." Joi looked away from Michael and said, "That life would be a dream."

Michael looked back at her and asked, "And it wasn't?"

She smiled. "I think we were talking about you."

Michael looked at the onyx ring he wore, rotated it around his finger, and then said, "To be honest, none of it has been like I expected."

"What did you expect?"

"To be happy. But I'm here. I am where I wanted to be, I guess. The book is doing better than anyone expected, but I feel like a fraud."

"Why?" Joi asked.

"Because," he whispered, and then the words faded. Michael hit the intercom button and said to the driver, "Do me a favor? Can you take us to the gulf?"

"No problem, Money."

"That's if you didn't have any pressing engagements," he said to Joi.

"Actually, I can't be out too late. My husband's home watching football, and I don't want him to think the wrong thing,"

"I understand. We'll have you back at the store by ten. Is that okay?"

"Sure," Joi replied, and sipped her drink. "But you were saying?"

Michael put his feet on the seat beside Joi, who sat across from him, and said, "I was not expecting every day to be perfect. I remember how hard my dad used to work. But in those days it was so much different. He wrote the book, and then he just sat back and enjoyed the results. I know it's more competitive today, but never did I expect it to be like this."

"But you said you feel like a fraud. Why is that?"

"What I mean by that is, I wrote this book," he said, looking at Joi, "and the reviews and public acceptance have been wonderful. But I know there are thousands of authors out there who are more deserving." Michael took the crystal goblet from the bar and poured himself another glass of wine. "I'm fortunate. But I guess I feel like Dub'ya in a way. I feel like a member of the lucky sperm club."

"I wouldn't say that at all. I read your novel, and you're

talented. And I am not just blowing smoke at you," Joi said, swirling her half-finished third glass of brandy. "I read a lot of books nowadays—at least two or three a month—and yours is one of the best I've read since *Another Country*, and I'm serious about that."

Michael's fingers slid over the smooth leather on the backseat, and he whispered, "Thanks." As Joi watched him, he looked as if he wanted to say more. He ran his fingers over his clean-shaven face and said, "When I was a little boy, you know the one thing I enjoyed most about my father?"

"What?" Joi asked as she continued to try to guess his age. *Twenty-five? God, could he be that wet behind the ears?*

"The man never kissed me good night. I don't even remember him ever saying good-bye. His father was a real hard-ass. Made him quit school and help support the family. So my dad never really got over that. His father left the family and never came back, and I think my father—well, anyway." Then Michael ran his hands over his chest as he reminisced and said, "I don't know how I got on that subject, but I loved the way the man held me. I would climb up on his shoulders, and he would wear me like shoulder pads. Never said get down. Never complained at all. I'd sit in his lap as he worked, ride on his foot as he walked, even sit on the toilet when he bathed. I just couldn't get enough of him, and I guess the words were never needed."

Joi could feel an attachment to Michael that went beyond the exterior. She wanted to reach for him and hold him in her arms. To comfort his head on her breast. To whisper to him that everything was going to be all right.

"Anyway," he continued. "Going back to what we were talking about, I have this friend. She's the best writer I've ever read. But she can't get a book deal."

"Is she that good?"

"Joi, reading her is—It's like eating chocolate. She's that addictive."

"So why can't you get her a deal."

"She's her worst enemy. She and I talk daily, and a part of her wants to be published; but there's something holding her back. A fear inside that she can't get over."

"Rejection?"

"No, that's too simplistic. She knows she's good. She knows her work is publishable. I think it's just the fear of success, which in many ways can be worse than the fear of rejection."

"I know. There were thousands of actors in coffeehouses all over this country I knew could perform better on stage than me. But it's not the best-qualified person who gets the book or movie deal. It's the one who is prepared and patient."

"True," Michael said. "Do you think Breidenbaugh's decision was a blessing in disguise?"

"In a way, yes. I was on the fast track, and it was killing me physically. And then I did a couple of roles in a few movies, and the Potts McGee thing jumped off. And then my life really got hectic. His decision may have saved my life in more ways—" Joi paused as she thought of the mysterious words she could not get out of her head the first day of shooting *Purchased Tickets:* "Today Joi Weston must die."

She had not thought of the words in years and had never shared them with anyone else. "Yeah," she said, regaining her composure. "It may have saved my life."

"The pressure of that career couldn't have been good on the marriage."

Hearing Michael say the word *marriage* caused her body to go cold. "It was rough," Joi said. "But I must say if it wasn't for Phillip, I wouldn't have made it. He was a rock. I mean, in that business you need that person there at night offering encouragement. He was always there for me when it came to the career."

"I'm glad to hear that."

"I love my husband."

"You mentioned that on the phone."

"So who's there for you?"

"No one," he said as his long, sensuous fingers ran down the crease of his pants, "except for Blair, of course. I know I need a woman in my life, but I don't know if I've found her yet."

"Have you ever been in love?"

"No."

Joi saw the opportunity to find out what she wanted to know. "How old are you to have never been in love?"

"Let me clarify that because to me love is like the wind. You can't truly describe it. You can feel it in your skin, your bones, and even if you never felt it, you'd know it was there. Love holds you," he said, and slowly interlocked his fingers as if he were cradling a baby. "Love. True love leaves *no* doubt. It's not something you look at from several different angles and wonder if it's there. I don't toss that word around, and if you remember, I never used the word once in *Season* because I didn't want the reader to read *love*, I wanted them to feel love. I want them to feel true love."

Michael looked into Joi's eyes and asked, "Is that what you feel when you tell me you love him?"

"That's exactly what I feel," she replied without a smile.

Michael smiled at her and asked as if he were Ed Bradley, "Really?"

"Yes really. You say that like it's a shock to you. Besides, I'm old enough to be your—"

"My what? My older sister's best friend?"

Over a nervous laugh, she replied, "Don't be cute." Joi looked out the window and noticed that the rain was starting to fall harder. She looked at the time displayed in the stereo above the seat as Michael slid in another CD, and said, "It's getting late."

"You ready to go back?" Michael asked. His lips formed a straight line, and his tone was even.

Once again Joi felt the excitement inside of her diminish. "Is something wrong?"

"Nothing," he said, and then leaned back on the seat.

As they rode, the driver asked, "Brockmier?"

"Yes?"

"You want me to park?"

Joi looked out the window and noticed they had arrived on a pier overlooking the Gulf of Mexico. The rain bounced off of the black waters like diamonds, and Joi wondered if she would regret what had happened already in the car, although all she was guilty of was intimate conversation. Michael reached up and turned off the jazz and asked, "Do you really love him?"

"Yes," she said before she could stop the words. "But wait a minute, where did that come from?"

"Just making conversation, that's all. We're talking about love, and I know a lot of women are in marriages and don't love their husbands. I know a lot of men don't love their wives. I'm talking about the love that goes beyond—"

"So what are you saying? Do you just go around asking people things like that out of the blue? How many times have I told you I—Is this for a novel or something?"

"Slow your roll, dear," Michael said. "Again, I'm making conversation."

"Well, that was not called for. I've been married eighteen years. I've been *happily* married eighteen years. I just wanted to ride and hang out with you. That's all. Now, if I sent the wrong message, I'm sorry. I'm not some young groupie, you know. I enjoyed the book and wanted to get to know you better. But that's all."

"Hey, I'm sorry."

"Don't be sorry. Listen," she said, and looked at the clock again, "I think it's time to go back."

Michael buzzed the driver. "Listen, bro, can you take us back to the bookstore?"

As the ignition started, Michael said, "I wasn't trying to imply anything. I'm nosy by nature, I guess. If I crossed the bounds of good taste or bad judgment, please blame it on the wine."

Joi sipped the last taste of brandy from the glass and slid it back in the hole designed especially for it.

Michael turned the music up again, and then Joi looked at him and said, "Listen, I'm sorry. I guess I went a little off the deep end. But I was trying to talk, converse with you, from one artist to another. And then I started getting these vibes from you," she said as Michael looked at her. As soon as he did, she felt her nipples get harder than they had all night.

In the back of Joi's mind when she had stepped in the car, she had thought about the possibilities. But as they headed back to the store, she knew allowing anything to occur would be the worst thing that could happen at this point in her life.

"Once again, I'm sorry. I was out of order, and I just, I guess, wanted to know more about you as a person. I was not trying to turn this into anything it wasn't." Michael turned away from her, but her yearning continued.

"I'm happy. Is that what you wanted to hear?"

"Good."

"I'm very happy."

"Wonderful."

Joi pinched her thighs together. In minutes they would return to the store, and all she would have was the memory of the moments they had spent alone. She folded her arms over her breast, allowed her thumbs to brush the surface of her fully aroused nipples and closed her eyes to allow the feelings to saturate her body.

"If you could have one thing in your marriage that you don't have now, what would it be?"

"You're a persistent young fuck, aren't you?" Joi said. Her own language shocked her, but she felt a heat in her panties she had not experienced in months. With a face that showed no desire for him at all, she imagined the curves and cuts of his nude torso. Joi imagined him taking her away, just for one night of pleasure, and making her feel whole and complete once again before letting her return to her reality.

"Sorry."

"There's nothing to apologize for. He doesn't kiss my feet, and I don't kiss his ass, you might say; but together we're happy. In my opinion that's why we've lasted. A marriage is not about losing yourself. It's about being strong and independent so you can be stronger as a unit. You follow me?"

Michael leaned deeper into the leather and gazed at Joi.

"What's wrong with you?"

"Nothing." Then he reached down and picked up her shoe. Although she could have stopped him, she did not. He removed her shoe, placed it behind his headrest and looked at her toes, which had recently received a pedicure.

"You got a foot fetish?"

"Just wanted to kiss your feet."

"That's sick," she replied. "Would you put my shoe back on?"

Michael looked deeply into her eyes and then kissed the arch of her foot softly. His lips felt like tulips grazing the surface of her flesh. Then he smiled at her again.

"Okay. Now, are you satisfied?"

"No," he said as he brought her foot between his legs just inches from his excitement.

"Listen," she said as she felt her body getting flush. "This is not right. Where's my shoe."

"I would just like to . . ." he said, and then stopped talking as his thumbs began a rolling motion between the bones of her foot. Slowly and deliberately he rotated his hands deeper into her flesh.

Joi swallowed and whispered, "That feels good," all the while wanting to point her foot just a few more inches into his crotch to feel him for herself.

She felt him stretch each and every tendon of her foot without tickling. He then covered her foot with his palm like a blanket and slid it up and down the surface, teasing Joi's flesh with his warmth.

"You know, I've never done this before," Michael said. "I won't lie; I've had women do it to me, but never have I taken the time to do it to someone else."

"I need my shoe now. Seriously," she said, reaching toward him without a smile.

"Okay." Then he reached behind him for her shoe with one hand, and with the other he slid her foot into the center of his wool pants. She could tell that under the wool there was a smooth silk lining. Joi could also tell that under the lining there was a throbbing penis that slid between her largest toe and its more slender companion. She knew she had to pull back, but was amazed by his size and stiffness. Just the feel of it made her heart hammer against her ribs.

Damn, Joi thought.

Michael retrieved her suede pump, placed it on the seat beside him and then, before she knew it, pulled her foot away from the spot, raised her pinky toe and covered it with his kiss.

Joi's skin screamed. She wanted to pull away, but for a moment could not summon the strength to even say stop. She felt her lips swell. She felt her back teeth clinch. And then Michael's lips covered the next toe, and he sucked it even harder. His wet tongue slid all around the surface, and as she opened her eyes, she saw a look of desire in his face to only pleasure her. Her mouth became desert dry; her nipples, air-conditioned-room-on-a-hot-summer-day hard.

"Michael. Listen, I won't lie and say I don't enjoy this but—"

He progressed to the next toe and slid it into his mouth even slower than before. Joi could feel the soft, slippery warm insides of his mouth as well as the hard, smooth textured edge of his teeth. She felt the softness of a singular loose dread sweep over her leg, the masculine touch of his hands on the back of her calf and his tongue sliding between her toes.

"Michael, once again you should really—" And the words died in the air as he slid his mouth to the next toe. *Oh, my God,* Joi thought. *If he can do this to my feet, what in the world would he . . .*

Michael brought his head up and smiled at Joi.

"Thanks. That felt nice," she said, "but I need my shoe now. Come on, stop."

Michael laughed aloud and then looked down at her big toe. He kissed the top of it. He kissed the nail. And then he licked the back of her toe and slowly allowed it to slide into his mouth. As he sucked without making a sound, he bobbed his head up and down, sucking soft pinkish brown skin never touched before by a man.

Joi allowed her defenses to fall and slid her fingers under the waistband of her skirt. Michael looked up at her, and she wanted to pull her hand out; but he immediately closed his eyes, and she allowed her fingers to stroke the pubic hairs of her peach.

They gyrated evenly in the rhythm of the motion he had set. While her fingers formed a *V* and moved up and down, Joi's thumb made tiny circles over her strawberry, and she imagined his lips on that special place. For an instant she wanted to grab him by his ears and pull his face between her thighs, but she restrained herself.

As she slid her shaking fingers inside her body, Michael reached down and grabbed her other foot, pulled off her shoe with one motion and placed her foot over his penis.

"We can't do—" was all she could get out on her third attempt to finish a sentence.

While Joi's toes found satisfaction in his mouth, her other foot massaged his thickness. It was as long as her foot, hard as steel, and with her toes she could feel the mushroom tip.

"Baby, I want to take you somewhere you've only dreamed of going. Not just in your mind. Can you do whatever you have to do to come—to come with me?" He begged her with his expression.

"I can't."

A tear formed in Joi's eye, and for a moment not only could she not remember the last time she made love; she could not remember *ever* making love. It had been months since she and Phillip were intimate. She had asked him to seek professional help, but he refused; so she resorted to polishing herself off until he built up the courage to face his problem. "I can't do this, Michael. I've never cheated, and I can't. Besides, I'm too old to be—"

"Joi," he said as he rubbed her foot and she continued to massage his penis. The mere utterance of her name made her tingle. "You're what, thirty-three?"

Too weak to wonder if it was a line or if he was being sincere, she replied, "Over forty."

"So what," he said, out of breath. "I'm damn near thirty. Big deal. I've never wanted a woman as bad as I want you right now. In this very moment. And I want to give you pleasure you will never forget. I'm not asking you to do anything you don't want to do, but all I would hope is that you allow whatever may or may not happen, to happen naturally."

"I can't. I want to," she said, and then moved her foot from his crotch, "but I can't."

Michael pulled her foot back into the seat of his passion and allowed her heat to slide between her toes. Then he continued to worship her body with his talented tongue and rotated his hips, which only made her want to make love to him in the limo before she could talk herself out of it.

Michael slid his hands up her calves and to the bend of her knees. With one motion, he pulled her hips toward him and allowed the flat edge of his finger to slide up and down the inside of her pulsating thighs.

Joi wanted to scream. She wanted to grab his fingers, but instead she opened her legs a little wider. And he stopped.

She opened her eyes. In her heart she could hear words from her first stage play. Words she had not recalled in years. *The first kiss is always the hardest.*

Michael stared at her as he tried to catch his breath. He didn't say a word, and neither did she as the car pulled to a red light two blocks from the bookstore.

Michael reached up and turned off the music. And then rested his head on the back of the leather seats. He brought his fingers to his lips as if he could taste her body and sighed.

Joi wanted to say something, anything. She prayed she was not going to allow the fire to die within the next two blocks. Her fingers discreetly slid from under her panties and from her skirt.

"We're almost here," he said.

"I know."

He reached up and buzzed the driver.

"Sup?"

Michael was silent as he looked out at the rain and then at Joi again as if he was trying to read her mind.

"Brockmier? Can I help you?"

Without a blink he said, "Do me a favor? Take us to my hotel."

"What!" Joi said with the fake look of surprise on her face. *The first kiss is always the hardest.*

"Just let me make you feel all over like you just felt."

"I want to, but I can't do that, Michael," she said. "I'm happy. I don't do things like this, so please tell this man to take me to my car."

Michael squinted at her as he continued to decipher her nonverbal body language. "Okay, okay, okay. If you want him to turn around, you tell him."

"Thank you. To be honest, Michael, it's not that I don't want to, and I know we'd have a nice time," she said as she tried to balance herself in the car, "but it's just not right."

Then the driver turned before her fingers could reach the buzzer, and she fell into Michael's body face first and found her hand holding his still-hard penis. "Oh, my God," she said. *The first kiss—is always the hardest.* It regained its natural beat, but she found herself locked in a passionate kiss. Michael pulled her roughly, almost violently, toward his warmth. She ended the kiss and allowed her face to slide down to the corded muscles of his chest.

As if he possessed her body, Michael's large hands held her face gently and guided her lips back to his. He kissed her just the way she wanted to be kissed. Not too sloppy, not too hard, tongues slowly circling, firm and in control.

Joi forced her body away from his as she ran her fingers through his locks. "I can't do this, Michael." She kissed him again, and her fingers moved from his hair, down his neck and around the outside of his shoulders. His chest was firm, stomach rippled, and all Joi wanted was to have him inside of her. If only for one night. Over a sigh, she whispered, "Get me home by one."

As they arrived at the hotel, Michael and Joi sat in the car holding hands as if they had just met. Joi silenced the voices in her head and thought of what she would tell Phillip. She could not imagine how he could ever forget the significance of the day her daughter died, and whatever happened that night would be retribution for his thoughtlessness.

"Why are you smiling?"

"Just thought of this joke my daughter told me one time. Where's the driver?"

"He went inside the hotel for something, I guess. So what was the joke?"

"Nothing. It would not be funny if I repeated it," she

whispered, not wanting to share the intimate memories.

"Kids can come up with the funniest things, though. My son still calls tattoos, tattoodals."

"Aw, how cute."

As the driver opened the door, Michael asked, "Listen, why don't we grab a cup of coffee or something in the café? I really enjoy just talking to you. I want you to tell me all about Angie. Okay?"

Joi immediately felt ashamed at what was about to happen. Hearing her daughter's name from his lips brought her back to reality. Then she looked inside the hotel lobby and thought she was dreaming again, but knew she wasn't. She saw Phillip at the registration counter. His back was turned; but he was wearing a windbreaker, and she knew without a doubt it was him.

"Close the door," she said.

"What?" Michael asked with a smile.

After she fell back into the seat, she repeated, "I said close the damn door!"

Michael got inside the car with her as the driver stood in the rain holding the umbrella.

"You look like you just saw a ghost. What's wrong?"

Phillip disappeared inside the hotel. "No," she said, "I just saw my husband."

"He works here?"

Joi ran her fingers over her mouth and shook her head. "No, he does not work here."

CHAPTER

8

Some days are just born ugly. Unappealing to the eye, ominous to the casual observer. In Harlem, this was not such a day.

From the vertical red neon lights spelling the word A-P-O-L-L-O, to the ivy-covered vermilion, burgundy and brown row houses, 125th Street blushed with pride on the most beautiful of beautiful Harlem dawns.

As was his morning ritual, Michael awoke before the sun, ran five miles, returned home and sat in his underwear writing words he prayed would one day be published. On weekdays he would wake Blair and help him get dressed for school. But since it was the weekend, Michael found himself in his study, at his computer, analyzing each word of his novel *Speaking in Tongues*.

Although Ani did not give him encouragement in regard to getting his work published, he had to at least try. He had to run it by the brass of Charisma to see what they thought about it. Living the life he was living had left him with an ulcer in his stomach, numerous sleepless nights and fingernails that were chewed to the nub.

Seven days had come and gone since he had spent time with Joi. Seven days had come and gone since he had wanted her so badly his body cried in pain. Seven days had come and gone, and still he tried to separate feelings from flesh and had no answers. And after seven days he wanted to speak to her again, but knew he couldn't.

After they saw her husband, at her request they returned to the store where she got out of the limo, slid away from his kiss, and drove into the night. Michael wanted to at least find out how she was doing, but decided that there should be a little time between their action and his reaction. So he poured his passion into page after page of the novel he felt he was born to write.

As he sat in the same room where his father penned *One Witness*, Michael lit candles, burned incense and did anything he could to summon the spirit of his namesake. For hours he would write and rewrite the words so they flowed smooth and poetic. Sometimes he was proud of the result. Other times he was ecstatic with the growth that was a result of his labor.

Michael hit print, stood from the desk, arched his back and then went to the printer. As soon as the first page fell to the tray, he pulled it out, verbalized the narrative into air and paced back and forth in the study. The more he read, the more he fell in love with the words. There was a cadence in the way they linked together—a symmetry that had not been displayed in the previous versions of the novel—and he knew Charisma would approve.

"Morning, Daddy," Michael's chocolate brown son

said as he walked out into his father's study. Scratching his backside, he said, "You up all night?"

"One second," Michael said, and continued to listen to the music in the words.

"Can I have Fruit Roll Ups instead of Froot Loops? They both fruit."

Michael did not reply.

"And I want some chocolate milk—"

"Blair? Go in the kitchen and get whatever you want."

"And I want some toast, too, and some eggs. We got eggs?"

"Not right now, Blair," Michael said, and started from the beginning of the page in an attempt to feel the words uninterrupted. "Give me a few more minutes and I'll cook you breakfast, but just not right now."

"But I want some—"

"Listen!" Michael shouted. "Give me a break already, damn! I have to get this shit completed by Monday, and I don't need you to bother me now!"

"Why don't you just let that lady write it?"

Blair yelled words that hit Michael like a wet baseball bat in darkness. Initially he was enraged to hear his son say what he had said, and then he sat down and calmed himself. "Come here a second.

"I've told you before, the lady, Ani, wrote the first book; but she didn't want to travel, so she and I worked out a plan. I'd—I would put my name on the book to *help* her, but the next novel would be mine and mine alone. Now, I've told you this before."

"I remember," Blair said as he walked closer to his father and sat in his lap. "So you just helped her do something she couldn't do?"

Michael wiggled his fingers in his son's hair and said, "Yeah, you can say that. But everyone needs help. It does not make you a weaker person. Actually, I believe it takes a strong person to admit they need help."

"Did Granddaddy help people like that?" Blair asked as he gazed at the rows of books against the wall.

"No. I mean Granddaddy was special, but he never—never helped anyone like I'm helping Ani." Michael looked at his son and said, "You make A's, right?"

"A couple of B's and a C, too," Blair replied with his lips perched as if he were awaiting a kiss.

"And you love math. Right?"

"Everything except trying to divide fractions. I hate trying to divide fractions."

"Well, I am glad you mentioned that, 'cause remember," Michael said, "when you did not understand fractions? You didn't understand what math had to do with pies? Remember I helped you?" Looking at the profile of his son's face, Michael said, "Well, for the rest of your life you'll need help. There is a saying that goes 'No man is an island.' Sometimes, no matter how old you get, you'll need someone to help you. Ani needed my help, and because I helped her, we have been able to help a lot of other people."

"So," Blair said, and closed his eyes as if he was drifting back to sleep, "when I get big and become a writer, I'll need to find someone to help me as well?"

"Mister man?" Michael sighed. "That's why you have a daddy." Then he rubbed his son's cheek, kissed him softly on his eyelids and sent him off to the kitchen for breakfast.

Monday

With anxiety boiling in his chest, Michael stepped off the elevator, dressed in a suit and tie with briefcase in hand. As he walked with Pam, several publishing executives came out of their offices to congratulate him on the success of his novel.

"So what's in the bag," company president, Vance Peters, asked as he passed Michael in the hallway. "Another best-seller I hope."

Michael smiled as he nodded. "I hope so," he said, and followed Pam inside her office with a view of Times Square.

"These people are just going crazy around here," she said, and closed the door. "I can't tell you how many times I've been asked about the novel. For example," she said, adjusting the picture of herself and Stedman Graham on her desk, "I was at a nightclub one night, literally on the dance floor, and someone from sales with *another* publisher asked me about your next release. Isn't that something?"

"That's something, alright." Michael felt the nerves bulging in his stomach. He wondered if he should just give her Ani's novel instead of his own because he was not sure he could take the rejection after the many hours of work he had dedicated to perfecting it.

"Now, if you were not"—then she rubbed the back of her hand, indicating the shared complexion of their skin tone—"it wouldn't be a problem at Charisma. I told them not to worry, that I had read parts of the book, and I knew it would be the bomb diggity when you finished it. So"—Pam sat and rubbed her hands together as if they were preparing to enjoy a meal—"let's see it!"

Michael reached into his briefcase and pulled out the novel that was wrapped in brown paper. Something he did because he remembered his father doing it when he was a child. He handed it to Pam, who sat across the desk from him. "Oh, yeah, before I forget," she said, and opened her desk drawer. "I went down to accounting and picked this up before it went into the mail. I spoke to your agent, and he okayed us cutting separate checks." Then with one hand, Pamela retrieved the manuscript and gave Michael the bonus check.

She immediately opened the manuscript as if it were a birthday gift. "I love the way you wrap these things up with twine. It's so—so Hemingway."

Michael stared at Pam to see the reaction on her face when she looked at the title.

Her eyebrow kinked upward, her smile twisted. "*Mule-Drawn Wagon?* Interesting."

When he had reached into his briefcase, he put his hands on *Speaking in Tongues*, but could not will himself to share it with her. He had no idea what he would tell Ani or how he would get out of the situation if he changed his mind about using her work. All he could feel was the gravitational pull of quicksand. "Yeah, I umm. I wanted to go into a slightly different direction with this novel. Something more—I don't know, eclectic."

"But, I thought you were going to do a continuation of Paula? Everyone wanted to know what happened to her."

"I was going to, but then I decided," he said as he watched Pam read the first page, "I would try to expand a little. I don't know if I want to write the same thing over and over again."

Pam was silent as she began reading the second page with her finger moving across the text as if it were brail.

"It's about," Michael said, and kicked himself once again for not having the courage to pull out his own work, "the journey of a family from the Mississippi Delta. But more so it's about many people who in the late 1800s migrated to St. Louis and Chicago from Louisiana and Mississippi. It's a novel with a number of intriguing characters, like Ernest Freeman who was a slave and had escaped to the North but returned to get his family. But in the novel we find him to be much older and very bitter. In this novel he narrates how—"

"I don't like it," she said after reading the second page.

"You don't like what?"

"I thought you were going to write about Paula. Sales has been promoting a sequel to *Season* for weeks now."

"I never told you that. You asked me to do it in conversation, but I told you I was working on several projects."

"Damn," she said, and then spun her chair around so she could look down at the Viacom Building below. Then she reached behind her, pulled off a few more pages, put her wrist to her lips in deep thought and said, "It's not that I don't like it, Michael. I'm sure the quality is there; but this is no *Season of Regret*, and that's just my honest opinion. I know a good manuscript when I read . . ." Michael could tell she had paused to read a few more passages. She stopped and let the pages settle on her thighs. "I know a winner when I read the first or second page. You can feel it in your gut. Those first few words will pull you into the paper as if you were ink. I'm not getting that here," Pam said as she gazed at New York. "I just wish we had a little more time, but I already have you scheduled for May." She ran her fingers through her hair. "Fuck me!"

"Listen," Michael replied, "I think—this is a wonderful novel, but if you like, just like before, I have something else you can read."

Michael had no idea where the words came from,

but before he knew it, Pam had spun around in her chair facing him. "Let me see what you got."

Michael reached into his briefcase, but before he could pull out the manuscript, Vance Peters walked into the room. "Well," he said loudly and looked at Pam, "I can smell a hit a mile away, and this entire floor smells like a best-seller!" As he cracked his knuckles, Michael looked at Pam for an indication as to if she wanted him to pull out the second manuscript. She screamed for him not to with her eyes. "So what have we this time?" Vance asked, and sat on the arm of the couch behind Michael.

"It's a little different," Pam answered, "but I think we got something we can—"

Before she could finish the sentence, Vance walked toward her desk, whipped off his glasses and picked up the first ten pages of the manuscript. "Different in what way?"

Neither Pam nor Michael spoke as he read. A thousand thoughts went through Michael's mind in what felt like milliseconds. Could he ask Ani to write a continuation of Paula's story line? Could he write it himself? Would Pam possibly see something in his writing that Ani did not? Maybe since Ani's latest creation was not held in the highest esteem, she was not the best judge of his creative talent.

Vance laid the pages down and returned his glasses to his pocket with a smile. "Way to go, son," he said as he looked at Michael and asked, "would you like to join me and Pamela for lunch?"

"Umm no, sir. I have to pick up my son from school, and I don't know if I could make it in time with traffic and all."

"Oh, yeah, that's right, you do have a son. Well,

Pammy, meet me in my office around a quarter of one, okay?"

"Sure thing," Pamela said, looking to be a fraction of the size she was when Michael initially said hello.

The small-stature executive looked at Michael and said, "Have a wonderful day," and then left the room.

As soon as the door closed, Pam laid her head on the desk and said, "My God, he hates it."

"How could you tell?"

"Damn, damn, damn. Well, let me see what else you have," she whispered as she sat up and ignored his question.

"Maybe I could do the continuation. It might take a few months, but if I push hard, I could—"

With her palm extended and fingers beckoning toward Michael like a 42nd Street pimp, Pam said, "Let me see what you got first."

Michael reached into his briefcase once again and pulled out the manuscript. It, too, was wrapped in brown paper; it, too, was gathered with twine.

As she retrieved the pages from the author who had single-handedly made her career, Pamela hunched over and read like a skittish kid eating her lunch in front of a bully. She smiled a smile that caught Michael's attention. Then he could tell she was looking for a spark that could tell her this was the one. All of a sudden she leaned back and said, "I love the title. But to be honest, Michael, this is shit on crack. It's almost amateurish. Now, if you and I had not gone back to the days, I would not tell you. I'd just put it out there and not sign you again. But I care for you."

"You haven't even read the entire first page."

"I know what readers are looking for, and it's not here. I mean *Speaking in Tongues* is a cute title. I love the

Christmas imagery thing you open with, but to be frank, it reads flat."

"It reads flat? What the hell does that mean?" Michael reached for the manuscript and put it in his briefcase. Then he reached for *Mule-Drawn Wagon.*

"I can't let you take this one. This is the one V. P. read. I gotta," Pam said, and then blew air in her cheeks thinking aloud. "I gotta turn in something yesterday, but I told you that." Tapping her long purple fingernail on her front tooth, she quietly said, "Maybe I can get a ghostwriter to help—"

"No!"

"No what?"

"No. I don't want a ghostwriter."

Pamela leaned forward on her elbows and said, "Well, here's the scoop, kiddo. A lot of people have a lot riding on this. They're not looking for a single. They want to clear the bases, and this is not home-run material. What I can do is get someone in here this week to punch it up a little so we won't hurt your name in the marketplace, and then that'll give you time to work on the next book."

"No," Michael restated. "I just can't go out like that."

"I know this novel was stressful to write," Pam said in a soothing tone. "Your father only wrote one, and he was almost the age you are now. I'm sure that's messing with your head, and that's natural. What I am suggesting you do is to let someone *help* you, fine-tune it, and we'll get your best effort in the third novel."

"Listen," Michael said as he stood, "the novel is what the novel is. You, Mr. Peters, you can't read the first page of a 491 page novel and know if it's any good."

"We're reading it like consumers. No one will give

you 491 pages to see if you can write—if you can't write the first three."

"The novel is what the novel is!"

"Why are you shouting? This is done all the time. All we need to do is—"

"Dammit, Pam, I'm not going to live like that!" he shouted louder than before. "The novel is what the novel is! I'm not going to . . . I am not going to be a fraud!"

After picking up Blair from school, Michael's plan was to return home, but he found himself in the Bronx and in the foyer of Ani's building.

"Hello," she said into the intercom.

There was a brief hesitation before he said, "Hey. Ani. It's Michael. I was in the area and thought I would swing by to drop off this package."

Dead air.

"Can you hear me?" he asked into the small grated slits in the wall.

Dead air.

"Ani? Are you there?" Michael buzzed again.

"I hear you. Why did you come here?"

"I was in the area."

"You told me you were going uptown this morning, and you were in this area?"

"Listen," he said, and spoke closer to the intercom, "there are a lot of things going down at Charisma, and I just wanted to touch base with you on a few of them. That's all."

"Michael, I've asked you I don't know how many times"—heavy breath—"not to come here unan-nounced."

"Ani? We've worked together for a couple of years,

live in the same city, and we have never met face-to-face. I don't want to e-mail you. I don't want to chat about it on-line. I know you have health problems, but I just would like to meet you face-to-face to discuss something that just happened at Charisma."

"What happened?"

"I'm not going to discuss it in the hallway."

Dead air.

"Can you hear me, Ani? I'm not going to——" Then he heard the buzz which opened the door.

As Michael walked down the hallway toward Ani's apartment, he wondered why she had not moved out of the building with the money they had made on the sale of the novels. *But then again,* he thought, *if she's going to write stuff like Mule-Drawn Wagon, it's for the best she didn't move.*

He walked up to her door and knocked three times before calling her name.

"It's open."

When Michael opened the door, the room was dark. Everything was neat and in place, which for some reason was not what he expected. Then he called her name. "Ani?" And his eyes followed the whistling sound that came from the corner of the room by the window.

Ani was a hefty woman and sat on what appeared to be a modified church pew that bellied downward like a contact lens. She looked away from him as if momentarily ashamed of her appearance. Dressed in a Hawaiian muumuu, she was within arm's length of a carton of Salems, an air freshener and a saucer filled with crumpled cigarette butts. Ani's silky hair was braided back into two neat ponytails, and she was fair complexioned with large rough patches on her cheeks. Michael noticed her legs were spread apart like a person playing a conga, her feet pointed outward, and between them were stacks of legal pads and journals.

"Come in," she said in the breathy tone he had heard so many times before, "and close the door."

"So how are you?" Michael said in an attempt to constrain his surprise at what he saw. "I'm so happy to finally meet you." He walked up to Ani and reached down and hugged her. She smelled of a mixture of witch hazel and Ben-Gay. Then he stood up and said, "There really is a person named Ani. I was starting to believe you were like the Wizard." Ani showed no reaction. "You know, like in the *Wizard of Oz*?" Again his words were met with no response, and as Ani stared at him, Michael found a seat at the dinette.

"Where's Blair?"

"I dropped him off with a friend down the block; then I came over." Michael reached into his briefcase and pulled out both the check and manuscript. He handed Ani the check.

As she opened the envelope, he listened to the purring sound of her breathing. Then she said, "Thank you. You didn't have to do this, you know."

"It's the least I can do. You don't know how much I have enjoyed this ride, you might say, across the country and hearing how people have enjoyed—well, your words."

"They're *our* words. We did make a few modifications," Ani said as she put the check back in the envelope, folded it in half and put it in her bosom. "Before, she was more of a victim, you suggested making her more amenable to her conditions, and I think that helped as well."

"Something I have been meaning to ask you for years

and I have no idea why it's taken so long. Are you Jewish?"

"My grandfather was. He studied in a yeshiva and taught my father from the Torah. My father, believe it or not, was half Jewish and half Asian, but he spoke Yiddish around the house. To make things even more complex, my dad married this sister from southern Georgia, and he moved the family up here to start over. I'm a regular old potpourri of races, you might say."

"See, I never knew that about you. No wonder you have such a distinctive voice as a writer."

Ani started to cough violently. Waves of flesh rippled from the jerking motion, and her stubby fingers formed a closed fist that covered her mouth. Michael was about to offer to get her something to drink from the kitchen, but then she stopped, cleared her throat and said, "So why did you come up here? I know you didn't come just to bring me this check."

"I did come in part to bring you the check, and I came in part to discuss the manuscript with you."

"I told you," she said, seeing the title page to *Speaking in Tongues* on his lap, "that you could use *Mule-Drawn Wagon*." Then Ani leaned back, rocked her body a couple of times, and with a hoist she stood. She wobbled momentarily as if she was about to lose her balance and then grabbed the back of a chair that appeared to be in its spot for just such an occasion.

Michael looked down at the pages he had poured his heart into and said, "Actually, I did."

"Okay. And?" she said as she picked up a foot and pushed it across the floor.

"They didn't like it."

Before taking another step, she strengthened her grasp on the back of the chair and said, "They what?"

"It was not rejected, but they wanted to see a continuation of the Paula story line."

"They expect me——" Ani took another step and then extended her hand to reach for the kitchen counter. Michael noticed her ankles, which were black and purple from the weight they bore, and the balls of her heels, which were crusty from neglect. "They expect you to write a frigging serial or something?"

"Not exactly. But it's a marketing thing."

"But what about growth? What about taking the reader somewhere—somewhere they have not been before?" Ani took another sluggish step toward the counter, followed by another. She had the look in her eye of a toddler holding anything in her reach to avoid toppling over.

"I know. I told her that before I left."

"So," she said as she reached the counter and leaned her upper body weight on her elbows. "What did Pam say? How did you leave it?"

"She promised to read the entire thing this week and let me know what she thinks. But unfortunately——"

"Unfortunately what? What unfortunately?"

"They can have a ghostwriter rewrite the novel if they like."

"A ghostwriter rewrite my novel? Are you serious?"

"I told them no—that they couldn't do it—but it's in the contract. It's in their hands, and they can do whatever they want with it."

"And you left it?"

"I know I should have taken it from her, but I wasn't thinking."

"You left it, Michael? What were you thinking?"

Michael ran his fingers through his locks in thought.

"You've got to get my novel back, and that's—That's the bottom line. You don't have a choice!"

"I can't get it back!"

"You left it; you have to get it back!"

"I can't, Ani. Damn, I told you it's their novel, and under the rights of the contract, they can—"

"Either you get my fucking novel back or I go to the press. If I do that, then they'll never change my words." Ani's head slumped, and she seemed to try to retain her composure.

"You wouldn't do that. Besides, if you did, they will want the money back. Then I would have to ask you to—"

"To what? Give you the money back? Michael, that money is stashed away in T-bills," she said with her head bowed. "I doubt we spent a thousand dollars of it. Nothing will own me. Not a man. Not money. And definitely not some dumb ass'd bitch like Pam Wilson!"

Michael closed his eyes and said, "Slow down a second, Ani."

"No, to hell with you!" She looked at Michael and said, "I'm not going to put a book out there and have somebody change everything I worked so hard to create!" Ani's face became flush red. "Look around you!" Michael continued to stare at Ani. "I said look around you, dammit!" Ani smashed her fist to the counter, causing it to make a cracking sound.

Michael looked at the wallpaper that was peeling in spots. The water-damaged ceiling and the glass in the window covered by duct tape.

"This is my world. This is my reality. This is all I have. I have a man who does not know his left hand from his right. I have a body that has not walked outside and felt the sun in years, and I have my fucking words. That's it. Nothing else. *Season* was my story!"

"I know that," Michael interjected.

"Well, if you know that, then you should know me. If

I let them change it, what is that saying about me as a person? I won't allow you, Charisma or anyone else to change what I've done, and I would rather"—heavy breath—"give them my last breath than to give them my soul."

CHAPTER

9

Everyone always said that Phillip had the goods. That he would make a great politician.

Phillip Evans was a former collegiate lacrosse player, had the right texture of hair, the right handshake and was well versed on state issues. Although his background was in mass communication, and he had spent the bulk of his adult life in the entertainment industry, many thought his political skies had no limitation. But that was before he had made an off-color remark at a party that was reported in the *Tampa Tribune*. After hitting the pothole on the road to the state house, many observers, including Joi, thought his prospects looked dim.

"You know I hate coming to these things." Joi pulled down the Range Rover's visor and applied her dark earth-toned eye shadow in the mirror as she tried to ignore her mate. "Nothing but a bunch of old stuck-up windbags with too much money, too much time and too little brains to put either of them to good use."

Joi thought of the close call when she had been in the limo with Michael five months earlier outside the same hotel to which they were headed. When she had seen her husband from behind, she had expected the worst, but later found out he had been there only to make last-minute arrangements for her surprise birthday party. The thought that he had done it in such a way that twenty-five of her closest friends were able to surprise her was what endeared Phillip to her. But on nights like this when he would whine incessantly, she wanted to be anywhere but by his side. As he continued to complain, Joi attempted to hum "Choosey Lovers" by the Isley Brothers so she could block out his voice.

". . . and then you'll have a bunch of jocks on the other side. They'll more than likely have a few of the Bucs there and a couple of the Devil Rays to impress these star-crazed people down here. I wish for *once* these people would hold something like this in St. Petersburg. I get so damn tired of coming to Tampa to do *anything* with a semblance of social importance. And to think," he added, "they had the audacity to want me to pay a hundred bucks per head *just* to walk into this shit. I'll tell you one thing. If they want a C-note from me, they got another thing coming. I bet'cha that!"

"Isn't the money going to the United Way?" she mumbled.

"Damn a United Way. I don't care if it's the Stop Slavery Fund! A hundred bucks is a hundred bucks!"

Joi opened her mouth to make a comment, but held her peace instead. She thought of the moments after her birthday party when she and Phillip returned home and she had opened a gift her friend Sandy advised her specifically not to unwrap at the party. Inside the box was a pair of red crotchless panties. When Phillip walked in the room and saw them in her hands, he said, "Leave it to Sandy to buy you some hooker wear. Have you seen my red-and-blue tie? I need it for tomorrow."

Joi ignored the comment and went into the bathroom.

At thirty she had had the opportunity to pose for *Playboy* and turned them down. At thirty-five when she had appeared on Letterman, he had stopped talking to her in the midst of the interview and said, "My God you're a beautiful woman. I know you're beautiful on screen, but in person you're just—just spectacular. Paul," he had said to his sidekick, "have you seen this woman up close?" Then he had smiled his huckleberry gap-toothed smile, and the crowd applauded as one.

But as Joi slid the panties up her thighs and took off the flannel pajama top, she wondered if she could still turn heads. While her breasts were not as full as they had been fifteen years previously, her nipples were not exactly pointing south due to gravity. Her stomach showed the effect of the miles of running she did each week, and her skin was a luminous sable brown from eating the right number of yellow and green vegetables, as well as leading the right lifestyle.

The night of her birthday, Joi wore her crotchless panties under her flannel pajamas to bed. At the right moment she complained about the heat, pulled off the pajama bottom and lay close enough for Phillip to notice the change in her attire. Her toes stroked the top of his foot. Her womanhood brushed his thigh. He never returned the touch. He never made a comment.

At a red light Phillip and Joi pulled up beside a brother with twists in his hair driving a lime green Escalade and bumping his head to the bass sounds reverberating from the walls of the truck. Seeing him sparked memories of a special night in Joi's mind. A night she would have cashed in all of their years for a few of his minutes.

There was something about Michael's touch that she could still feel months later. The way he kissed her body. The way he looked into her eyes. When she went to sleep, she would touch herself and allow Michael to mentally slide between her and her husband. She felt guilty, because of the vows she had taken, but she could not stop the feelings that boiled inside. Her marriage for all practical purposes was dead. They had become an almost couple. They were married almost two decades. Almost happy with each other. Almost content with their lives. Almost over Angie. Almost ready to turn the page. But as she sat in the truck and listened to Phillip complain about the noise from the Escalade, Joi realized for the first time that the marriage was not almost, but completely over.

"So," Joi said, and closed the mirror as they rode toward the Hyatt, "do you intend on making at least a donation tonight?"

"I thought we donated money every year?"

Joi was fascinated how *her* syndication money for the show he said was beneath her was always *their* money. "I have Nina send them something each year, but I assumed you would give them a little extra since they are having this big drive and all."

"Drive my ass. Listen, I have to raise about seventy thousand to get some TV ads going. Plus we need to get a few ads cut and in the can in a few weeks."

As they drove toward the hotel, Joi decided to ask him something that had been churning in her mind for days, but since he was always either on the road campaigning or at work she never had the time. "Phil?"

"Yes?"

"I got a call from Breidenbaugh's office Monday."

"Jerk. What does he want?"

"They wanted to know if I would consider taking a

teleconference. Since I don't have an agent, they wondered if I would be interested in a few ideas they have."

"You did tell them to go to hell, right? Since *Purchased Tickets* bombed, what's he trying to make now? *Purchased Shit II?*"

"Only in Hollywood can a hundred million dollars be considered a bomb. But actually, it's an ensemble piece. Me, Glenn Close, Ally Sheedy, Alfre Woodard and Nicole Kidman. Just a movie about five women who are stranded in this cabin."

"Are you," he said, and then looked at his wife. "actually considering doing this? Considering working with Breidenbaugh after he called you the *C* word?"

"This is business and this is Hollywood."

"No, honey. That *was* Hollywood, okay?" he said as he pointed his thumb over his shoulder. "That *was* Hollywood, and we *made* our bones there. We accomplished what we wanted, and we got out alive."

Joi squeezed a dollop of moisturizer into the center of her palm and applied it to her elbows.

"I'm glad to see there is some interest for you in L.A., but to be honest, if you are asking me for my thoughts, I think it'd be the worst mistake ever."

"Why is that?"

"Reeve's name in that town is shit nowadays. Yeah, he had a few big techno flicks that made it; but now that he's in the Church of Scientology, he's trying to make these warm and fuzzy movies, and the public's not buying it. If this thing gets distribution, I'd be surprised. Especially if he's trying to do it for eighty or ninety million again." Joi was silent. "You know, you've been acting strange ever since you returned from California." Joi held her tongue. "I don't know what's going on, honey, but all I can tell you is this. This business runs in cycles. You don't want to be attached to a dog when your time comes around. I mean, look at *Purchased Tickets*. It was one of the biggest bombs of the year. It pulled a few dollars but not nearly what they expected. Now, when the right vehicle comes along, you don't want that baggage." And then Phillip reached over and held his wife's hand and said, "And this is not the right vehicle."

Joi refused to ask him how he had become psychic.

"Phil, I'm an actor. That's what I do. If you lose your dreams, you will lose your mind, and I swear, sitting in that house every day, I'm losing it."

"So what do you want to do?" he said, still holding her hand. "You want to run off and audition for this part or whatever when I need you here with me?"

"It's not about this part. It's about my life. I have *no* life."

"Ohhh, so the truth comes out. When I was in L.A. supporting *your* dreams, when I was working two jobs so you could run casting calls," he said, and released her hand, "that was not a problem. When I was handing out head shots to directors and pitching you while I was waiting tables, that was not a problem."

"Jesus Christ, here we go again," Joi said, as she stared deep into the night.

"You're damn straight here we go again. What about the wind beneath my wings? I supported your dreams, and now that it's my turn to do something I want to do, that I am compelled to do, you don't have a life? Leaving my parents' business in White Plains to move to L.A. with you is not a life. Parking cars at Spagos, although I have two degrees, is not a life. Being Mr. Joi Weston is not a fucking life!"

"Phillip, it's not about that, and you know it. I sit home all day crocheting like I'm seventy years old. No matter what the calendar says, I'm in the prime of my life, and I know I can——"

"You're forty——"

"So?"

"Joi, you know what time it is. You knew that when you got in the business. Why don't you just hold out a few more years until you get around fifty? Your face will age a little more, and then you can get different types of roles. I'm not telling you this because I want to keep you under my wing, although I know you think that. I just don't want to see you having to audition for these minor roles. That's something that I think is beneath you to be honest."

"I'm an actress, Phil," she said as they entered the lighted circular drive of the hotel.

As soon as the truck came to a stop, the doorman came to Joi's door and the valet to Phillip's. He graciously smiled and held up a finger to indicate that he wanted to sit in the truck a little longer.

"Actors act. That's what we do, and we do it for the same reason we draw breath. And if you take it from us, there's a void."

"Can't you do something here in Tampa at the Jaeb Theater?"

"I can't do that, and it's nothing against people who do. I played in the pros. I can't go back and play in college. Acting with Laundromat attendants and people who sell cars by day and act by night. I just can't."

"Well, the answer is no."

"No?"

"No! I have to put my foot down somewhere, Joi. I love you," he said, and looked at his wife, "and because of that, I'm not going to let you go out there and hurt yourself. Besides, once again, I devoted years to making you a success, and I think the *least* I can expect is five months."

"No?" she repeated, trying to come to terms with the two-letter word.

"That's what I said. Now, I hate to be a hard-ass about this thing, but—"

"You did *not* just tell me no."

"Joi, if you go through with this—just don't go through with this. Not now. It won't look good with me campaigning here, and you off in L.A. Just don't."

Phillip got out of the car, walked around to her side and, before the doorman could return, opened her door, smiled at her and repeated, "Just don't."

For years Joi had faked a smile to the world. When they lived in San Francisco fifteen years earlier and he had had an affair with a stripper, she had smiled. When he slapped her so hard one of her teeth came loose, after the swelling went down, she had smiled. So as she got out of the dark blue vehicle and noticed several people looking at her, once again she smiled, slid her forearm under her husband's arm and walked inside the cocktail party like the perfect high society couple.

After Phillip and Joi exited the elevator, they went through the usual motions of working the room. It was something they had perfected since their early days in Hollywood. Phillip would walk in one direction; Joi in the other. And both would grin and shake hands for hours. On the top floor of the hotel, Phillip held court with a number of businessmen while Joi talked to a gathering of mostly women about her days working on the small screen.

Occasionally, if she met someone who seemed to be of substantial worth, she would personally walk them over and introduce them to Phillip, and when they made a connection, she was off to continue her wifely duties. As she spoke to one woman who said she had watched each and every episode of "Potts McGee and Me," Joi's mind drifted to the previous conversation. *I can't believe he told me no. Just plain no.*

"I read a few years ago in *Ebony* that you were married to the same man for over ten years," the woman said.

"Actually, it's a little more now." With a smile Joi graciously held up her fingers and said, "Can you give me one moment? I need to go to the ladies' room." As she walked away, she saw several men who were so large they physically seemed to fill up the room by themselves. There was also the normal quantity of women who appeared to be there on a mission to find a mate, and men who were on a mission to find satisfaction. As she walked toward the ladies' room, Joi passed the bar, which overlooked a pool that was darkened. All she wanted to do for a quick moment was to order herself a glass of Armagnac and sit near the pool to watch the water. To contemplate what that she should do with the next half of her life.

"Joi," she heard Phillip's voice, which for a moment made her wince, but she was determined to give a stellar performance. And just as she did when she acted, she whispered to herself the word, "Purpose."

"Yes, dear."

"This is Sam Addison," Phillip said. "He's the president and C.E.O. of—"

"Belkin Foodway. How are you, sir?" Joi said. "I've seen your TV commercial. You have a wonderful presence in front of the camera."

As she spoke to the tall, lowbrow man who wore white shoes to the formal affair, Joi noticed her husband's expression as he watched her roll the man as if he were putty. After she finished talking, he looked at Phillip and asked him to call his secretary to set something up for them to play golf. Translation, a sizeable donation to the Phillip Evans congressional campaign was in the offing.

When Mr. Addison turned to walk away, Phillip smiled at his wife and disappeared into the crowd to find additional prey.

Son of a bitch, Joi thought, and then continued walking into the ladies' room. Since it was empty, she spoke aloud to herself. "He must think I'm a fool. How in the hell he gonna just tell me no. Like I'm some kinda dog. No—No, this shit is definitely over. I have half a mind to call an attorney tomorrow. But he's so scandalous, he'll more than likely want alimony or something." She ran her fingers over her forehead as she walked back and forth. The night he had told her he was cheating was the first strike; the night he had hit her the second. And she had promised herself that on the third strike it would be over. Before she knew it, she pulled out her cell phone and called Michael. She could count on one hand the number of times she had called him, yet she knew his number by heart.

"What in the hell do I say if he picks up?"

"Hello. This is Michael and you know the deal. Peace and blessings." *Beep.*

Joi opened her mouth to speak, but hit the end button on the phone to terminate the call. "That flat-feet bastard trying to control me like that? Telling me when I should roll over," she said as she called her brother, "and fetch? Well, after all these years he don't hardly understand!"

"Speak."

"How are you doing, sweet cakes?" she said in an attempt to stifle her anger.

"Oh, it's you," Joe replied.

"Well, don't sound so excited."

"I thought you were G.G. She left about eleven this morning, and I haven't heard from her."

"What?"

"Another fight—shit ain't right—what else is new."

"Tell me about it," Joi sighed, "sounds like a Teddy Pendergrass song."

"Don't tell me, you're having problems with Phillip."

"Unfortunately I am. But I don't even feel like talking about it. Actually, I called you to talk about anything else but Phillip."

"So what's going on in your world? Did you make it to that charity function?"

"I'm here now. In the bathroom no less," she said, walking into the stall, "sitting on the john. It's just another get-together where everybody wants to show how important they are."

"Next weekend I'm going to a symposium in—"

"It's over, Joe."

Joe paused before speaking, then said, "I was afraid you would say that. Did he cheat again?"

"No. This time, to be honest, it's about something bigger. I don't know if I even love him anymore. I know we have a lot of water under the dam and all of that, but I feel disgusted when I look at him. I want to bathe when he touches me. At times, honestly, it's torture just holding his hand."

"So if you leave him, then what?"

"I don't know. I might go back to L.A. Maybe I can find something to do in the business besides act for a while. Maybe I'll move back to New York. Possibly do some off-Broadway stuff. I just need to learn how to breathe again 'cause I'm dying in this relationship."

"Isn't Michael still living in Harlem?"

"Please, as big as that city is, he would never know I was there."

"Have you thought about the possibility of—"

"Nothing is going to happen between him and me. Please. I don't need that drama. I've been with one man over half my life. Think about that. Do you really think I want to just jump into another relationship?"

"I was just asking. Does he still call?"

"He's called a few times in the past. But that's about it. Actually," she said softly, "he called several times yesterday, but as soon as I saw the number on the caller I.D., I turned off the ringer."

"Have you been intimate with him?"

"NO!"

"Are you sure, Joi?"

"*Hell no!* How can you ask me some shit like that? You know that's not my style."

"I was just wondering. I know you said Phillip had his little problem in the bedroom, and that has to be tearing at the marriage."

"It's not even about that as much as it's about him. I'd rather be in bed with a man I loved who couldn't, than one who could go all night that I couldn't stand. And frankly a brother who cannot," she whispered, "sex me and is an asshole, has gotz to go."

"Let me give you a bit of advice. I know you have thought long and hard on this, 'cause you've never been the type to go off half-cocked. But I heard a saying today that fits your—our situation. It goes like this. 'The product of a failed marriage is not that adults produce children, but that adults become children.' You have almost twenty years. I have five. We have people who drive us crazy, but you know what? It's easy to walk away. It's easy giving up and saying it's over and I want a divorce. Mom always knew about Daddy. I'm sure it embarrasses her even now, but she ain't leaving. She has more character than anyone I have ever met in my life."

"Joe, I love you, and I know you love me. I appreciate the advice, but let me tell you something. I value my marriage. But more than anything else, I value myself. If I die, if I'm not whole, what can I give to Phillip—if I have nothing left for myself?"

"Tell me this, and I will not beat you over the head with it anymore. How in the world can you stop loving someone after all you've gone through for all these years? The good and the bad."

"For two hours, as he snored next to me in bed, I looked at the ceiling of our room last night and asked myself the exact same question. I asked it in the exact same words you just used. It's not the sex, Joe." She swallowed nothingness. "It's not the affair. It's not even his temper." Joi opened the bathroom stall and looked at herself in the mirror over the basin. "It's me."

A woman walked into the bathroom as Joi approached the door.

"Do me a favor?" Joe said to his sister.

"Yes?"

"Before you make a decision, get some professional help."

"We can't. Phillip is very antipsychiatrist since the man we spoke to before seemed to do more harm than good. He always says no one can tell him anything he don't know about me after all these years together."

"Yeah, I remember you telling me that. Well, call me tonight when you get home."

Joi hung up the phone, slid it into her purse and willed herself to grab the doorknob. *How in the hell does he get off telling me no? And what kinda tasteless bastard makes a joke about slavery on top of it. The older this man gets*

. . . *anyway. This shit is over. Finished. Done.* She opened the door to the restroom and scanned the crowd for new faces. She looked for anyone to talk to who would not come up to her and ask the same questions. Then over the crowd she heard the familiar hyenalike cackle of Phillip's laughter. "Just keep on laughing, Phillip. You just keep on laughing."

Hours later the social event was winding down, and Joi was looking through a high-powered telescope at Tampa Bay by night. She could see the lights of the Florida Aquarium as well as St. Petersburg in the distance. She could also see the moon, which was as round as a dime, as pale as beach sand and as honest as a Sunday morning. Phillip had led a nonstop battalion of individuals to meet her one by one and collected so many business cards he had asked her to tuck them in her purse on several occasions.

She knew if she was going to take the meeting with Whisper Films, she had to agree to do so by the next day; therefore, as soon as they returned home, she would tell Phillip. She would not tell him she wanted a divorce, but she would tell him that she was going to pursue the role. He would be upset, but she knew he would get over it.

"Joi," Phillip said. "I have one last person for you to meet."

Before she pulled her eye away from the ocular of the telescope, Joi whispered, "Purpose," and prepared her face as if she were about to hear the click of the slate marker before hearing the word *action!* She turned around and saw his face, which looked Rembrandt beautiful.

"This is the guy you've been reading over and over

again. I think you went to one of his signings a few months ago. Michael Brockmier, this is my wife, Joi Weston-Evans."

Joi was shaken by the image of him. Her knees felt mushy, but she maintained her composure and stayed in character. "Yes, I enjoyed the book immensely. I went to see you at a signing in Tampa. A small store outside of town? You might not remember," she said to him.

Michael was visibly shocked and stammered before saying, "Ahum, I do so many signings, I don't remember."

"I told my wife that she fell in love with that book so much it almost makes me want to read again. I think the last book I read was something by Walter Mosely, but that's been at least fifteen years."

As Phillip pontificated about his literary inadequacies and segued into how he was running for office, Joi watched her husband, but could see only Michael.

He seemed taller than she remembered and smelled like the forest after the rain had fallen. His hair was once again pulled back, and a single thick, yarn-like strand hung over his eye. He looked at Phillip as he spoke as if he was listening to everything he was saying, but Joi could feel his spirit.

He was dressed like a number of other men in the room in a white dinner jacket, red tie, crimson carnation and black slacks. But none of the other men in the room could set her body to aching by the way he simply held a glass of champagne to his full lips and wiped the residue off with the rim of the glass.

"Now, I know your father was involved in New York City politics back in the day. Do you have any ambitions as such?"

"Actually, no. My dad was the total Renaissance man in the family, and I'm just trying to concentrate on the words." He looked at Joi and said, "Just trying to write the best novel I can write."

"And it shows," she said, and then excused herself. "I have to get something to drink from the bar. Can I get you something, honey?"

"No, I'm okay."

"Nice meeting you, Mr. Brockmier. I'm definitely looking forward to that next novel coming out as well."

Joi wanted to melt into the carpet as she walked toward the glass-enclosed bar.

"Can I help you, madam?"

"Yes." She stood before the bartender, who was storing the liquors in a locked cabinet. "I would just like to have some club soda and orange juice if you don't mind?"

As the woman poured the mixture and added a few ice cubes, Michael walked up behind Joi and said as he looked in the opposite direction, "Now, isn't this something right off the silver screen? Me meeting you here?"

Joi looked at the bartender, who handed her the drink and seemed intent on returning to secure the bar for the night. "Excuse me," Michael said to the middle-aged woman dressed like a penguin. "Can I get a Jack Daniels?"

She looked at her watch and then said sure as she searched for the key to open a previously secured cabinet.

"What're you doing here?" Joi asked. Then she turned around to look for Phillip on the other side of the glass wall and found him sitting on a pool table talking to a football player undoubtedly about sports.

"I flew in last week. I've been here all week long doing a little writing, some media stuff, but mostly thinking about you."

The bartender, who heard the last line, looked at Joi

and then Michael and said, "Sorry, we're all out of Jack. Actually, the bar closed ten minutes ago."

"Thanks anyway," Michael said, and allowed the woman with a pack of Marlboros in her vest pocket to finish her cleanup for the night.

Joi turned to walk away, and Michael said without looking in her direction, "Don't do that. Okay?"

The bartender glanced at the awkward couple, but then took her black order pad, placed it under her armpit, wiped off the counter and headed toward the exit of the bar. "If you all don't mind," she said, "I have to turn off the lights in this area to let people know the bar is closed, but you're welcome to stay if you like."

Joi finished her drink and said, "Ahum, no, I am leaving, too."

"Don't do this," Michael said, and grabbed her hand.

Joi looked at the bartender, who saw what happened, then turned and walked away. Joi shot daggers at Michael with her eyes and said, "Don't do that. Are you crazy? People know me here!"

"Yo, I called you what, ten times, and you never returned one of my calls. I wanted to tell you I was heading down, but you turned off the voice mail on your phone."

"Yes, I turned it off. Have you forgotten that I wear a wedding band?"

"Yeah, you don't have to tell me again."

"Tell you what?"

"You love your husband. You keep saying it, you *might* just start to believe it."

"Fuck you!" Joi said between clenched teeth.

Michael paused, rubbed his fingers through his banana locks, which now hung loose and partially in his face, and said, "Listen, I was wrong to go there. It's been a long and exhausting day, and I was afraid I would be in town and not see you. That's all. I know you can't give me what I need or want, and I'm cool with that. But when I was calling, I just wanted to hear your voice. Sometimes I would just call and hang up. I know it's childish, but I just wanted to hear—anyway."

"We really should not be having this conversation."

"I have *never* been attracted to a married woman, Joi."

"You're not attracted to me, Michael. You just want to—"

"You can't say that. I feel something, and I know it's sincere. Maybe it's the fact that we've both lost something near and dear. Maybe it's because you are the only person who I can tell how I felt all those years not talking, who does not look as though I am making them feel uneasy. I just know that from the moment I first saw you in Atlanta, I had to take this chance. Tell me to go to hell if you like. You think I care? I had to let you know what I feel."

Frozen in her steps, she asked, "Why are you here? At the function?"

"Trust me, I've asked myself the same question all night long. The publicist thought it would be a good idea for me to show up and mingle a little. It's not my crowd, but it's a good cause, so—"

"We can't talk like this," she said, and continued walking. As she opened the door into the main room, she looked at Phillip again, who was this time making gyrations with his hands, apparently recreating his feats of prowess on the lacrosse field for the athletes.

"Why can't we talk? Your husband already introduced us, and no one will know what's going on. We can just sit at a table and talk about our careers."

"I don't have a career. Or have you forgotten that

also." Joi adjusted the pleat in her skirt and said before she walked away, "Good night, Michael."

As she stepped through the gathering of mostly drunk attendees, Michael weaved through the crowd like a fish in a stream behind her and whispered so only she could hear, "I'm headed back to New York first thing tomorrow. I know I was out of line earlier, but I'm in room 3118, right here, in this hotel."

"Are you brain dead?"

"Just wanted to tell you. Just call me? I am not asking for anything. I just want to talk."

Joi looked at Phillip and heard the word *no* echo in her mind as if shouted from Mount Rainier. "No, we can't talk. Take care," she said, and looked at Michael with complete sincerity. "And please, do not call me again." Joi walked over to the woman who had never missed an episode of "Potts McGee and Me," and asked her, "What other TV shows do you enjoy?"

As the woman counted off the shows with her fingers, Joi inhaled the scent of Michael's cologne as he passed by her and headed toward the door. While the woman spoke, all Joi could think of was being intimate with the novelist, lying on her back and the tops of her knees touching the top of the mattress. As the woman spoke she saw Michael leave, and felt she had made a mistake.

As he moved through the crowd, the woman turned and looked at him, then looked at Joi and said, "I hate to ask like this."

"Ask what?"

"Is that—is that, ahum."

"No," she said as the door closed. "He's not the singer. It's Michael Brockmier."

"Oh. Yeah, I studied his book when I was in high school. He's good."

* * *

"Phil," Joi said as she stood in the darkened bar area alone, looking out at the pool. "I need this role." She said the words several times to prepare how she would tell him later that night. Each time she said it, she emphasized a different word. "Phil, *I* need this role. Phil, I *need* this role. Phil, I need *this* role." The more she said it, the more her confidence grew.

Although the bar had been closed for a couple of hours, Phillip was still in the pit of the recreation area with the celebrities doing what he did best, and Joi needed the time to stand in the same spot she had spoken to Michael and prepare herself for the fork in the road of her marriage.

Behind the counter she saw what appeared to be a bound galley. On the cover was the title *Mule-Drawn Wagon*, and under the bold print were the words "From the New York Times best-selling author Michael Brockmier II." "What in the hell," she said to no one as she picked up the book and thumbed through the pages. On the front were the words "Uncorrected proof. Not for sale or trade."

And then she saw him. He walked toward the darkened bar across the patio area beyond the pool.

First instinct made Joi want to retreat and leave the bar, but her body could not move. She looked back at Phillip again and thought of the roomful of black balloons he had bought for her birthday party. She thought of the 'you're not getting older; you're just getting more miles on you' joke he had made during her toast. She also thought of her solo voyage to California and how she had picked the weeds from her daughter's headstone alone, and she knew somehow, someway, she would make love to Michael that night.

Joi slid the galley into the cabinet over the bar and

positioned her back to the door so it would be the first thing he saw when he walked in.

"I see you're still here."

"Yeah. Just waiting for the old ball and chain to get enough of telling his war lies out there."

"He seems like a nice guy," Michael said in a singsong voice. "Listen, I left my galley here earlier. Do you know if anyone mentioned seeing it?"

"No."

"Umm. Let me go out here and ask," he said as he walked toward the recreation room, "if anyone saw it. I need to do a reading tomorrow night."

"Wait a minute," she said, and then squatted to look in the cabinet under the bar. "I think I saw the bartender with something earlier, now that I think about it."

"Did it have an orange cover?" Michael asked, and walked around to the other side of the bar.

"Maybe it's in one of the cabinets up there. You check up there, and I'll check under the bar," Joi said as she watched her prey walk into the trap.

As soon as Michael reached for the cabinets, he saw the book—and felt Joi unbuckle his trousers. She saw his eyes bulge, and then he looked toward Phillip and said, "Baby, are you sure you want to do this?"

Joi pulled his manhood free, which she could feel hardening in her hand. "I want to do this," she said, and felt utterly in control of her life for the first time in weeks.

Michael rested his back against the refrigerator as Joi took a moment to admire him. Just inches away from her tongue, she inhaled his scent. She held him in her hand as if she were holding his heart and one wrong move would send his body into convulsions.

Since Phillip was an average-sized man, when their sex life had been active, she never desired the feel of another, but the absence coupled with his change in demeanor had driven her to gazing at something so close to her lips she could smell it. She could taste its sweet, musky, yet masculine scent without ever bringing it to her mouth. But then she did, and she felt the rest of his body harden as well.

With both of her hands at the base, she slid them up and down his fully aroused body, and watched as the tip turned into a glorious shade of coffee brown and came just a hairsbreadth away from her lips. She grabbed the backs of his thighs and allowed him to slide between her kiss.

The salty taste of flesh in her mouth turned her on to a level she could not remember experiencing. Her fingers ran up and down the rolled line of material that was his black bikini underwear positioned at the top of his thighs. For this moment, she was not going to worry about being caught. This moment was all hers, and she took pleasure in indulging.

She could feel Michael's hand over her head as if it were an erogenous halo, and she did not mind if he grabbed a fistful of her hair and directed her in how to pleasure him. She didn't mind because in giving up the control, she knew she was the master of everything that would happen.

Faster and faster, the fold of skin covering his hardness, she stroked his shaft, trying to feel him explode, and then Michael begged, "Baby, stop. Please stop." Joi massaged him faster and faster. "No, baby, seriously. Please don't do that," he said, and then the back of his cupped fingers slid over the softness of her cheek and sent a warm shiver throughout her body. "I don't want it like this. Can you come back to my room?"

Joi squeezed him softer, so her fingers were barely sliding up his shaft, yet she allowed her thumb to drag stiffly over the head and moved her fist like a kid on the monkey bars, making his body flinch with every stroke.

"Baby, please, let's not do it like this. I want you. But I want all of you."

Then she stopped. "Csistst!" She heard his breath vacuum from his body and looked up to see his eyes staring blankly into the recreation room.

Michael relaxed and looked at her as he gripped the edge of the bar like a first-time swimmer in a pool.

"Baby, what are you doing to me?"

Joi stood, turned and looked at Phillip. He was attempting a trick shot with the pool stick behind his back, and as soon as the ball went in the hole, the others applauded his mastery of the pool table. Joi felt Michael walk up behind her and press her body against the bar. As she closed her eyes, she wondered if she had locked the door and remembered that she had not. She wondered what would happen if anyone walked in at that very moment. But those thoughts were trampled by the size, thickness and weight of Michael's penis, and her imagining how it would feel inside her wet body.

She felt him slide it up and down the crease of her butt and felt like a nineteen-year-old virgin.

From nowhere Michael's voice became Barry White deep and authoritative as he said, "A thong?"

A quiver passed through the blades of her shoulders, and she nodded as his hands slid around her and stroked her swollen nipples. Michael's large, strong hands were slow; his touch was firm and even. He tasted her earlobe, and the sucking sound made her toes curl even in the four-inch stilettos.

Then he said, "Baby, if I can't take you to the room, can I—"

Joi reached over her shoulder and without looking placed her hand over his mouth. Michael took the cue, moved his hand to the center of her back and firmly bent her over the bar.

Her eyes closed, Joi's heart took a perilous leap. She moved her hips in a circle and swallowed slowly. The excitement in her body was palatable to her lips.

"This will be a night," his voice rumbled as he raised her skirt over her bottom, "a night you will *never* forget." Then he slid aside the red birthday thong that her husband had all but ignored and grunted, "Baby . . . baby . . . baby."

Joi's hands eased over the smooth black surface of the bar, and she looked at Phillip one last time, then closed him out of her night. If only for the moment.

Michael slid his hand over her bottom and rubbed his body around and around her wetness. Teasing, taunting, tantalizing her flesh, he moved himself closer to the spot and moved away. She wanted to back toward him. Joi wanted to force its entrance inside a part of her that had been neglected, but she did not. Then she moved her fingers to her nipples and prepared for whatever the moment would bring.

Her eyes opened. And although she was in heels, she tiptoed higher, and her mouth formed an *O* as he entered her domain.

"Baby," he whispered. "Don't let me hurt you. Okay?"

She shook her head no to grant him permission to explore deeper, as she rose to her tiptoes. Michael gave her a little more love and pulled her body upward so that her back was against his hard nipples.

"Show me with your body, baby," he whispered, and guided his hands down to her freshly shaved triangle. He moved the rest of her thong to the side and leisurely circled her swollen cherry as he slid his body in and out of her slowly, evenly, passionately.

"Baby, I want you to fuck me," she whispered, "like

I've never been fucked before!" She felt fire in her eyes that transformed into tears. She could feel her body start to shake. Joi could feel the ribs of his penis inside of her with every stroke, and occasionally the groove of the head would slip out and cause her stomach to stir as it reentered. Although her eyes glistened, she looked at Phillip, laughed and felt nothing but contempt. "Say no to this," she whispered. "Say no to this."

After she climaxed, Michael allowed himself to explode inside of her, and she closed her eyes. She had forgotten the sensation of how a man felt settled all over her love. How it felt when it rolled down her upper thigh, making its way inch by scintillating inch to her knee. She had forgotten the feeling of her lips being so aroused it felt funny walking afterward, causing a sensation that would excite her all over again. But this was what she was feeling, and as he kissed her good night, gave her his number again and pleaded with her to call him, she tucked it under the strap of her thong and watched him escape out the pool door. To her utter surprise, there was no regret.

As Michael disappeared into the night, she prepared herself for the role of Mrs. Wifey. She went into the private bathroom and checked her makeup in the mirror. After a few minor adjustments, her hair was almost perfect. Her makeup for the most part, except for the lipstick, was still in place after a quick touch-up. She gave herself one last look over, closed her eyes and leaned against the wall, remembering how heavy he had felt. Remembering what he had touched inside of her. Remembering—Then she shook her head and smiled a smile she knew would be hard to remove, no matter what Phillip said to her on the ride home. "Phillip," she smiled, "I want *this* role and I'm going to Hollywood."

She clicked off the light with fingers that were still

experiencing the shakes from aftershocks and looked one last time toward the pool. Michael was gone. Just an unforgettable memory she could not believe she had experienced. As she left the restroom, she remembered that she should clean what was left of him from her thighs, but there was something erotic about wearing him home that would not allow her to do so.

Before Joi went to join her husband, she saw the orange-red embers of a cigarette being smoked beside the pool. She walked a little closer to the window and saw the bartender gazing back at her.

"Holy shit."

CHAPTER

10

Everyone always said that Michael had the goods. That he had the voice, coupled with the looks and breeding, to not be a marginal, but a great novelist.

The words in *Season of Regret* were "as smooth as an autumn breeze and as comforting as a baby's bottle," one reviewer wrote. But then he submitted *Mule-Drawn Wagon*, and Janessa Harvey, who happened to see it by accident on Pamela's desk, told Pamela this would be the one that would put Michael in the class with his father.

In spite of the fact that it was not as commercial as *Season*, Janessa saw the bigger picture and asked Pam if she could assist her in tweaking it for a broader market. After a few modifications, Vance reread it not with an eye toward commercial, but for literary success. He enjoyed what he read, committed the financial support of Charisma behind the project, and Janessa and Pam found themselves with a novel on the brink of greatness.

Nearly a year later, Michael sat in the green room of the "Today Show" with his editor waiting for his cue to be interviewed. As he thumbed through the pages of his latest work, Pamela returned her cell phone to her purse and said, "Well, it's almost official."

"Really?"

"Looks like *Mule-Drawn Wagon* is on the National Book Award short list of nominations. If we can get you nominated, I know we have an excellent shot at the Pulitzer."

"That's great. And to think. This is the novel *you* did not care for."

"Hey, I grew up on Putnam Ave. in Bed Sty. What I know about a damn mule? But I'm glad it's getting some play, and from what sales is telling us, the buzz is incredible nationwide."

"It's about trust," Michael said with a smile.

A young brother walked in and said, "You have five minutes."

"Thanks." After he closed the door, Michael said, "You didn't trust me before. But I want you to trust me this time."

"What do you mean?" she asked as she took out a portion of a solicited manuscript to steal a few moments of reading time.

"I know this young lady. Her name is Ani. She has a physical ailment which would not allow her to tour and stuff like this, but she has the goods, Pam. Sister can write," he said as he brushed his fingertips over the red cover of *Mule-Drawn Wagon.* "She can write the most incredible stories. Now, as you know, I don't like referring a lot of people to you, but this one is a can't-miss. She's the real deal."

Pamela continued to scan the pages in front of her, then looked at Michael and said, "If I had a dollar for every time I've heard the words *can't miss,* I wouldn't have to work."

"But this time it's true. She is working on this novel. It's entitled *The Seventh Day*, and I saw it last week. It's amazing, Pam. I kid you not." By giving her the title, Michael knew he could never use her third novel. He knew that the journey through deceit would end with *Mule-Drawn Wagon* and a calmness came over his body.

Pam looked over her glasses at him and asked, "Why are you smiling like that?"

"Because I want to help this sister out. Trust me, you won't regret signing her."

"Well," Pamela said as she turned to the next page of her manuscript, "what's wrong with her? Why can't she promote?"

"She's sick."

"In what way?"

Michael smiled as Katie Couric walked past the green room door. He looked at Pam and said, "She has—she's obese."

"How obese?"

"She's heavy. Not morbid, but she has trouble walking, and she has a respiratory problem also."

"You know how I like keeping authors on the road, and that could be a problem."

"Her words are like liquid fire. She can—"

"She could write as poetic as Rita Dove; if she cannot promote her work, we have a problem. Once again, I don't look for singles. You know that. I look for home-run hitters," Pam said. "This is an image-driven industry nowadays. Just like any other segment of entertainment. Look at the big boys. Look at King, for instance. Do you think he would be as big as he is if he lived in Malibu and was a surfer dude? His image plays into his popularity. Same thing for Alice. You look at her and see the embodiment of wisdom. If Toni wrote just how she writes now but did not look, did not ra-diate the aura she does, I'm not saying she would not be a success, but I am saying it perpetuates her success."

"I understand that, but there must be something you can do with this young lady."

"I hate to be so frank with you again, but yes, you can write. But it's also your looks. We play you up because you have the goods and you pull asses into stores. Now, your friend could be wonderful; but this is commercial fiction, and the word *commercial* comes first for a reason. We're looking for books with a big upside, and if she's too big to leave the house, that means we can't put her on the cover. She can't do book signings. Only thing she can do is radio interviews by phone. That's a tough sell in today's competitive market."

"But think. Wouldn't that—"

"Two minutes, Mr. Brockmier," the page said.

"Thanks." Michael continued. "Her disadvantage *may* prove to be her advantage. Because no one can see her, it will only heighten curiosity about who she is and what she looks like. If anything, this business is about hype, isn't it?"

"That's a cute premise on the surface," Pamela said, and tucked away the pages from the manuscript, "and that may work in the movie world, but rarely in real life. Don't get me wrong; I know a lot of people who can write, yet never get published. You have the name. You have the looks. You have mad connections in New York. You have the ability to write unlike any of your contem-poraries, and with this novel you will be in a class by yourself. I would love to help your friend, but with her having just one of the four things I just mentioned, she's severely limited."

"Damn that's messed up. You won't give the sister a break because she's overweight?"

"No." Pam returned the manuscript she was reading to her briefcase. "Look at me. I'm no skinny minnie myself. I would not hire your friend to be a police officer, nor would I hire her to be a lifeguard. I won't give her a break—as you say—because this is business. It's nothing personal, and at the end of the day, that's all that counts."

The day after the NBC interview, Michael returned to Midtown with Blair. His plan after eating at McDonalds was to go shopping. After finishing his burger, he sat and watched his son. The years had seen Blair grow several inches taller, his minilocks fell over his ears and for the first time Blair seemed content with life in Gotham.

"So, Daddy, how did you like being on the 'Today Show'? How was it?"

"Just like any other interview. Only difference is millions are watching instead of a few thousand."

"Were you nervous?"

"Not really. I used to come to the studio years ago with dad, so I didn't feel—" Michael watched his son's lower jaw drop as if he saw a ghost behind him. "What's wrong with you?" he asked as he turned and looked over his shoulder. He saw a young lady dressed head to toe in red leather and buckles. Her hair was braided with what looked like orange yarn, and her fingernails and lips were painted black. She was signing an autograph for a brunette girl with pigtails.

"Who is that?"

Blair looked at his father as if he had just dropped in from another galaxy. "You don't know who Momma Cilk is? Man, Daddy, you old."

"Oh," Michael said with a half smile on his lips. "What song does she sing—rap?"

"A lot of them," Blair said as he picked up his napkin. "She has this song called "Momma's Kitchen" and another one called "Sound So Fulla Pound.""

"Sound so fulla what?"

"I know you done heard that song. Angie Martinez play it all the time on Hot 97."

"Yeah—I umm, I heard it, then."

"You got a pen? I can't believe Momma Cilk is in McDonalds in New York. She's west coast. What's she doing here? Just wait 'til I tell everybody in Montgomery. You got a pen?"

"Yeah, yeah," Michael said to his son, who had stood from his seat, ready to get the rapper's signature.

As Blair jogged toward the rap star, Michael looked through the window at Manhattan on the picturesque day in New York. A red, double-decker tourist bus plastered with advertisements on the side and tourists clumped together on top passed by. He could see the gigantic JVC sign flashing down the street as well as a woman who appeared to be homeless, next to a man handing out yellow ad sheets next to a woman speaking on a cellular phone and dressed in business attire. Just another day on Forty-sixth Street and Times Square.

"Excuse me," someone said behind Michael. He turned his head and saw her. My name is Cassidy, but your son knows me as Momma Cilk. How are you?"

"Fine." Michael looked at his son, who stared at his father so hard he didn't appear to be drawing breath.

"Dig, I can't stay long, and I know if I sit down you won't be able to enjoy your meal. I wish I had brought my book, but I left it at the hotel. I just wanted to tell you that I saw you on the 'Today Show' yesterday, and I'm not the type to read *anything*. You know, they keep me pretty busy whatever-whatever, but dig, I walked out the hotel, without my security, and went over to this brother on the street who just *happened* to be selling your shit—stuff. Well, I bought a copy to read while they were setting up for this photo shoot I'm in town to do. All I have to say, dawg, is this—You the bomb. You the shit," she said, holding her hand over her nose and mouth as she smiled. "I mean like yo—from the first page, right? I'm reading you, right? And I am feeling this sister. Paula, right? I mean, like I have never been in that situation, but word, she was deep. I mean deep deep."

"Well, umm—thanks. I'm glad you're enjoying it."

"Enjoying? Who said anything about enjoying? Yo, I read your book last night, player? Word. I called my assistant, and today she's going out to buy twenty copies. I told her we are going to start sending your shit out like welfare checks. Ya dig?"

Michael glanced at Blair, who looked as if he could use an I.V. to resuscitate him. "Thanks. I know my son is a big fan of your work and all, so you must be doing something right yourself."

"Yo, like Master P said, 'I'm gonna ball 'til I fall.' But on a serious tip, I *know* I got one maybe two more albums max, and this shit is ova like a four-leafed clova. So I'm trying to develop a few acts, get my wax on that way, and also doing some investment shi—stuff," she said as if she just remembered Blair was at the table. "I got a broker on the street, and I'll be hooked up investmentwise. But what I want to do is something like you. I know I can't write, but I want to create something," she said with a different expression in her eyes, "that will help people. You know dawg? Something that will say I've been here, because I don't want to leave a mark, Mr. Brockmier. I want to leave a dent."

* * *

Moments after the young lady left their table, Blair was still in shock.

"What's wrong with you?"

Blair shook his head. "I can't believe you were acting so goofy around Momma Cilk?"

"Goofy in what way?"

"Like a nerd. Face it, Daddy, you're old."

"I'm in my thirties."

"Maybe that's young in another country or something. But here thirty-anything is ancient. Momma Cilk is nineteen. You're almost twice her age. Man!" Blair said, shaking his head. "But I have decided one thing."

"What's that?"

"I might want to be an author."

"So, since you see me on television now and celebrities know me, you think you can get with this?"

"Yeah. Before I was scared, but I can see myself doing it. If the NBA don't work out, I'll just write books."

"You said you were scared?" Michael asked his son as a pregnant mother passed by with two Happy Meals for her children.

Blair looked at the tray in front of him and asked, "You want my fries?"

"No," Michael replied. "What do you mean by scared?"

"Well, maybe I shouldn't say scared."

"But why did you say it?"

"Let me just say this. I'm glad you didn't name me Michael Brockmier III, 'cause then everyone would want me to be a writer, too."

"I understood that a long time ago, which is why I told your mom I wanted to name you anything else but Michael. But what did you mean by scared?"

"Because Granddaddy was a writer and he killed himself. You write and you do it a lot, I know, but you don't like it. I mean to say you don't like it like you like playing the piano. I just want to do something I enjoy when I get big. Like playing in the NBA or putting tattoos on people. You know, fun stuff."

"Can I tell you something?" Michael said, looking into his son's eyes. "I made some mistakes. I made a very big mistake. I, umm—I took credit for writing that novel, and I really should not have. And it's been a living hell for me ever since. But your grandfather was a true genius. I wish I had a fraction of his talent. He could say more in a sentence," Michael said, looking at the backs of his hands, "than I can say in a paragraph. That's genius. Yes, he took his life. But maybe, Blair, he did it because . . ."

Blair looked at his father for answers. "Because of what?"

"Sometimes in life, when you have given all you have, when you can no longer find answers, you just give up. Maybe he was at that point. Maybe the true genius in him was too much to be restrained by this world. Do I think he was right or wrong? It's not for me to say. I spent too much of my life hating him, and I'm over that. But I do know this. Going through that situation prepared me for raising you, 'cause there is no way I will ever give up, on anything I do, as long as I have you in my life. No way." Michael reached across the table for one of his son's cold french fries and popped it into his mouth.

"Do you think you will ever get married again?"

"Why do you ask?"

"Just curious."

"Do you want me to get married?"

"Yes."

"Why?"

"Because," Blair said, and pulled his fingers away from his father's grasp. "You're lonely. I can tell."

"How can you tell?"

"All you do is work on the computer. You used to tell me bedtime stories. You used to play basketball with me in the afternoons. We used to hang out like this all the time and just"—he looked up at his father—"just talk. Now all you do is work. And watch 'Potts McGee' reruns."

"It's not easy, Blair. The career and raising you is like having two full-time jobs. I may be weak at both of them, but I try. And trust me, it's not easy."

"I know. And I still love ya," Blair said as he sucked from his straw. A cherry red Hummer with Momma Cilk's picture emblazoned on the side pulled in front of the restaurant. "Even if you are old and decrepit."

CHAPTER

II

Dear Phillip,

I can start this letter by saying I love you, but that is a given. You are without a doubt the most important thing to happen to me. I know if we had never met, I would not have achieved many of my dreams. And you were big enough to allow me to fly in the sun. I can never thank you enough for patiently standing in the shadows.

But something happened last weekend that even as I think about it now, I'm amazed it happened. I am amazed that I allowed it to progress.

There has been a divide in our marriage for a while. It would be easy to blame it on our shared tragedy, but I will not. I think age has pulled us in opposite directions, and I am told that is normal. I noticed you wanted to seek your dreams even before Angie died was killed, and I applauded you for doing that. But your dream has sucked the winds from my sails, and I feel myself on dry land unable to move forward in my life. Phillip, I had an affair. It's not easy to even write the words or necessary to say with whom. But I will say I am sorry. I wanted to tell you and not have you find out the way I found out about the error in judgment you made at Fisherman's Wharf. It hurt me to know that you sought comfort in the arms of another; but more than that it hurt to hear it from someone else. To have her call the house while I was nursing our child to tell me how you went to her because you did not find me attractive during the pregnancy.

I will never share the details with you. It's not important. I remember when you sat in the living room and told me A to Z about your six-month sexcapade. It made me ill even thinking about it today. But I will tell you that the old saying about men always doing it out of lust and women always doing it with their hearts is not true. I did it because I felt empowered. I was weak, but felt stronger at that moment than I have ever felt. It's something I have never done before. I can honestly say because of the hell I am living now, it's something I'll never do again. But the human part of me will not live a lie. We have too many miles on this road together, and that means more to me than a single act of indiscretion. We do not have a perfect marriage, and we have both made mistakes. I do not say this to minimize my transgression, but to only say at the end of the day, I still love you, and the thought of living my life without you is unbearable.

I apologize,
Joi

She reread the letter she had written and torn up four times. The third draft was condescending. The fourth seemed to put her in the position of being a martyr. But the fifth one struck the balance between all the feelings Joi held inside.

She asked herself, if she had not seen the bartender outside, would she be so bold as to tell her husband, and the answer was always no. But maybe the woman sitting by the pool and smoking Marlboros was the impetus she needed to do the right thing. So in a way her presence was a blessing. *But what type of blessing?* she wondered as she looked down at the letter on her personalized ABC Network stationery.

"Hey, I was wondering if you were still coming down to go fishing with Phillip next weekend."

"I told him I was going to try," Joe said, "but it's not looking good. G.G. doesn't want to come down with me, I have to attend this function Friday night and getting a weekend flight out will be murder."

"Well, I was going to keep my schedule open until you made a decision, but since you guys are not coming down, I guess I'll book something."

"Very funny. Listen, I wish I could sit home all day and enjoy life after working all these years. You have to be careful what you—"

"I had an affair." Joi closed her eyes as she said the words into the cordless phone. It was almost time for dinner, and she stood on her balcony and listened to kids playing in the neighbors' yards next door. For a moment the air was eerie and still as she awaited her brother's reply.

"I knew it."

"That I had an affair?"

"When you started talking about leaving him, I knew it. You guys have had problems for years, but you were never considering walking out the door. When you said that the other night, I knew you had to have someone else."

"The two situations are totally unrelated. If I were to leave him, I wouldn't go to this guy."

"It's Brockmier. Right?"

Joi paused. She softly whispered, "Yes," as if it pained her to be so predictable.

"I've known of the brother for a while. I remember he had Cynthia tripping big time. She stopped eating, stopped talking to her friends, even went up there to see him, and he made her stay in a hotel 'cause he didn't want her around his son. He's rough on women," he said with a sardonic laughter in his voice, "but the bad boys always get the girl."

"You have blown this *way* out of proportion." Joi went to the recliner, picked up her crochet yarn and partially completed afghan to keep her fingers busy as she tried to decide how much to tell her brother. "He's not some Don Juan who I couldn't say no to, and I'm definitely not chasing after him. He had been calling, and by some stroke of luck—or misfortune—he was at this party we attended."

"Damn."

"And we did it in the bar."

"Double damn."

"And umm—Well, he didn't use protection."

"Triple-stupid fucking damn, Joi, have you *lost* your mind?"

"I know it was stupid. I went to get tested for HIV. I have no reason to believe he would have anything, but I've just had a funny feeling about—"

"I have this discussion with my students. When you were out there twenty years ago, it was a different world. I remember you having the tubular ligation, but today a pregnancy is the least of your problems. How could you have casual—"

"Joe, if you don't mind," Joi said, letting the crochet needles and afghan come to rest in her lap. "I've tortured myself long enough in that regard, so I don't need any help from you, thank you very much."

Joe was quiet, and Joi could picture her brother with his fingers massaging his temples, which was what he did when he was in deep thought. "Have you ever done anything like this before?" he asked softly.

"Joe, come on. You know me better than that."

"I was just wondering. I remember you telling me about the wild parties when you were in L.A. Just wondered if—"

"I have never cheated on Phillip. Not even once. Yes, there were a slew of opportunities, but I was always faithful—until now."

"Then, why did you do it? Why this guy? Why now?"

"It had nothing to do with Michael, to be honest. He's an attractive guy and all, but it could have been Bookman off of 'Good Times.' It could have been almost anyone else. I was fed up with Phillip. Not the husband—the man. I was hurt about things he said in the past. I was tired of my life here. I was upset about going back to L.A. alone. I was, I was, I was, you fill in the blank."

"Don't tell Phillip. Michael would never tell. I don't think that's his speed, but I know you."

"Why do you say that? That you *know* me?"

"Joi, just don't tell him. That's really why you called me, isn't it? To ask if you should tell him?" Joi was silent.

"You couldn't steal a piece of Bubblicious without wanting to tell Momma. You've always been that way."

"With all we've gone through, I don't know if I can

live this lie. I'm not Phillip. I can't sit at the table and have dinner with someone every night knowing that I've been unfaithful. I tried to sleep in the bed with him and not tell him as I remembered how it felt to be with another man. And to be honest, I felt dirty. I must have taken three baths a day since the night we were together." Joi pinched her tear ducts to retain her control. "All I keep asking myself while I am in the tub is, if I am that weak of a person that after all this time, I can screw just anyone. That I could put my life at risk because I was bored? Because I was upset? I let myself down, damn Phillip. He has his faults—we all do—but I let me down this time, and that's the thing that's so hard to live with," she said as she removed her fingertips and allowed the tears to flow unabated.

"Whatever you do, do *not* tell him. I can hear your emotion, and I know you're upset. But a woman cannot just walk up to a man and say, 'Listen, I had an affair.' That shit's not going to fly."

"So I'm damned if I do and damned if I don't. If I don't tell him, I'm a liar he can't trust, and if I do, I'm a whore and a liar he can't trust."

"Joi, you made this bed. I hate being so blunt, but you allowed this to happen. It's not an easy choice, but let me tell you something. I would never want G.G. to tell me she had an affair. Now, I'm not going to tell her that shit, but in all honesty, lying in bed with her at night and thinking about it would kill me."

Joi could hear Phillip's car pull into the driveway.

"Do me a favor?"

"I can't talk right now. He just got home from work."

"Before you do anything, do me a favor."

"I can't talk right now, Joe."

"There's a sister down there who attended Clark

Atlanta College. I know her family well. She's only about twenty-eight years old, but she's one of the most respected young psychiatrists around from what I hear. Call her and—"

"I can't talk about it now," Joi said as she stood up, ran her fingers over her face and prepared to meet her husband. "Call me tomorrow and we can talk about it, but I know Phillip would never go. It would just be me, and I don't—I really don't know if I *want* to save the marriage that badly anymore."

"But just—"

Joi closed her eyes and said good-bye.

As the screen door closed, Joi heard the garage door open, and before he had cleared the threshold, Phillip said, "Hey, my lovely bride, how are you?" For some reason his mood had not seemed so bright in weeks. His dark eyes reflected sparkles of light.

As he danced through the doorway, Phillip held both of his fists pent together in the air and rotated them around as if stirring a large pot. "Have you ever noticed how when a white person wants to act cool, they always start doing the cabbage patch or the running man?" Joi could only smile. "I had a meeting with Rabbi Hazelstein, and I apologized for the Rotary Club joke. He told me that not only would he make a joint appearance to resolve this mess in the media; get this, he said he would *formally* endorse my candidacy."

"Oh, really," she said, dressed in a blue floral tank dress he enjoyed seeing her wear.

Phillip took off his coat, laid it on the couch, removed his cuff links and jiggled them in his hands as if they were dice. He walked up to Joi and said, "What's for dinner?"

"I made"—then she paused as he put his arms around her—"lamb chops."

"My favorite." Phillip backed away. "And also, I finally did it."

"Did what?"

"I finally talked to the doctor." He put the silver cuff links in his pants pocket and reached into his shirt pocket and pulled out a blue tablet. "He gave me a few free samples to use."

"Viagra?"

In a poor Austin Powers imitation, he smirked devilishly and said, "Yeah, bay'beee." Phillip stepped closer to his wife. "Seriously, I noticed how you were acting lately. And I've been thinking about you being held captive in this house all day. I'm sure it was wonderful the first few years, but it must be getting a little old now. Isn't it?"

"You might say that."

"And on top of that, things have not exactly been great in you know where either. So I went to talk to him, and he said tomorrow *I* might be walking funny," Phillip said, laughing aloud. Joi could only offer a polite smile. Then she backed away and went into the kitchen. "Is everything all right?" Phillip asked, and then resumed dancing.

"Just fine, honey."

"I thought you'd be happy. I finally took your advice."

"No, I am. I'm glad you went through with it. I'm fine," she said, and pulled down the hexagon-shaped plates for dinner. On her desk, ten feet away, was the letter tucked under her *Upscale* magazine. She started to retrieve it, but a part of her wanted him to find it so she would not have to tell him herself. She rubbed her hands together and felt the perspiration.

"You need any help?" he said, and took off his tie.

"I'm fine."

Phillip walked into the kitchen and said as he walked toward the refrigerator, "We have any beer? Heineken, Ice House, anything."

"Do you think you should drink alcohol with those things," Joi said before she caught herself. He stood next to her desk with his fingers inches from the letter.

"He didn't mention a side effect," Phillip replied, and poked his head inside the refrigerator. "All he could tell me was how hard I would be the first time I took one. Said it would be so hard my mouth would feel like cotton." Rubbing his hand along the outside of the steel door in a slow, circular motion, he said, "I'm so hungry, I could pull out one of these little blue fucks and screw the fridge." Laughing, he pulled out a beer, twisted off the cap and shot it into the trash can as if he was shooting a fadeaway jumper. After sensuously licking the long neck of the brown bottle he said, "Maybe you and I could recreate that love scene from *Disappearing Acts*. When Wesley had Sanaa Lathon on the refrigerator door?"

Joi opened the oven and slid out the robust-scented lamb chops. Their pungent smell floated upward to fill the kitchen. As she lifted the double broiler to the top of the counter, she knew she could not rest until she came clean. Phillip looked at the cover of *Upscale* and said, "You know, they know how to sell a magazine. Just put Maxwell on the cover, and they're guaranteed to push another fifty thousand."

As Phillip looked at the cover, the open-faced letter stared up at him. *Just let him read the letter*, she thought. *Just let him read the letter for himself.*

"Honey," Phillip said as Joi pulled off her green and white oven mitts, walked over to the desk and retrieved the letter. "After this election stuff is over, would you like to go on vacation? A real vacation, like Africa or something. We can go on one of those safaris or maybe finally go to Marrakesh. Remember we used to talk about that when we were teenagers? Making love and seeing giraffes and shit walking around in the distance? Doesn't that sound nice?"

"Phillip, we need to talk."

"Sure thing, bay'bee," he said in a late sixties beatnik voice. "We'll *talk* a little; then we'll *shag* a lot!"

"Can you sit down?"

"Aw hell," he laughed, and did the moonwalk to the breakfast nook. "I've never gotten good news when someone said sit down. Let me brace myself." Phillip held on to the edge of the table as he smiled.

"I have some news you might think is good, some you may consider bad. You'll have to make the call."

He took a stiff swallow, clenched his teeth and said, "Shoot."

Joi thought. *Just give him the letter, then you can answer the questions.* But as her nervous fingers traveled the outline of the stationery she held under the table, she tightened her hold on the paper and tore it down the middle. "The reason I wanted to talk to you"—she tore the paper once again for good measure—"was to clear the air. I got a call from Whisper Films earlier today." Joi saw Phillip's shoulders settle, and he rested back in his chair. "In fact, Breidenbaugh called himself this time. Asked me to audition for the ensemble piece I mentioned before. He said if I couldn't decide by Monday, they would have to offer it to C.C.H. Pounder." Joi could feel her heart stop beating from the nervous tension she felt, but knew she had to continue. "He apologized and even told me it was a big mistake not keeping me and trying to find another actor to play the lead. But," she said as the pieces of paper fell to the floor, "I told him I was not interested. To be honest, Phillip, I am interested in acting again, but not now while you need me here in Florida."

"Thank you," he said quietly. "I think we can win, baby. I know we're not doing that good in the polls or whatever, but I know we can win with Hazelstein's endorsement."

"Also, honey, I have to tell you something else." As she spoke, Joi felt as if she had left her body and watched from above. She watched herself say, "Phillip, you know I love you and would never do anything to hurt you." She watched Phillip nodding with a confused semi-smile plastered on his face. Joi watched herself say, "Well, since you know that, you'll understand why I am telling you this. I had an affair." Joi watched Phillip's face crumble like hourglass sand. He looked as if he wanted to say a million things, but could not form his lips to utter one.

"It was not because you had one. It was not because I loved or even cared for the guy. It was because I was weak for a moment and—" She watched Phillip stand on shaky knees and wobble to the sink as if seventy-pound weights were on his feet. He grabbed it with both hands and held on to it as he tried to calm himself.

"I love you, Phillip. In a morbid way, it took this to see how much I love you, and it's been killing me not telling you about it."

Phillip looked at the lamb chops, picked them up and flung them against the wall on the opposite side of the kitchen. *Crash!* The Pyrex glass shattered to pieces, and the lamb chops left a greasy inkblot stain on the wall that dripped to the floor.

"Phillip!"

He walked over to the plates she had taken out for

dinner and one by one smashed them on the Italian marble floors as if he had just scored a touchdown. Joi shook in fear. She knew he would be upset, but had not seen him react in such a manner in years.

"Who was it!" he screamed.

"It's not important. What's important is—"

"God dammit, I asked you, who was it!"

"Baby, I don't—"

Phillip pulled out the drawer with so much force he ripped the knob from the wood. He threw the knob to the floor and snatched out the knife and screamed again, "*I asked you to tell me who . . . it . . . was!*"

"It was—It was Michael."

"Michael. Who the fuck—is Michael. I don't know no damn Michael."

"Brockmier."

Phillip's voice went up an octave as he said, "The writer? You fucked that faggoty ass writer?"

Joi was silent.

"You fucked that punk motherfucker, 'cause I couldn't fuck you?"

"It had nothing to do with that."

"*Bullshit!*" He said as he paced back and forth gripping the knife. "Bullshit," he repeated as the knife fell to the floor. "*Bull-fucking shit!*" He screamed at the top of his lungs. Then he walked to the sink and held it again. Looking at herself from above, Joi watched how she sat pensively not knowing what to say or what to do. She watched herself rest her elbows on the table, hold her head and openly sob by saying, "I'm sorry," repeatedly. She watched Phillip reach into his pocket, pull out the pill, turn on the water and wash it down the drain. He reached into his other pocket as he stood on a lamb chop, took out the bottle with the other pills and flushed them as well.

She heard herself say, "Baby, I wish to God I could take it back. I'm sorry."

She saw Phillip rest his head on the countertop as he stood in the shards of black broken glass and cry like a baby.

To Joi, Michael's words proved to be prophetic. It was indeed a night she would never forget.

CHAPTER

12

Dear Michael,

I just wanted to drop you a note to say that I'm sorry for what happened. Sorry. Damned if that's not the most overused, least understood word in the dictionary. But I know I vacated my "motherly" duties, and that's a cross I have to bear. I'm not perfect but guess what? Neither are you.

When I was in Cleveland, I had a coworker (who loved Season of Regret and plans to buy your new book) tell me I should take stock and recapture my life. I never really understood what he meant by that, but I do know that in the last few weeks, I've reevaluated everything that has happened to me in the past six years. I've decided that I will make a few changes in my life that will, in fact, change my destiny.

I miss my son, Michael. I know you said if you leave, you leave. But there is something about having something taken out of your body that you can't touch. It's hard to describe. I thought these feelings would die, but they just get worse every day. I don't expect you to agree with me, because to understand a mother, you would have to be a mother.

I read an article about you in Ebony, and they showed you at home with Blair. I had my friend blow the picture up, and I am looking at it as I write this letter to you. You seem to have done a wonderful job with him, but now I think that I should have some input in regard to his future as well.

Why am I coming back after all these years? I'm a changed woman. I've learned from my mistakes, and I want to reestablish a relationship with Blair. You can't change that, because no matter how big you get, your son will always be our son. And that's just the way it is.

Call me and let me know when I can see Blair.
555–1789.

Robyn Porter-Brockmier

Michael refolded the letter he had received in the mail the previous day as Blair walked downstairs, and stuffed it into his pocket.

"Why aren't you working?" he asked his father, who sat at the dining room table.

"Geez, you make it sound as if all I do is write." Then Michael whispered to himself, "At least try to write. Besides," he said louder, "I just wanted to fix you some breakfast before school. Is that okay? Can I hook my son up once in a while?" Michael smiled.

"Cool. So what we having?"

"Just eggs, toast, sliced fruit and sausage."

"That's what I'm talking 'bout," Blair said, and sat at the table, rubbing his fists into his eye sockets as he yawned. "Daddy, when can we go back into the city? I want to have lunch at Mickey D again."

"We can go anytime you like, but don't expect to see Sister Cilk there again."

Blair stared at his father. "Momma, not Sister. Momma Cilk. See, you are decrepit."

"Oh, yeah, that's right. Momma Cilk."

"But I want to go and do some shopping on Broadway."

Standing from the table, Michael picked up a spatula, then turned over the sausage, which filled the air with its sweet, savory aroma, and put two slices of raisin bread in the toaster. "You know, you've become a regular old clothes hound. When you moved up here from Bama, I had to make you stop wearing them skips. Now you want to go shopping almost—almost—" Michael looked over his shoulder at his son. "What's her name?"

"What's whose name?" Blair asked, as if he did not know what his father was getting at.

"Has to be a girl. What's her name? Why are you wanting all these new clothes?"

Blair blushed and then replied, "Natasha."

"Oh, really?" Michael asked as he cracked an egg on the counter and emptied the contents into a bowl.

"Yeah, she just moved to Harlem World from Michigan, and she was scared. Had heard all the bad stuff about 125th. So she and I would talk almost every day, and soon we were going together."

"Cute."

"Daddy, word, she's the prettiest girl at school, too. Everybody was up on her, but she liked me. She *loves* my dreads. She likes to play in my hair."

Michael held his fist toward his son, and Blair pounded his fist on top of his father's. "It's a well-known fact. Women love the locks, my brother."

"I know. Do we have any orange juice left?"

"Get up and see," Michael said with a smile. "And hurry, so you won't be late for school."

Blair walked over to the refrigerator and passed the stove. "Man, this smells good. Did Granddaddy used to cook you breakfast?"

"Naw," Michael laughed. "He was afraid of anything having to do with cooking. That's why I'm so surprised he was able to write that scene in *One Witness* that was in the kitchen. But anyway, Momma was always there to—" He knew he had already said too much as he watched his son's smile dissolve. "Listen, umm, do we have any juice in there?"

"Naw, and guess what, Daddy," Blair replied as he closed the door to the refrigerator. "You don't have to trip. I used to want to talk to *her* all the time, but not anymore. That's over and done with. I guess I've outgrown all of that."

Michael poured the eggs into the frying pan, adjusted the temperature as the toast popped up and asked, "Have you really?"

"Yeah. I mean, she left. That's the bottom line. She dropped me off," he said with the look of anger behind his eyes, "like it was Tuesday and left me like I was a bag of garbage. So now I don't even care anymore."

"Blair, your mom and I have had our differences. But one thing we agree on is the fact that we both love you. Now, for years—,"

"Man, please. How many times has she called me in the past five or six months? How many times has she written me? She don't even e-mail anymore. Is that love?"

"What I mean is this, Blair. She's going through a lot. Has been through a lot. I don't want to judge her, but one thing I know for sure is the fact that she loves you to death. That I know. When you were a baby, I watched this woman stay up with you one time twenty-four hours when you were sick. I tried to alternate with her, but she would not leave your room. The first time you took a step, if Robyn called two people, she called two hundred. People all over the country knew about Blair's first step. She loves you; there is no doubt about that. She just has to overcome a few issues." Michael pulled down a plate for his son.

"Why are you telling me this?"

"Because—Well, because," Michael said, "she wrote me a letter about you."

"And?"

"She would like to see you. I guess she wants to be a part of your life again. I know she has done some things that are——"

"Where's the letter?"

Michael reached into his hip pocket and handed the letter to his son. Although the only sound in the room was the clack of the spatula putting eggs on Blair's plate, Michael could feel his son reading each word and tried to think of a way he could put his son's mind at rest. He did not want him to hate his mother, because beneath all the layers, Michael saw Robyn as essentially a good person.

"Daddy?" Blair said quietly.

"Yes."

"I, umm—I want to go down south this summer."

"Really?"

"Yeah. It's been a long time, and I want to see a few people in the family," he said and refolded the letter. "Is that all right?"

"Yeah—sure, umm, let me call your grandmom and see what she says."

"Okay."

Michael brought his son's breakfast to him. Blair looked at the food and then walked over to the phone with the letter in hand.

Although it was obvious, Michael asked, "Who you calling?"

"Mom."

After Ani finished reading the letter, she folded it in a neat rectangular square and returned it to Michael.

"She kept your last name, huh?"

"She wanted an identity she never had before. So she stole it from me."

Michael sat across from Ani in a room that smelled like used sweat socks. The bed where Ani lay consisted of a box spring that had exposed coils piercing from its sides and a mattress that was only half its original intended thickness. She was positioned on her stomach as she laid her face on her lace pillow to think about the content of the letter.

"So, why do you think she's coming back, after all these years?"

"I have no idea. Well, I take that back," Michael said. "I do have an idea," he amended, sitting on the dinette chair with the back sawed off. "I can't tell you how many people have come out the woodwork for money since the book blew up. Everyone's trying to get on the gravy train."

"You think it's as simple as that? Money?"

"Why else would she return all of a sudden?"

Ani rubbed her face deep inside the pillow and asked, "What are you going to do?"

"He called her this morning, but she wasn't up—or

maybe back in yet." Michael sighed. "I'll talk to him tonight if she doesn't return his call, and if he likes, I'll let him call her again."

"Jesus Christ, Mike. You sound like you'd rather stand in a pit of alligators than let him talk to her."

"She was right about one thing. She will always be his mother. No matter where I go or what I do in life, she will be attached to my ass like a canker, and I just have to come to terms with that. To be honest, I always knew she'd return. She was just biding her time to spring up, and voilà, here she is."

"If she is such an ass, then why did you marry her?"

"I don't know. I was young, stupid, wanted to get married. Wanted a family. Wanted something I never really had. I guess I was trying to be the man I wanted my father to be, in a way."

"I thought you said your parents were happily married?"

"I may have, but, no, I don't think they were ever really happy. Daddy worked like a dog. Always sitting upstairs typing. This man had a typewriter so worn all the keys, even the Z and Q, were rubbed off. Every morning, it almost sounded like someone playing on a snare drum, he'd be pounding the keys so fast. Then around lunchtime I'd hear him," Michael said, closing his eyes, "walking back and forth and reading to the walls. From nowhere we would hear him burst out in laughter after something, as he would say, tickled him that he wrote. Around dinnertime, he'd finally shave, put on two or three handfuls of Aqua Velva and smoke a cigar." Michael looked across the room at Ani, who appeared to hang on his every breath. "That's a day in the life of a genius. He did this every day of his life. *Nothing* interrupted his writing. Not his agent, Christmas, snowstorms . . . not even me. And after all the years they were married, I don't think Momma ever came to terms with her role as a second fiddle in his life."

"So, if he worked that hard on his novels," Ani asked, "then why only one? Writing that much, I would imagine he would've had three or four at least."

Michael waited before answering and said, "There was another one. Actually a full-length novel and a novella. I found them after Momma died, and the first thing I did was wrap them up and find his agent's phone number. I knew the advance would be serious, and my plan was to live off the interest."

"You *are* kidding me, right?"

"Robyn was there the night I found them. They were in the attic wedged in a corner and covered by old magazines. Why he saw fit to hide them, I'll never know. The novella was entitled *Light in My Son's Eyes.*"

"You're kidding me. Please tell me there's not a full-length novel that no one has ever seen by Michael Price Brockmier."

"Seeing this story about how much he loved me gave me closure in a number of ways. And in hindsight, I think that's why it was so hard to sell them. They were too personal."

"So, do you still have them? I would love to—"

"Burned them up."

"You did what?" Ani said in wide-eyed amazement. Michael cleared his throat as if he could see the manuscript once again with his mind's eye. "I reached into his desk drawer . . . pulled out one of his Have-A-Tamp cigars . . . sprinkled a little Aqua Velva on them . . . and watched them burn in the fireplace."

"That's a sacrilege."

"Not really. Had he wanted the world to see them, he would have had them published. So, to publish them would have been wrong. Robyn was upset, but she didn't leave because it was a sacrilege. She left because she had already gone car shopping, and the car salesman was sitting outside the house in a brand-new silver convertible, waiting for me to come out and test drive. When she came in, she flipped out, and two days later she and Blair were headed to Penn Station to catch a train down south."

"I never knew that."

"I've never told the story before because I know what I did was wrong. But it was all I had left, and by burning them, I was able to keep them. It helped me to forgive him, and I needed that more than anything."

"Forgive him for committing suicide?"

Looking at Ani, Michael appeared to think aloud as he said, "There's still not a day that passes that I don't hate him. Not a day that passes that I don't think of him as a god. He did it in his office on his typewriter. Can you not see the symbolism in that? Blood, on the typewriter keys?"

Ani did not respond.

"He did it in a place where my mother was bound to find him. You just don't do that to people you love. He did it without leaving a note. Who does something like that," he continued with his palms extended like a crucifix, "without leaving a fucking note?"

"Maybe the books were the note."

"I would like to believe that, but I can't." Michael pulled down a lock and twirled it around his finger as he gazed down at the dingy brown carpet. Ani continued to stare at her houseguest without saying a word.

"I never played catch with the man. Never went to an amusement park, never even went to church with him. All I remember him doing was working, smoking, drinking and working."

"I'm sorry to hear that."

"It's a wound that never heals," Michael said in a stoic tone. "No matter what you do or achieve, you'll always be that little kid running up the stairs looking for his father and finding him dead."

Silence dripped in the room like water from a faucet, and then Michael rubbed his fingers over his dry lips.

"I've thought of joining him more times than I am afraid to remember."

"Doing what?"

"Just got tired of living, Ani. Tired of being here alone, you might say. Tired of searching for a purpose in life. Just fucking tired of being fucking tired." He stared at a spot on the floor and continued. "So, one night I took out a butcher knife and decided . . . Anyway, I guess that's really why I got married so young. I wanted to reinvent myself, and when the marriage failed, I just devoted my time and efforts to the two things I loved more than anything in this world. My music and, when she brought him back, Blair."

"Do you miss playing your music?"

"I miss it. I've called the owner and asked him if I could play every now and then, and he told me I could. I just never have time to get over there."

"So, what is it about music you enjoy so much?"

"What *don't* I enjoy? I would spend every moment I'm awake creating something that floats in the air and disappears if I could. Music frees me. That's the best way I can explain it. It pulls something out of my soul too deep to be touched by words.

"I started playing right after my father died. Right after I stopped talking. My mom, who at one time considered having me sent to Bellevue, later understood, and although the psychiatrist told her not to, she gave me this little small piano like Schroeder in the *Peanuts* comics. I had never touched a piano before, but I would just stare at it initially. I would admire the wood. The design. The curves," he said, and closed his eyes. "I'd admire the symmetry of the keys. White, white, black." He paused. "White, black, white, white, black. Everything was perfect. Exact." Michael stood and walked toward the window.

"There was an order to it. Not like my world. Things made sense. And then I'd hit the key, listen to the sound, and it occurred to me that I was connecting to my father by hitting these keys. Much like he had played the keys of the typewriter. We just made different kinds of music. And when that correlation came to me, and in effect drew me closer to him, I was hooked. I played until my fingers were raw. I wanted to play until I left grooves in the keys like he did with the typewriter. I wanted to find a deeper meaning to my world, to my life, in those notes." Michael looked at his friend and said, "I knew I could find it in music. I knew all my questions would be answered if I played long and hard enough. But that was taken away from me, too, I guess, when I got into the publishing business."

"Do you think you would ever be able to be your best, to create your masterpiece, you might say, if writing is not your true passion?"

"I have two things going against me big time. First of all, it's not my first love. Second, I have a name that will always dwarf me. No matter what I do, I will always be the son of. The name opens the door, but once you're in the room, damn you feel cold. You feel . . . like you don't deserve to be there."

"You, umm, mentioned that your father had a novel and a novella. What was the title of the novel?"

Michael looked at Ani and sat on the windowsill. *Speaking in Tongues*. It was not the same story line I have been working on, but I wanted to use the title because it was as if it was a parting gift to me."

"I can understand that. We're going to get *Speaking in Tongues* up to par. I really think they will like this version, and then you'll not have that added pressure on you. I know you're concerned about that."

"I am. But more so, I'm trying to come to terms with how my son will react if this is ever made public. If this gets out, what happens to him if he decides to go into the publishing or music or another entertainment industry?" With raised eyebrows he said, "It's hard to sleep sometimes thinking about the corner I've painted myself into."

"You say *myself* a lot."

"Because all my life it's been me against the world. Being an only child, there were no brothers or sisters there for me. When I went to school, I never had a relative there. After Daddy killed himself, I was the only man in the house, and when Momma died—Well, it's always been just me against the world."

"Do you think you'll ever remarry?"

"Do I seem that pathetic? Blair asked me the same thing. I would like to in the right situation. I am one of those people, I guess, put here to serve the masses. Maybe that's why God placed me here alone."

"Why do you say that?"

"I have had serious feelings for only one woman in my life. I married Robyn 'cause she was pregnant, and I thought I was in love, but was more in lust. I've been infatuated since the divorce, but I've never before had a woman that I thought about constantly."

"Cynthia?"

"No, Joi."

"Who's she?"

"I've known her for a while, and I can't get her off of my mind, Ani. I dream about her, I smell her body at the most unusual time of day for no reason at all and I can't even call her."

Ani looked as if she was going to say something, but withheld her comment.

"I know it was wrong to even get involved, if you can call it that, with a married woman who happens to be *ten* years older than me, but she has me strung out. Maybe I wanted her even more because I couldn't have her. During the tour, women were giving me nude photos of themselves, panties, you name it. And I went back to my room each night and thought about her. Thought about a woman I could never have."

"Why do you think she touched you so deeply?"

"We had a telephone conversation that did not last very long, and in that conversation I saw how much we were alike, yet totally different. We've faced tragedies few people can understand. We have both dealt with a fair amount of celebrity and all of its ups and downs. But she has a passion to perform, and she cannot do it. I have a passion for music, and I, for whatever reason, can't do that either. Both of us would love to do what we do best, but we're stifled by circumstances. And I think that's one of the things that draws me to her."

"Is that all?"

"She's beautiful," he said, scratching his scalp with his pinky. "She's also intelligent and intriguing, but I see something dying inside of her. Something she had that she's losing in her marriage. So, a part of me would like to replenish it." Michael looked down at his father's onyx ring and slowly rotated it as if deep in thought.

"So, having sex with her is helping the marriage?"

"I'm not saying that at all."

"What are you saying?"

"I'm lonely, Ani. You have Johnny, and you all seem to be happy. I'm proud to have Blair, but to be honest, I've achieved a lot in the past few months. Not only monetarily, but in many other ways as well. And I have no one else to share it with besides my son. It feels empty, I guess. Hollow."

"Is that all?"

"What more do you want?"

"Michael, a preacher once said if you and your friends poured all of your problems on a table and let everyone see what you had, you would be fighting to get yours back. I have lost two children during childbirth, and I have a third one in a mental hospital in Queens. She's retarded because of lack of oxygen to the brain that she lost due to having an obese mother"—heavy sigh—"and an OB GYN who did not know how to handle a patient so large. Let me tell you about my happy relationship. Johnny has slept with damn near every woman in Tracy Towers. Since I can't leave this place, few of them even know I'm here. Have I ever told you any of this? No. Why? Because you have your own burden to bear, and I respect that. But life has no guarantees."

Michael looked out of her window once again as her words bit at him like vipers.

"I look at it this way. I have had to shoulder more than my share of pain in life because I've been given more than my share of talent," Ani said. "That's the thread of hope that keeps me hanging on. That's why I've never considered suicide, because in spite of what you see around you, I've been blessed in more ways than you can ever know."

"I just wish," Michael whispered, "there was something I could do."

"I knew you would say that, and that is not what I am

looking for. Pity is a cheap emotion; so keep it to yourself. I don't go around telling this story to get pity. The reason I shared it with you was to help you find you."

"Meaning?"

"You're lost. I've known that for years. You're searching for something, and unfortunately you don't know what that something is."

"Please," Michael said with a smile. "You make me sound like a mental patient or something."

"Then, tell me this," Ani said, are you a writer? A musician? Are side. "Who are you? Are you a father? Are you a man in love with something he *can't* or *shouldn't* have . . . and I am not talking about Joi now." Pause. "Who are you?"

In a cracked whisper, he replied, "Sometimes I really don't know."

"People live their entire lives wearing a mask. We go to the same church our parents go to. We live in the same physical and mental states where our parents resided. We even find ourselves pursuing the same careers as Mom and Dad. Is that who we are? A lost generation, indebted to a past generation? Tonight, before you go to sleep, challenge your heart. Ask yourself, 'Who am I?' And if you find the answer, you will find peace."

"Who are you?" Michael asked.

"I'm Ani Bella Ginsburg," she said with a beaming smile. "I'm big-fat-piss-the-bed Ani, and I love myself to death." Her smile faded as she said, "I'm a Rangers fan. I can write one hell of a story, and in six months to a year"—heavy breath—"I'll be dead."

"What?"

"I've known about it for months now. This old body has been abused enough, and for me to get thirty-one years out of it is a minor miracle."

"You serious?"

"Of course I am. You think I'd kid about something like that? I don't have a glandular problem. I don't have something that slows my metabolism. I don't have a thyroid problem. No one molested me when I was young so that now I am trying to change the way I look. I just eat too fucking much, and I've dug my grave with my teeth. But as you can see, I have no fear of death whatsoever. And when I say none, I mean *nada*. I'm ready to get out of this body, Michael. I'm tired. I'm so tired, and I'm ready to go to the next phase in life, whatever it may be.

"You know something," she continued. "Since the day the doctor told me, I have not shed a tear. I wanted to cry, I guess, because you're supposed to, in that situation, but I didn't. Sometimes I don't think I can even cry anymore.

"But the tears did not flow because for one, God had granted me a reprieve and to sit here and complain would be blasphemous, and two, I know that fifty years from today, I'll still be here. As long as someone reads *Season of Regret*, a part of me lives and breathes. You can't ask for a hand as good as the one I've been dealt."

Michael bowed his head and allowed his locks to hang toward the floor like a wet black mop. "I had no idea."

"I have no regrets, and I did tell you that for a reason. Your glass, my friend, is way past half full. Stop bitching and start living. Life is so beautiful if we *allow* it to be."

"Ani?"

"See, Michael. You heard what I just said, but you were not listening. Let me say it once again. Life is so beautiful if we *allow* it to be."

Michael listened to the words and then looked at his friend and said, "Thanks. But tell me this. You told me you have not been out of this apartment in years. Have not seen Midtown since high school. How can you say that? With all due respect, you look out the window and read books. How can you say that life is beautiful, when you're not living it?"

"Is that what you think? I'm letting life pass me by. I close my eyes, and I can go anywhere I want to go. Do anything I want to do. I can see the pyramids, and I can sit and talk to Dr. King at a disco if I want to. If I close my eyes, there is no place—"

"You can't feel the sun on your skin, Ani," Michael said shaking his head.

"What?"

"You can't feel the surf between your toes. You can't," he said, and pulled out his cellular phone, "smell how it smells after it rains or watch little girls with pigtails run after the Mr. Softee truck as though their lives depended on it. Get that Mickey Mouse bar, bite that ear off and smile as if they are literally experiencing heaven right down here on earth." Michael dialed Blair's school. "To truly experience any of that, you have to be amongst that, and all I am asking you to do is let me take you out of here for one day. Hell, one hour."

"I can't. I'm too weak."

"I'll pay for a few nurses to help us. They can bring your oxygen, and we'll just sit outside. And instead of living life . . . we'll spend a few moments feeling it."

"Thanks, but no thanks," Ani said, and turned her head toward the wall as he put his phone to his ear.

"Hello, this is Mr. Brockmier. I am running a little late, but I wanted to let you know that I'll be there . . . excuse me . . . what? But who authorized—"

Ani turned toward Michael, whose face had lost its color. "I'll be right there!"

Startled, he looked at Ani and said, "She took my

son . . . and told the school to transfer his records to Alabama."

Life had dealt Michael a card he did not know how to play, and five days later it had not run far from the center of his heart.

While he worked on *Speaking in Tongues*, he was thinking of Blair. In the years since the boy had reentered his life, Michael had evolved from a man who looked at his son living with him as an obligation, to a father who looked upon his son like the sun he needed for survival.

Michael longed for the noise in the house, so he played the television louder. He missed cooking dinner for two, so he would inevitably throw away more food than he intended. He missed the light of Blair's eyes when he would ask him questions.

After hitting print, Michael retrieved from the basket the words he had crafted and looked at them on the page. He ran his fingers stealthily over their surface, feeling them as if they were a woman's cheek. He knew his first one hundred words had to be stellar. He knew he had to pull his reader into the world he had created for them quickly or they would not pick up the book. This was the thirty-third rewrite of *Speaking in Tongues*, and in his heart he prayed there would not be a thirty-fourth.

Speaking in Tongues

by Michael Price Brockmier, II

Poems make wonderful songs. They attach to music like a cool summer breeze over blades of grass. They speak, they cry and at times even scream. When they work as one, they ignite the soul. When they do not, they are like pieces of glass at the bottom of a river. Simple words that cut the very breath from which they emanate.

Michael read the words with emotions he never felt when he read *Season of Regret*. As he read them, he could imagine himself in the midst of readers, answering their questions, asking them what they would do in the same situation and hopefully challenging their morals.

He read the opening paragraph once again and again. *Could it be better?* He asked himself. Possibly, but he knew this was as good as he could get the words. He knew he had poured his soul into the words just as he had in the past with his music.

As he read the poetic verses, he instinctively looked up and noticed the time. It was ten of two, and Michael laid the sheets of paper on his desk, while he pictured the character in his mind and headed for the door to pick up Blair from school. He was at the top stairs when it occurred to him that Blair was physically no longer a part of his life. He leaned on the banister and looked into his son's room. It was just like he left it except for a box in the middle of the floor, which contained his clothes. After a meeting with his attorney, who advised him that his chances of winning in court were slim, Michael had brought home a box, packed Blair's clothing and waited for his ex-wife to call him with a physical address.

He left three messages a day the first week. He never heard from her or Blair.

Michael pulled himself from the memory of his son and returned to his office in an attempt to refocus on his manuscript.

"Dawn touched the sky," he read aloud, "on a day

that would change his life forever. Percy Stallings woke up ten minutes before his alarm clock disengaged. Most mornings, he would be jarred awake by the patter of the "Wake Up Posse," on WLCV, but not this day. When his eyes opened, he gazed at the clock and then pushed the covers from his body."

After reading the paragraph, Michael smiled. So much had happened in his life, but in spite of it all, he could see the growth and maturity of his writing. He had no idea if it compared to Ani's; but it didn't matter because it was his moment, and he would share with the readers a story he had wanted to tell for several years.

After the printer published its last sheet of paper from his manuscript, Michael gazed at the labor of his work in amazement. Then he took out one of his father's cigars, placed it between his lips and looked at himself in the mirror. He had never smoked a cigar in his life, but this was a moment he wanted to share with his dad. A moment when he wanted to feel close to him. A moment when he wanted to feel he had made his father proud.

After the first draw on the cigar, Michael coughed intensely. It seemed his entire body rejected almost twenty years of stored tar and nicotine. Michael pulled it from his lips, wiped his mouth with the back of his forearm, looked at the cigar and wondered how anyone, including his father, could enjoy such a disgusting habit. But being the persistent soul he was, he slid it between his lips once again and allowed the vapors to envelope his being. He closed his eyes to control his reaction and heard the phone ring.

"Hello?"

"Michael?"

"Yes?"

"You sound hoarse. Are you sick?"

Michael attempted to clear his throat and said with a laugh, "No, it's okay. Who's calling?"

"Harvey, Janessa Harvey from Charisma."

"Oh, hey," he replied. "I'm glad it's you. Dad used to smoke a cigar every day to christen his pages; but I am not a smoker, so since I just finished the last page of *Speaking in Tongues*, and trust me you all will love what I've done with it, I wanted to smoke a Cuban. It just felt like a very Brockmierish thing to do for some reason."

Janessa was silent.

"Are you there?"

"I'm here, Michael. I have a friend of mine in the office from legal." As soon as she said the word legal, Michael knew the odyssey had come to an end. "Listen, I know you and I rarely talk on the phone, but I needed to speak with you about something. Pam Wilson resigned two days ago."

"No. Really? She, umm, she never called to tell—"

"Her departure was quite hasty to be honest. She didn't give us two weeks or anything, and they had big plans for her—after the success of the first two books. But anyway, this morning—"

"One second," Michael said in an attempt to delay the inevitable. "Where is she working?"

He could hear Janessa place her hand over the receiver as if she was speaking to an advisor, and then she said, "She's working for Galaxy Books. They specialize in doing electronic books or something like that for the Internet. But anyway, the reason I'm calling is—"

"Have you heard from her?"

Pause. "Excuse me?"

"Have you, umm—heard from Pam. I know you two were pretty—pretty close," Michael said as he sat in the chair his father sat in for years.

"No. No, I have not heard from her. Listen, Michael, I got a call this morning from a reporter with the *Times*. Apparently he received a phone call from a Mr. Johnny Freeman concerning *Season of Regret* and *Mule-Drawn Wagon*."

Although Janessa paused to offer him the opportunity to come forward, he refused to take the bait. "Okay."

She continued. "He indicates that a friend of his, whom he refused to name, actually wrote those stories, and you paid this friend a portion of the advance and—"

"He's lying." Michael had no idea why he denied the accusation. He had no idea what he would say next.

"People used to try to extort money from Daddy all the time. That's all this is. He saw that ad in *USA Today* you guys did for me, which I want to thank you for, and he wanted to get paid."

Pause. "Well, Michael—"

"It's a game, Janessa. Pure and simple. If I had a dollar for every time people asked me for a buck," he said with insincere laughter in his voice, "I wouldn't have to write another word." Michael could feel the lies about to topple over on him.

"It's more than a game, Michael."

"Excuse me?"

"The call came through to me this morning. Apparently this Johnny guy sent the *Times* reporter the handwritten pages from his friend's legal pad. According to the reporter, he sent him three legal pads from the novels, all filled with handwritten text.

"Now," she continued, "this could be some elaborate scheme or whatever to extort money. Things like that have happened in the past. You have a great name in this industry, and someone doing that is not too farfetched. I don't know why Pam resigned, and she doesn't return phone calls; but I'll deal with that later. What I need to know from you, Michael, is this. Did you write those books?"

"Of course I did!" He hated lying, but consoled himself in the fact that she had given him the legal pads and original manuscript, and he had re-typed them into his computer.

Pause. "Are you sure, Michael? I have thirty plus years in this business. I have clout with everyone from the president of this company to the editor in chief of the *Times*. I will go to the wall to save this book, this company and your reputation. I don't mind doing that. I've dealt with first-class pathological liars like this before. But before I make any move, I have to know the truth. I'm asking you once again. Did you write those novels? Yes or no."

CHAPTER

13

*T*he immature lover loves a woman because he needs her, but it's the mature lover that needs her because he loves her.

Joi thought of the wedding advice received from her mother. For years the tautology had bounced in her head and never made sense until she told Phillip of the affair. It had been over two months since the night he stared through her for a couple of minutes that seemed like hours. Over two months since he walked out of the kitchen and looked as if he was demoralized and small. That night she knew he wanted to get physical. She knew he had passed the boiling point. But all he could do was shake and brace himself, and then he drove away.

Days later, Joi suggested they go to counseling, but Phillip refused to do so. He told her if he was going to see anyone, it would be an attorney.

Weeks after contacting Joe to get the counselor's information, Joi made an appointment to meet with her. She sat in the small, nondescript office alone, awaiting the doctor's return. Although she busied herself by scanning magazines, she would find herself looking at the wall and reading the woman's degrees.

Dr. Vanessa Field's office was not on the best side of town, nor did she have a receptionist. While Joi knew she was approaching thirty, she appeared to be around the legal drinking age. The spartan office contained a chair, a love seat, a coffee table, and all of the items had a thrift store appearance about them.

"So sorry, Mrs. Weston—I'm sorry," the counselor said, reentering the room and sitting in front of Joi, "I should say, Mrs. Evans."

"That's okay, I'm used to it."

"I hate interrupting our sessions, but trying to do this without a secretary is the pits. But I called the service, and they'll answer any subsequent calls." She crossed her legs, tilted her head to the side and said, "So, where were we?"

"Well, umm, I was telling you about—Don't you think," Joi said, raising her voice an octave, "that it would be best if you took notes?"

"Not really. I know that's what Bob Newhart did on television. I never missed an episode. But I find I'm distracted. I never took a single note in college."

"Soooo, why don't you use a tape recorder . . . and then transcribe to notes later."

Vanessa ran her fingers along her thighs as she looked at Joi and said, "Why don't we just pick up where you left off?"

"Okay," Joi said, shaking her head. "Just making a suggestion."

"And it's appreciated."

"What I was saying is, he did dirt, and then I make this one mistake and boom. You would think the world has come to an end."

"Does he know about the pregnancy?"

Joi paused as if she could not draw breath. "Actually, no one knows. Well, no one but you, Joe and my OB."

"Do you think that's wise, Joi?"

"I am doing—the best I can. This was not supposed to happen. I had my tubes tied years ago." Joi looked at the doctor for a comment, but she sat silent. "When I was late, I was thinking I was facing menopause, and here I am looking at damn babypause. At my age? From a man I hardly know? No, I've not told him, 'cause I have not come to terms with it myself. 'Cause I don't know what I'm going to do."

"Telling your husband and deciding what to do with your body are two separate issues. But I follow where you're going."

"But," Joi said as she rubbed her forehead as if she was trying to massage away the onset of a headache, "can we talk about what we were talking about before?"

"You want to talk about Phillip's transgressions, right?"

"Exactly. I mean for years he—"

"Did his dirt, and you made a single mistake, and boom you would think the world had come to an end. I think you said that four times now."

Joi allowed her mouth to close as she listened to the youthful counselor regurgitate her words.

"Listen, I know your brother well. He's a great teacher, and he's crazy about you. I looked at your picture in his office every time I visited him. So allow me to be a little more candid than I might be with most of my clients. Okay? What's over—is over." Vanessa smiled a smile at her that showed far too much gum and not enough teeth and leaned back. She had a look on her face that said she had just decoded the secret to life itself.

"What?"

"That's right. What's over," she said more dramatically this time, shaking her curly black hair, "is over."

Joi looked at her watch and said, "I hate to be short with you, but can I say something?"

Giggling like a teenager, Vanessa said, "By all means."

"Joe thinks the world of you, too, but do people actually let you get away with saying 'what's over—is over' and then pay you a hundred dollars an hour to sit in here? And also—"

"Actually, it's one-fifty," she said, smiling. "I gave you the hook-up rate, and in answer to your questions—Yes, they do." She continued to smile.

"Well—"

"Joi, you have been the victim too long in this situation. You have done a wonderful job playing the role, and I applaud that. What Phillip did was wrong. No one will deny the obvious, so why should we sit here for an hour and say he was wrong. He was wrong to do it fifteen or twenty years ago; he would have been wrong if he had done it last night. Makes no difference. But having said that, Phillip is the target patient." She leaned toward Joi and swiveled back and forth in her chair. "He is the re-act-tion to something that was festering in the marriage."

"So, you're saying I'm just as much at fault?"

"Let me say this. See these shoulders?" Vanessa said, patting her shoulder with her fingertips and continuing to smile. "My fee does *not* include crying on them. I'm tough, but I know what I am doing. Please follow me.

"Men do not cheat because they are dogs, as many would have you believe. Women have been duped for years by saying men will be men and given the opportunity all men will cheat. And guess what? That thinking comes from men, so don't buy into it. Even saying that is defeatist. It's almost akin to saying the sky will be blue, the sun will be hot and water will be wet so accept the obvious. Once you've convinced yourself that a man is a dog and a slave to his primal urges, you have convinced yourself to be content with a lifetime of unhappiness, a life of fearing that any time he is out of your sight that opportunity might arise. A lifetime of regrets. A lifetime of being a victim.

"Want to know why men cheat? Men cheat because something is missing. Maybe not in the marriage, maybe not in the spouse. It may be something inside of them. Let me explain.

"If a man is suffering from poor self-esteem, like possibly your husband was when you were climbing the ladder of success, the affair was not done because he loved or even liked this woman. He did it to find something to fill that cavity in his chest. Have you ever been in the hospital and you were being given a drug for the pain? And you lay there when all of a sudden the pain seems to come from nowhere, and it's overburdening? You grind your teeth; you kick your feet back and forth because you need relief. Joi, that's what he was feeling. Whatever this thing was inside of him grew and grew, and then he reacted because he needed relief from it.

"Now, if he has such a hole in his chest, what could you have done to help him? Possibly nothing. Sometimes we have to be mature enough to heal ourselves, and if we don't know what's wrong, that can be difficult. To the best of your knowledge, has he had an affair in the past year?"

"No."

"The past say, five years?"

"No."

"Let's go back ten years. Has he done anything in ten years?"

Joi shook her head.

"You told me that after you got the show he became a producer, correct? So, that in turn empowered him. That may have filled the void he felt. I don't know unless I speak to him, but that may be the solution."

"I still don't trust him, though," Joi said over a stiff sigh. "I know everything you just said makes sense, but you're right, whenever he's away, I think he's with someone."

"So, when I asked you at the outset if you forgave him, you did not tell me the truth?"

"No, no, I forgave him. I said I have not *forgotten* what he did."

"Joi, we are playing with semantics. You are a half step from saying, 'I have forgiven him, but I have *not* forgiven him.' Think about that. It's not a gray area. Either you hold anger inside about the affair, or you let it go. You don't let it go and hold a little bit in reserve in your heart."

Joi's fingers traveled the leather of the couch.

"When you found out about his affair. Did you all talk about it?"

"Well—" Joi was interrupted by a knock at the door.

"Please continue," Vanessa said. "I have a sign on the door."

"Well, what I was about to say is when he told me about it—or rather when I found out—"

Another more forceful knock emanated from the door.

"I'm sorry, Mrs. Weston, let me see who this is."

As Vanessa walked toward the door, Joi replayed her

words in her mind and decided that she had to make some changes in her life regardless of whether her marriage succeeded or failed.

"May I help you?"

"You called her Weston. Her name is Evans—at least for now."

Joi looked toward the door and saw Phillip. "What are you doing here?"

"I just want you to know that when this is over, we need to talk. If you like, we can meet at Vito's and do it or—"

"We can talk now. That is if Vanessa doesn't mind."

"No," he said, shaking his head. "We don't need a third party to interfere in our business. Whenever you would like to talk, you know where I'll be."

"Mr. Evans. I understand you're upset, sir. I really do. But—"

"Who are you?" Phillip asked incredulously. "The receptionist?"

Vanessa smiled at him. "If you like, I would really appreciate it if you stayed for a few. I think it would help Joi a lot."

Phillip stared down at the petite counselor, looked inside the room again at his wife and then walked through the door.

"Okay," Vanessa said. "Looks like the gang's all here. I was asking your wife a question before you walked in, Mr. Evans, and she was just about to answer me." Vanessa looked squarely into Joi's eyes and asked, "Have you all talked about Phillip's affair?"

"He—Well, he talked about it, but I wouldn't say—"

"We talked about it," Phillip said point blank.

Vanessa looked at Joi again. "And you were going to say?"

"I was going to say that we talked about the times, places, the things that happened. But he never told me why."

"What do you mean why?" Phillip asked, turning his body toward his wife.

"Why? As in why did you do it?"

"Aw, hell, here we go. I made a mistake. Okay? It's as simple as that. She was there. I did it one time and got away with it; then it became a challenge. I've told you this what . . . a hundred times or more? It was a fucking mistake! And every time I tell you—"

"Freeze!" Vanessa said with her previous smile but a memory. "First of all, in this room no one raises their voice but me. Second of all, no matter how many times you come with that it was a mistake . . . I made a boo-boo . . . excuse, it ain't washing. Why? Because it's bull-shit."

"What?" Phillip asked, seemingly shocked by the change in her demeanor.

"Total bullshit. If you want to bullshit yourself, your wife and your life, then, sir, you can leave now. I don't have time for it. Let me explain something to you. This woman was hurt." She paused as if she wanted him to feel the words unlike he ever felt them before. "I know what she did scared the hell out of you, and we will ad-dress it later; but you cannot imagine what you did to her. Your sin . . . was the original sin. Okay?"

"I've *tried* to make it up to her. What am I supposed to do?"

"Talk about it."

"*We have talked*—" Phillip gained control and said, "We have talked about it."

"She says you have not, so obviously the wound is still open. There's a cliché I swear I wish people would never use again. Time does not heal shit. Okay? Time makes things fester. Time makes us angrier. Time gives us ulcers, and time will kill us; but it don't heal shit. You can give her a strand of pearls in a royal blue Lexus if you like, but if you don't tell this woman why you cheated—and I mean the *real* reason why—it means nothing."

Phillip relaxed his shoulders as Vanessa continued. "As bad as her infidelity made you feel, Phillip, trust me, hers felt worse, and this is not gang up on the man time, 'cause I don't subscribe to that thinking.

"You violated the trust. The sex thing was bad, don't get me wrong, but it was a matter of trust. And when a partner can no longer trust the other partner, it's not a matter of if, but when, the marriage will come to an end. Trust is the foundation; trust is the core." She emphasized her words by tapping her fingertips together. "Trust is earned, trust can be regained, but without it . . . sex, money, anything else in a relationship is secondary." Vanessa rocked back and forth as if she was ready to deliver another salvo of words, "You violated that trust, you violated your vows, you violated this woman and you destroyed the essence of your marriage."

"Then, what am I supposed to do? She has a ticket to fuck anyone she likes now 'cause I made a mistake years ago?"

Vanessa looked at Joi and smiled again as she said to Phillip, "You like that word *mistake*, don't you? Joi, what do you need to do to find closure?"

"What do you mean?" she whispered.

"What will truly bring this to an end? It might not be talking to him in front of me. It might be writing a fifty-page journal and having him read it to you. It might be going on a long drive and not playing the radio and allowing it to come out that way. It might even be grabbing a handful of skin on his face with those beautiful fingernails and getting it out. But—"

"I know you are being sarcastic," Phillip interjected, "but you would recommend someone being *violent* if it released their aggression? Where did you get your degree? Please tell me you're joking."

"Well"—she smiled—"maybe not with lamb chops and dish plates. But, yes. If she has to punch you to feel better, and if that truly makes her feel whole and complete, I wish she would hit you as hard as Mike Tyson, sir. You have a cancer in your relationship. I'm telling you how to treat it. There are less painful ways to do it; but in three years you may or may not be together, and it will be as a result of this cancer killing you day by day." She paused for a moment, and her eyes narrowed to slits. "You made this bed almost twenty years ago. It's time to go to sleep."

"To be honest, Vanessa, I just wish he would—"

"I love my wife! You hear me? I made a mis—Things did not go as planned, but I love my wife. I would give . . . I would give my life for Joi right here and now. So don't you imply that—"

"No one is *implying* anything, Phillip," Vanessa said with her smile still present. "And no one is *asking* you to die for her. You die once. You live every day. Live for your woman. You guys have all of these shared memories. I'm single. I'd give my left arm to be in a long-term relationship. Years of disappointments. Years of happiness. If this doesn't work out for you, it will be like losing a part of your anatomy. You have *too* much invested at this point." She focused her attention on Joi and said, "There's another cliché I dislike that talks about doing bad all by yourself. Let me tell you something. Both of you may look back and wish someone—anyone—were there. Because when you have the memories you have, someone or anyone beats the hell out of no one.

"Losing Angie was hard enough. Don't let her death steal something else from you. If anything, let her memory make you stronger. That's all I'm asking."

Phillip opened his trembling hands and rubbed them over his face. And then Joi looked at her husband and debated if she should tell him now or wait until later. She chose the former. "Phillip, I have to tell you something, and I know—Well, there will never be a good time to say this."

There was a pause as Phillip turned and looked into his wife's eyes for the first time that day.

The pause of a few sentences seemed to last forever "I'm pregnant."

The hum of his sports car disappeared into the night, and Joi looked at the phone. She wanted to call him, but could not find the courage. It had been a grueling day in more ways than she ever imagined. A day that tested her will as much as it tested her spirit. So as she listened to Vanessa's voice remind her, "This is not the time for cowardice", she took another sip of brandy and made the phone call.

"Hello?"

Joi spoke softly. "Is Michael there?"

After a weighted silence, he whispered back. "You don't know how many days I've waited to hear your voice. How have you been? It's been what, three months?"

"Ten weeks to be exact. So how have you been?"

"I don't want to talk about me. What's going on with you? Still in Florida?"

"Yeah. I was thinking about going to L.A. to work on a particular project, but decided not to. I don't miss it anymore, though."

"Acting? You've gotten rid of the bug?"

"I've come to terms with the fact that life goes on, and I accomplished more in my fifteen minutes than most actors accomplish in a lifetime. I'm fine with that. Now, I'm sure," she said, looking at the brandy but seeing Michael's face, "that I will never watch a movie and not wonder if I could have delivered the lines better. But I think that's natural. I had a nice roll of the dice, you might say."

"You don't sound like yourself. Here I am sounding like we've had a hundred conversations, but you just don't sound like Joi. You sound different."

"Well, seeing that I was very conflicted last time we spoke, I will take that as a compliment. But I was watching "Book TV" on C-SPAN II, and I heard about your situation."

"That was embarrassing and hard to swallow, but to be honest, I don't even feel the pain yet."

"What do you mean?"

"I lost Blair."

"I'm sorry to hear that."

"I often wondered who I was under these dreads, and I found out. It was not a writer; well, I guess everyone knows that now. It was not a pianist. It was a father. I did that better than I did anything I have ever tried to do in my life. It took a while to get the knack of it, but I know that's what I was first and foremost."

"Sounds like you've found your center, and that's always healthy. In the *Times* article, they said the young lady has not made a comment yet. Is that right?"

"No, she has tried to avoid the media. It's a long story, but she's terminally ill and her boyfriend is of little support. He thought if she passed away, it would stop his gravy train. He asked me for some money, but since I gave her most of the advance from the book, plus all the bonus money, I thought I did my share. He wanted me to agree to giving them the royalties also, and when I said no, he went to the *New York Times*."

"I'm sorry to hear that."

"In a morbid and sick way, I'm glad it's over. I lived that lie for years, and it's like being a dealer, I guess. You have the riches, but you can't sleep at night. You're always looking in the mirror, and that was me. When the editor called I had my opportunity to get out of it, and I lied. I lied and lied and lied again. Then after she hung up, I just went running. I ran from my house to Central Park and back. My heart was pounding, but I was looking for answers, I guess. Well, the answer came to me. The next morning I went to the office and told them everything. Fortunately, Janessa had not made a move, so she was able to avoid getting tarnished."

"We all make mistakes. God knows I have. But once we do, it's up to us to stand up and do the right thing."

"I know. I'm going to issue a public statement apologizing to the National Book Award nominating committee as well as to the readers. Charisma has, of course, opted out of publishing my next book that was actually going to be a book I wrote myself. They say there's no interest at all because I've ruined my name, and I can't fault them for that."

"But couldn't you have it published under a pseudonym and then let the public know it's you after the book is——"

"No. I don't want to do anything that has even a hint of dishonesty attached to it."

"So what's next?"

Joi could hear the sound of labored breathing on the phone before Michael said, "I don't know. I called the bar I used to play at, and although the emcee would like me to return, the owner now thinks I'm too controversial to even play there. What this situation has to do with my playing in a piano bar is beyond me, but—Well, I don't want to talk about it. So, what made you call?"

"I'm sorry to hear about all you're going through."

Joi hesitated and looked at Phillip's picture on the wall. After she shared the news of the pregnancy with her husband, he had promptly stood and walked out of Vanessa's office, and the two had not spoken in three days. "I've wanted to call for a while. But I had to take care of a few odds and ends first. I often wonder about things and why they happen to people, because life is just a series of lessons, which we repeat over and over again until we pass them. What's happened in your career, to your son, us meeting, it was meant to intersect. I wonder sometimes, what was the lesson in what happened between us? Why did we do what we did? Was it just passion, lust, or could it have been, under the circumstances, something more?"

"I think—"

"So I asked myself," Joi continued, "this morning, could I have fallen in love with a man like you? In a different day, if you were a little older, if I were a little less married. I like to think I could have. What we did was wrong. But you know something? I don't regret it for a moment. Since we moved to Florida'—and for the first time in months, Joi allowed herself to shed a tear in regard to her situation—"since we moved here, it's been too secure. Too safe. And I'm reminded of the saying about ships being safe on the shore but being built for the seas. I've lived my life chasing rainbows, and after you catch them, can you ever go back to just gardening and sitting at home—crocheting?"

"Must be hard. I'd imagine——"

"And that's why I can't regret what happened. We took a chance and lived on the edge. And I like that. What we did renewed my life in a number of ways." Through the tears, Joi smiled and said, "You're a father."

"Excuse me?"

"I said, you're a father, and I know one day you will get your son back again. No parent who wants and takes care of their child should have to live without them. Trust me, I know. But I think the thing that attracted me to you more than anything, Michael, is the fact that you can see the artist inside me. People see me and see Potts McGee's stepmother, or they see the woman who did bit parts in movies. But you saw more. You saw past the fame, the money and all the material stuff into why I had to do what I did. I know Phillip can never understand me"—she wiped her eyes—"on that level."

"Baby, I wish I were there for you. I don't know what to say. All I know is——"

"I'm ten weeks pregnant."

"You're what weeks what?"

"I told Phillip a couple of days ago, and it's definitely not his because, well, I know it's not his."

"What?"

"Yeah, I knew something was wrong after a few days. Nothing physical, just mentally I knew I should have never let you do it without protection. But at that moment, at the second, who's thinking like that. It was stupid and immature, and I guess since I have not even seen a condom up close in years, it just did not click in my mind for some stupid reason. I took an HIV test, so on top of everything else, all of a sudden I'm worried about that as well."

"Joi, I've been tested. You don't have to worry about—"

"Well, Michael, it's my life." Joi paused and said, "I started to take care of this without him knowing; but I guess I'm too damn honest, and I told him. He's running for office, and I know this would leak, and it'd be an even bigger mess."

"Take care of this?"

"I started to. It seemed like a quick and simple solution to the problem. But I know this is my last time being in this situation, so as much as I don't want to have it, there's a part of me that wants it. So until I'm one hundred percent sure, I guess I won't do anything at all."

"Damn," Michael whispered. "You're pregnant?"

"Yes, I'm pregnant."

"How did Phillip handle this?"

"What do you expect? If I abort and it gets leaked, he can kiss his political future good-bye. If I have the child, he will get the slaps on the back and cigars, but every time he holds the baby it'll be a reminder, I'm sure. If we split up, it's going to hurt. If we stay together, it's going to kill him. Sometimes, Michael, there really are no quick and fast solutions."

"But, Joi, can't you at least tell me what you're going to do?"

"If I had to decide at this moment, I would terminate. I have a lot to think about. Most importantly, I have to decide if it's something I can do by myself physically and mentally. Right now I don't know the answer to that question. Secondly, if he's going to be a part of my life, I have to think about what Phillip wants to do."

"Well, I would think the answer to that would be obvious."

"It may be. But a friend of mine once said, You've made your bed; now it's time to go to sleep. Good night."

CHAPTER

14

Without love, life is like a year without spring. A ship without a rudder. A body that has no soul. This can all be said of a man without love.

When Michael read the last line of *Mule-Drawn Wagon* he paused and read the words over and over again. Initially he had not liked them, assuming they were too soft for the character in the tale, but after asking Ani about the words and where they came from, he knew no other words could better capture the essence of the Gaines family and their travels to Chicago better.

After he had spoken to Joi, all he wanted to do was see her. To wipe away her tears. But he knew his being there would only cause more problems, so he waited for her to call him again. She assured him that she would let him know how the situation with Phillip was resolved and what she decided to do in regard to the pregnancy. But seven days had passed, and he had not heard from her.

Michael's attorney had called to advise him that the court had made a decision in regard to his case. The decision was an order for him to pay his ex-wife's legal costs in the custody battle. Michael was adamantly opposed to it, but since she was earning an income that was far less than his, his attorney advised him to pay the costs and move to the next phase of regaining custody of his son. But seven days had passed, and he had not heard from his attorney.

Michael had given his publisher a letter through his agent. The publisher issued an official announcement decrying his action and denying any knowledge of such. He had called Ani, but seven days had passed, and there was no word from her.

Sitting in his home and surrounded by pictures of his namesake, Michael wanted to talk to someone. In the past, these were the times he would talk to Cynthia, but she was no longer a part of his life. Or he would call Ani, but she was not accepting his calls. Or he would talk to Blair.

"My God," he wondered aloud. "What have I done? Everything and everyone that mattered to me is gone. How in the fuck did I get here?"

Michael rubbed his hands together like a raccoon and rocked back. "What do I do now?"

He walked into his living room and inserted a Sade CD, then pressed play on the player. Then he went into his son's room, picked up his red-and-blue Giants football and lay in his son's bed as the silky voice blanketed his body.

Her words took him beyond the level of grief he was experiencing into a deeper realization as to who he was and how he had come to this moment. Michael curled into a tight ball as he wondered if there was any way he could turn back time to the days when he would be so busy working he couldn't take out the time to play with his son. How he had become what he hated most about his father. He lay in the bed thinking of the mornings his son would walk into his office before school, and Michael would shout, "Not now, Blair, I'm in my zone." It had never occurred to Michael until that moment how cold he must have sounded. And on top of everything else, unlike his father, his had only garnered bitter fruit.

"Hello, Dr. Weston speaking, may I help you?"

"Joe, how are you?"

"I'm fine," Joe said with a tone in his voice that indicated he had no idea who was calling.

"Sorry to call you at work," Michael said. "I just wanted to call to say hello."

"Mike?"

"Yeah. How are you? It's been a while."

"A couple of years to be exact."

"So what's going on in A.T.L.? I haven't been down there since——"

"Atlanta is Atlanta. Listen, my sister told me everything. I'm not one to cast stones, my brother, but I will say it was fucked up you not using protection. I've been out there, and God only knows I've done my dirt. But I've never gone in uncovered."

Michael lay in Blair's bed looking at his poster of Momma Cilk as he once again was admonished in regard to his misjudgment.

"Now she's worried sick. Phillip is tripping. It's just a big mess that could have been avoided had you made the right decision."

After holding his breath a second, Michael said softly, "Listen. Can you do me a favor?"

"Depends."

"I need you to call Joi for me. I don't want to call and—"

"Freeze, freeze, freeze. You want to call my sister's home even after everything you've done?"

"Joe? I've known you for a while. And trust me when I say I'm sorry things did not work out with Cynthia and me. But I have never loved a woman like Joi. It's hard to explain. She moves me, man. It was not a one-night fling as far as I'm concerned, and now that a part of me is growing inside of her, it's hard to sleep."

"Bro. I can't do that. Maybe she needs some more time."

"Joe? Please, man. Just call her on the three-way. If she doesn't want to talk, she'll hang up. I just don't want to call and cause any more problems."

"You're serious, aren't you? The answer is no. Now, what you should do is try to get your name cleared up. I heard about that book shit and—"

"I don't give a *fuck* about a book man! I can't move on with anything until I come to terms with Joi." After a beat of silence, Michael added, "I love her, Joe. I know that sounds stupid, but I do. Please. Just let me talk to her, okay?"

Michael held the phone to his ear and the first voice was that of Phillip's. "Hello?" Silence. "Hello? Anyone there?"

Michael started to speak.

"Oh my bad, Phillip," Joe said. "I didn't hear you. I'm here grading papers. What's going on?"

"Nothing. Just in the midst of this damn campaign, and it's not looking good at all. They did a little poll in the local paper, and out of five candidates, I came in fourth."

"No, that's not too good. But how reliable is the polling data?"

"Not very. They've never called an election correct, so I'm not going to get too caught up in it. What's going on? When are you and G.G. coming down here again?"

"I'm teaching Summer A, so it'll be a while for me. You guys should come up here for a few days after the election."

"We might just do that."

As they caught up, Michael lay listening and wishing Joe would just skip to the chase.

"We're going to this black tie thing tonight, and then tomorrow I'm headed to Tallahassee for some party business. Then it's back to shaking hands and pounding the pavement until October. If I lose, it will not be for lack of effort." Then Phillip said, "Joi? Your brother is on the phone. Listen, Joe, I have to shower and shave before we head out; but it was nice hearing from you, and you should really come on down after the election. We'll take the boat out and do some deep sea fishing or hit a few balls."

"It's a date," Joe replied.

Michael could hear Phillip drop the phone and then listened to the sounds in the background. The steady flow from the shower and the TV voice-over that said, "Tragedy on the high seas. Details at eleven." He heard a sound that sent joy through his body and closed his eyes to visualize her answering the phone.

"Hello?"

"Hey, baby girl . . . how are you?"

"I'm fine. What's going on?"

"Well, first of all, Dad said call him. Said he's been trying to catch up with you."

"I will. So much is going on right now. But he's been on my mind the last few days because—but wait. Is that why you called me? What are you now, a page boy?"

"No, listen, I know we spoke this morning about—well, about Mike."

"Don't tell me you told him. Is that why Daddy's calling me out of the blue?"

"No, he's—on the phone?"

In an angry whispering tone, she asked, "Dad or Michael?"

A pause with no end entered the conversation, but Michael held his tongue. "The latter," Joe answered.

"Don't get upset with him," Michael blurted out. "If he had not called, I was going to call myself. Joi, I know I am not acting mature, but I just had to know."

"Can we talk later?" she whispered.

"Just say yes or no."

"Honey," Phillip said in the background, "do we have any Irish Spring?"

"My bathroom. Third shelf on the left."

"Joi?" Michael repeated.

"Yes?"

"I know it's your decision, but I should at least be told what you're going to do. You already made it clear that I don't have a voice in the decision, and I respect that under the circumstances; but can't you at least tell me what you're going to do?"

"Joe? Are you there?"

"Yes. I'm here," her brother sighed.

"I know you hate being in this position, but if you would put the phone down a second, I'll call you tonight, okay?"

"Sorry I did this. I just didn't want shit to escalate. Good night."

Michael heard the sound as if Joe had laid the phone down on a desk, and then Joi whispered, "What you are doing is totally fucked up. I know you are going through a lot right now, but you know something? So am I. You are being publicly humiliated, but I am humiliated every night I go to sleep. I rub *my* stomach . . . my very own body and feel shame. I look at this man get up and go to work at seven A.M. and I feel shame. You want a decision? I can't give you one, 'cause I have not made one."

Michael was silent.

"I found it," Phillip shouted in the background. Joi did not respond.

"I could have loved you," she continued. "You know that? I could have loved you in the right time in our lives, but we started out so wrong we could never find right."

"Can I at least come to Tampa or St. Pete or wherever you are? If you make the decision that I fear you're going to make, can I at least be there for support? I don't want to pressure you. I just want to be there for you."

"Ab-so-lutely not."

"Joi, I have nothing." Michael could not believe he had shared the words that had encircled him for days, but continued. "I'm dying on the inside. I don't want this, I need this more than I can tell you with words. I look in the mirror and see nothing. Not you, not Blair, not my father, not even myself. I see nothing, Joi, and I need this to happen, to save me." Michael waited for her reply but heard Phillip talking in the distance, so he continued. "Joi, I love you. How we could get back to right is beyond me. Why I feel this way about a married woman I will never understand, but I know that—"

"Let me understand what you're saying. You want me to have a child . . . that you will more than likely *never* see . . . then you'll have two kids in two states . . . but you will feel whole. Is that what you're saying?"

"No. What I—"

"Michael, you are in love with Michael. What you're going through is self-inflicted. I know you have caught hell in the press; but you created this beast, and you have to deal with it. But instead you're feeling self-pity and looking for a place to fall, and I can't provide that. You're looking for picket fences and a fantasy, but what's inside my body is real."

"I know what I feel. You can do your five-dollar psychological analysis if you like, but I know what's in my heart."

"It takes no courage to be a victim, Michael, so stop playing the role."

"What do you mean by that? I know what I feel."

"You know something," Joi added. "In hindsight, I'm glad you called because it helped me to make a decision about me and about this—this child. But I know what I need to do to get on with my life, and now it's just a matter of doing it."

"What's that?"

CHAPTER

15

Joi lay in bed with the phone pressed to her ear after spending Saturday night alone. When she awoke, she had opened her eyes and felt the heat of the sun needle her skin and had known she had to speak to her father. As she waited for him to return, she felt fortunate she had escaped the dreams.

The last image on a person's mind stands the best chance of engraving itself in his or her head at night. With this knowledge she had feared closing her eyes because she would see Phillip, Michael and Angie. But she had seen only darkness in spite of the decision she had to make within the next few days. While the night had encouraged bitter tears, it also brought sweet relief, because it was the calm spot in the ocean that followed the titanic wave.

"I'm back. So what were you saying," Mr. Weston said, as if he was not in the mood to be bothered by the early morning call.

"Now that you know what happened, I just wanted to call and—well, get your thoughts."

"What would you like me to say?"

"Daddy? I just want you to say what's on your mind."

Joi could hear her father clear his throat after a pause. "Does your mother know about this?"

"No. To my knowledge just Joe, the gentleman, of course, and you."

"And Phillip. Phillip knows, correct?"

Joi rolled onto her stomach. "Yes, Phillip knows."

"I don't know much of anything to say. You have to make a decision, and you know what my stance is on—"

"Dad, I just need you to be my father. I'm not looking at you as a person who'll provide all of my answers and make it better. I want you to—"

"It's hard, Joi."

"Hard?"

"It's hard knowing that—I just think most of this is my fault."

"Why do you say that?"

"Numbers," he quipped. "Numbers fourteen and eighteen. The Lord is long-suffering, and of great mercy, forgiving iniquity and transgression, and by no means clarifying the guilty."

Joi remembered how her father seemed to have the entire Bible on index cards in his mind ready to use whenever necessary. She stared at the silk sheets on her bed as he continued.

"Visiting the iniquity of the fathers—*of the fathers*," he emphasized, "upon the children unto the third and fourth generation."

"Daddy, this had nothing to do with you."

"I was not there. I should have been. I allowed Joe and your mother to pretty near raise you. I wanted to support you back then; but I was too busy sowing my own seeds of shame, and now it has come back upon my second generation."

"What—What you did hurt me. It hurt all of us. I will not judge you, and I have tried never to do so. But I will say that it has shaped my relationship with every man I've known. It's bigger than just the infidelity. I never felt I was good enough as an actress, so I always felt insecure. I never felt I was whole as a friend, so I would abandon friendships and just cling to Joe. And of course I never thought I deserved a husband who was faithful to me, and only me, so I *allowed* things to happen. If you could step out on Mom, the one man, who was the epitome of a man, then who am I not to expect the same thing to happen to me."

"I can feel your heartache, Joi'de-ve," he said. "And for a lifetime those indiscretions have disturbed my mind. I am sad to report that long after I'm gone the fruits will still be here."

"The mistake I made, Dad, I can honestly say had nothing to do with you."

"I should have been there for you to talk to me. That's why it's sometimes hard for me to call you now. When you were a child, I was always too busy, and I missed that whole chunk of your life. You're a big-time movie star now. What do you need with a rough-neck, tobacco-chewing deacon now that you're grown and—"

"I need you even more, Daddy."

"What?"

"As a woman, I need you to show me how a man can make a mistake—and redeem himself. I've never seen that. Show me how he can do it not for his wife, not for his children, but for himself. God, I need to see that in you so I can make a decision I have to make for me."

* * *

After saying good-bye to her father, Joi thought of different numbers. As of Tuesday, she would be eleven weeks. *Two months, three weeks, four days of pregnancy*, Joi thought as she lay in bed.

She had made her decision.

There was no way she could go through with an abortion. There was no way she could take a life because she had made a mistake living her life.

Breathing heavily, Joi snatched the sheets from her body and rubbed her stomach in a slow, circular grind. She moved her feet as if she was running backward in an attempt to find comfort, but could not. Closing her eyes, she thought she could feel a kick inside of her. She could sense her breasts swelling and her body going through a metamorphosis, but she knew at this point it was just a figment of her imagination. "I have to do this," she said. "I have to do this now."

Joi sat up in bed, put her feet in her slippers, arched her back in a catlike stretch and proceeded to go downstairs to where Phillip was watching a cable news show. She knew he heard her enter the room, but he chose not to say anything to her. So she stood behind him and watched him watch the television. His pillow from their bed was on the floor. The sheet and blanket he had used from the guest bedroom the previous night were folded beside it.

Phillip picked up the remote, scrolled through the channels and laid it to rest beside a bowl of cereal.

"Good morning," Joi whispered. He did not reply. With her first instinct being to return upstairs, Joi turned around, but then placed her hand on the banister, looked at her husband and thought to herself, *Not this time.*

She reached over his shoulder, picked up the remote and turned off the television. Phillip did not move.

"Listen," Joi said meekly. "I know this is hard; but you're flying out in a few hours, and I wanted to settle this before you left. That's if you don't mind."

Silence.

"As you heard last night . . . I made a decision, and I wanted to tell you—"

"Really?" he growled. His facial expression was muted, but his eyes showed the rage he felt in his heart.

Joi smiled as fear glittered in her eyes. But her smile faded, and a question mark appeared on her face as she said, "I'm having the baby."

The silence mushroomed, and Joi saw his chest rise and fall at a faster pace. Yet he refused to make eye contact with her.

"I know this is messed up, and I would never have thought it would happen to me—to us—even three months ago. Like I've told you before, it was not something I wanted to happen. I didn't go to meet him for any other reason but to get the book signed. I'd met him before." Joi noticed her husband's foot tap as if it were a fuse headed for a two-hundred-pound block of TNT. "What I mean," she clarified, "is I was in the airport—he used to date Cynthia, I guess—and Joe introduced us. We didn't exchange numbers, and until the night of the signing, I had not seen him."

"You expect me to believe that?"

"No. Actually, Phillip, I do not expect you to believe anything I say at this point, but I will say this. I have told you the truth, and if I were going to lie, I think I could do a better job than that."

"Truth? It's funny you should use that word." Phillip looked up at his wife and said, "I don't know which is worse, Joi. Me thinking you're a *whore* or me thinking you're a *slut*?"

For a moment all she could see was his face was red. His face was red. The paneling on the wall, red. The oversized blue leather sofa he sat on, red. Joi opened her mouth, and the only thing that could come out was, "What?"

"If you slept with him for one night, you're a slut. A slam-bam-thank-you-ma'am slut. If you were fucking him on a continuous basis, then you're just a Saturday night garden-variety whore. So which is it?" he asked as he turned away from her gaze.

Joi scratched her head in thought and said, "I can't believe you just said that to me." She looked at the back of his head and added, "I'm your wife for God sakes. How can you sit there and say something like—"

"Joi, let me tell you something. You can come with that condescending shit if you want to. But you don't see what I'm going through. Do you know what it feels like for me to go to sleep thinking about some man inside you?"

"Phillip, I—We don't have to go there. I made this decision, and I have to now come to terms with it."

"Let me get this straight. We are *supposedly* a couple, yet you made a decision?"

"In regard to my body," Joi said, "you're damn right. Besides, Phillip, are we a couple? Every time we start arguing, you break plates and leave. What happens when you break and don't come back? How do I know you will be here in six months one way or the other? Are you staying because of the image?"

Phillip remained as still as an oil portrait.

"Is that what keeps us together?"

As she spoke, Joi remembered the dialogue from the last day she had acted professionally. "If you're staying because of the time we've spent together, you wanna know what all the years count for? Almost two decades . . . we'll never get back."

Phillip reached for the remote and turned on the television.

"I have to know where we stand," she said. "If we are a couple, then I want to know what you want to do, but if not, then I have to do what's right for me and me only."

"Joi it's *always* about you and you only. From the moment we met," he said, and turned off the TV, "it was always you and you only. You're carrying another nigger's child! That's the bottom fucking line. Another nigger's child is in your stomach!"

Joi ran her fingers over her lips and then said, "Phillip, that's not the real problem. I know that's a part of the problem, but what's at the core of the situation?"

"Other than the small fact that you are *pregnant* from another man, let me think."

"You can patronize all you want; but it's deeper than that, and you know it. You know this is the surface. This is about control. You're losing it, and that's what's killing you."

"This . . . has nothing," he said through locked teeth, "to do with control."

"It has *everything* to do with control! Yeah, you supported my dreams from day one, but the trade-off has been that you have controlled me from day one. You told me what scripts to read, what auditions to attend and everything. The one time I went my own way was the biggest break of my life. You were the one who said I should never play in a comedy. No wait a minute; you called it a coon'medy.

"Damn straight and it stereotyped you forever."

"And it *paid* for this damn house, too! Let's not forget that!" Silence. Joi had never called in question his ability to provide for the family, and she watched the news roll through him like an awakened volcano.

"So that's how it is, huh? You supporting me, too?"

"That's not what I'm saying at all, Phillip. I'm saying—Listen, why don't we just try to see the counselor again. Then we can both vent."

"Why you wanna talk to Vanessa, when you don't fucking wanna talk to me?"

"*I can't talk to you!*" Joi screamed so loud she felt her eyes bulge outward.

"*And whose fault is that?*" Phillip retorted as his wife shook her head out of frustration. "Your wounds are self-inflicted, unless you're saying it's my fault I can't—I can't fuck!"

"Where in the hell did that come from? I'm saying stop pointing the finger at the world and point it at yourself!"

Phillip leaned back on the sofa, but Joi was not going to show her fear.

"So are you saying it's my fault I can't fuck?" he asked.

"I'm saying it's your fault that—It's your fault that . . . " Joi lost the words and the courage she had before. She looked down at the floor and with a shaky voice said, "Listen. I can't deal with this now. I just can't. When you're ready to talk, we'll—we'll talk."

"That's always your answer. Isn't it?"

"What?"

Phillip looked at his wife with contempt in his eyes. "When I lost my fucking daughter, where were you? Huh? When she asked for me with her dying breath, did you have to tell me that five *hundred* fucking times? You had to let me know that I let my daughter down? Huh? Was it that important to tell me that you were there for her and I wasn't? You wanna know where I was? I was parking the *fucking* car. I was trying to avoid the media. I was trying to be the wind under your wings, once again. That's where I was, Joi. But all through this marriage, I've been parking the damn car." Phillip reached down for the remote, picked it up and tried to turn on the television with his thumb. When he could not, he flung it across the room and shattered it against the wall. "I can't deal with you and I can't deal with this. Okay? You talking to this nigga on the phone and having your brother call me to put him through? What kinda middle school shit was that?"

Joi held her tongue to avoid losing her composure.

"Yeah. I fucked this woman almost *twenty* years ago. Okay? I messed up twenty years ago. I messed up once!"

"You messed up for about four months if I remember correctly."

Phillip stood and walked closer to Joi. She could smell the fury that radiated from his pores. "I was young, it was L.A., it was the eighties, I was stupid and I needed someone. Was it right? No. But you were pregnant and—and you acted like I was not even a part of the shit. You shut me out completely. She was there."

"I shut you out? What in the *hell* does that mean?"

"After you got pregnant what is the first thing you did?"

"I went on a vacation for a few days."

"With who?"

"With Joe, so what?"

"Who was the first person you told you were pregnant with our child? Who was the first person you told you were pregnant with this—whatever it is? When you got the Emmy nomination live on TV, who did you call from the "Good Morning America" set? Who flew down to pick out this fucking house with you? Who did you call when—"

"Are you saying you're jealous of my brother? Is that what you're saying?"

Phillip backed up two steps from his wife and said softly, "When Angie was killed, who did you turn to, Joi!"

"Because," she replied, "you were not there."

"I was *not* there 'cause you left me!"

"You can pretend you were the neglected, hardworking, ever-suffering spouse if you like. If that's what you must do to get through the night, then go with it. But it's not that simple. When you *parked* the car in this relationship, you did other things, too."

"Like what?"

Joi had never wanted to say the words she felt coming from her lips, but she had no choice. "You had other affairs."

"What?"

"You can call me a slut if you want to, but I knew. I always knew!"

"Knew what?"

"You had another goddamn affair, you son of a bitch! You fucked the receptionist on the show. Carlota Winfield. I still remember that hooker's name. And I know you did because the bitch left her lipstick on your drawers to let me know she did you, and plus one of the extras saw you together. Did I say anything? No. Did I ever tell anyone else? Including the only person in this world I can talk to, Joe? *No!* You're upset about Michael. I understand that. But what's worse is you're thinking, if you did this to me and got away with it for all those years, what could I have done to you without you knowing it. It's not what I did that's getting to you; it's *your* guilt that's killing you. It's your own dirt that has come back to haunt you!"

Phillip returned to his wife, and she could see his jaw expand from grinding his teeth. She could feel the heat from his nostrils, and he was on the verge of exploding. She refused to take a step backward. She braced herself for anything, including his becoming physical with her once again. She felt better for finally releasing the words she had held inside, so there was nothing he could do or say that would bring her harm.

"I'm not afraid anymore," Joi said over a nervous laugh. "I'm not afraid of what you will do to me, or what you won't do for me. I've lain in the bed alone too many nights to allow you to take my soul. I've apologized to you in *every* conceivable way, and now my knees are sore and my back hurts. But I am willing to do it once again."

Phillip looked down at the carpet.

"I'm sorry," she said with her fist over her heart. "I'm sorry," she repeated once again, this time shaking her head. "Phillip, I—am—sorry for what I did." Phillip remained silent. "You don't have to answer, but let me tell you this. The *only* difference between what you and I did is not the number of times we did it. It's not the number of people we did it with. It's the fact that I'm a woman and you're a man. If you were a woman, you could be in the same position I am in now.

"I'm not a slut. I'm your wife—at least for now. If you're not a big enough man to deal with this, then I don't want you. You can leave now," she said as she wiped away tears she tried desperately to hold back, "because I don't need you, either."

Phillip threaded his fingers together as if even thinking of the words he was about to utter pierced his soul.

"Joi, I'm a man," he whispered. "But what is a man if he can't provide for his wife?"

"Phillip, everything I have accomplished you have accomplished right beside me and—"

"What," he said, and raised his voice, "is a man if he cannot have sex with his woman? What is a man if he cannot save his child from harm? By doing what you did, you emasculated me with a man who is younger, better looking and more successful than I will ever be. You could never replace what you've killed inside of me." He sighed. "You could never be in my shoes. I know you had pain in your heart for years, but does it really make what you did . . . right?"

"Let's not compare wounds, Phillip. I, too, lost a child," Joi continued. "I lost my angel. The little girl who I used to sing to every night before she went to sleep. Gone. The little girl who never tired of dressing as a clown on Halloween. She's gone. The little brown face that liked to dress like me. Gone. The beautiful young woman that I should've—that I wanted to stop that night and tell her she could not go out. I wanted to take her keys away, but I didn't. I was weak," Joi said, and lifted her chin, "and now she's gone. And I have to wake up with that, and go to sleep with that, every day for the rest of my life. Everything I accomplish for the rest of my life will be framed by the thirty seconds I was weak."

Phillip put his arms around Joi, and as she laid her head on his chest, she said, "You are the only man—I have ever loved. I always knew that, and I especially know it now. I know this is not a perfect situation; but it's the situation I'm in, and I don't want to lose it. I don't want to lose another child. And I don't want to lose you. I'm sorry,"

"I want to leave, but I can't. I know that sounds terrible," Phillip said quietly, "but it's just the way I feel. I know we have something left. Maybe not a lot, but something to work with. We've had a lot of bad things happen, but we've had our share of good times. There is no way to wipe the slate clean in a person's life, but you endure. You look at what's important to you, and you endure.

"I lay here last night, and in spite of everything that has happened, all I could think about was the night I proposed to you. All I could think about was the night we made love in the restroom, and the woman in the next stall started to masturbate just listening to us. Or the time at the Oscars when you thought Morgan Freeman was me, and you pinched his butt. No one else will ever find the humor in that," he said, and wiped her eyes. "And I don't want them to because I don't want to begin again. I just want, somehow, to begin anew. I want to leave you. God knows I do. But I saw on the news the other day a house that was burned down to the ground. Everything these people had worked for was gone. The clothes, pictures, all just a memory. But the foundation was still firm. It survived the fire, and it left them something to build on.

"Even though we went a while without having—without being intimate—you stayed." Phillip looked into her eyes and said, "I know you've been miserable. I know you miss the caresses more than the sex, but that was something I didn't feel I could do. I know you may have even done this because you were tired of sitting home and making afghans. I knew this and I was not there. I was too wrapped up in trying to overcome my shortcomings as a man, you might say. You might say I was out parking the car. But you were there. You were supportive, and although I never said it"—he held her close once again—"I thank you. You loved me when I didn't love myself. But more importantly you found a way to like me when I did not like myself."

"Phillip, I—"

Joi could feel the hand that caressed her back start to tremble. "God, it hurt to hear his voice last night. I wanted to scream, and if I had a gun and could find him"—and the shakes left his body as he said—"but I heard your voice. And I heard how much you loved me in spite of all of this.

"Joi, this shit is hard. This shit is harder than anything I have gone through except losing Angie. But I— We survived her death for the most part, and I can't imagine any fire being worse than that. We grew apart; but we're still standing, and in the end that's what it's all about. If we can survive that even though we turned away from each other"—Phillip's voice reduced to a whisper—"we can survive this. If we turn toward each other."

"I needed to hear you say that."

"I know we can. Because nothing in this world can teach you more about life than losing something you love."

"Phillip?"

"Yes?"

"I love you."

"I don't want another woman," he said with tears in his voice that were not yet visible in his eyes. "I don't want to see what's on the other side of the fence. You can make me so angry, but, Joi, I've never stopped loving you. In the darkest moments, when you told me what happened, I wanted to hate you. I wanted to hate you so bad I couldn't sleep, but I could never see myself leaving. And one of the reasons is because before I loved you, I discovered that you're my friend. And as your friend, I could never leave you. No matter what, I'm here," he whispered into her ear. "This will be our child."

Joi covered his mouth with a kiss as gentle as a winter sunset. Phillip looked at his wife, brushed a kiss across her forehead and in a broken voice repeated, "Joi, this will be our child."

CHAPTER

16

Michael gazed down the block from Ani's third-floor apartment as the sun glistened upon the façade of Tracy Towers. With her speaking to the landlord about the possibility of renting a larger unit, he absorbed the looks on the children's faces as they played in the snow.

He could see the subway train stop at the corner and watched children prepare their ammunition and wait to thrash their unsuspecting victims with snowballs. Other children built forts behind cars and battled each other as if recreating a scene from *Saving Private Ryan*. Little girls insulated by layer upon layer of coats, shawls, jackets, hoods, and windbreakers made angels in the snow untouched by passing trucks, buses and cars. And in the park Michael saw a little boy who played alone. Other children built igloos or tried to slide down the gently sloping hill on *borrowed* garbage can lids, but this child did not join in. He seemed to pace in a world guided by the sound of a different drummer. A world where he was preoccupied with things more important than playing.

"What if we do this, David? What if I sign a four-year lease"—and then she winked at Michael—"and give you a double deposit. Can you then modify the apartment and give me the reduced rate?"

Michael smiled politely, yet his eyes were reserved. He then redirected his attention to the playground, and the child was gone. He scanned the monkey bars, the merry-go-round, and did not see him. He looked at the basketball court and on the black tires that stood in direct contrast to their white environment, and there was no sign of him. Michael turned his attention away from the scenery outside the window because in his mind Blair was all he could see.

After retaining the rights to their son through the courts, Robyn decided to return to the Heart of Dixie and purchased a home just a couple of miles from her mother in the city of Montgomery. The court approved liberal visitation for Michael, which equated to three weeks in the summer, a week at Christmas and a week at spring break. The judge, who let it be known he was an avid book reader, showed his disdain with what Michael had done, not with words, but with the amount of child support awarded. Against his attorney's wishes Michael refused to appeal the decision, and after court he asked Robyn if he could take Blair across the street for a sundae.

Blair, whose locks were shaved, looked at his father as they sat in the small booth and said, "Don't worry, I'll be back next summer. Cool?"

"Are you enjoying the South?"

"It's different. When I lived there before, you know, I was just a Shorty. Now they laugh at the way I wear my clothes, the way I wear my Tim's, even my hair. That's why Momma made me cut it, but it's cool. They say I try to talk proper, but I'm not. This is just the way I kick."

Michael smiled. "The way—you kick?"

"Yeah. This is just how I am," he said as he enjoyed a spoonful of the dessert. "You have to have a car to get anything. You can't just walk to the store on the corner And it's so quiet, too. I forgot how quiet it was in Bama. You don't never hear a police car round there."

"Well, that's a good thing."

"I know, but I miss being here."

Michael ran his fingers over the damp freshly cleaned table and asked, "Do you really?"

"Yeah. You need someone to be here with you," Blair said without looking up from his treat which was smeared on the tip of his nose. "Someone to keep you in line."

"I'll be fine," Michael said.

"No, you won't, because you're still lonely and I have to come back and take care of you."

The acidic words bathed Michael's soul, but he smiled and outwardly enjoyed dessert with his child.

"Oh yeah, Daddy, check this out." Blair took off his jacket and rolled up his sleeve and formed a muscle in his bicep.

"What," Michael asked.

"You can't see it?"

Michael looked at the outside of his son's arm and saw the temporary artwork.

"I finally got a tattoo."

Michael stared at the picture of a skull and cross-bones and then started to laugh out loud with his son.

*   *

*

"Well," Ani said, pulling Michael away from the memory, "it looks like I am not going to be moving out of this place after all. They're going to approve me for a three-year lease!"

"I'm happy for you."

"Yeah," she said, looking out the window. "I can't move from these apartments. These are my people. I've been in this complex most of my life, you know. Besides, if I move, I may not be able to write anymore. Every story I've written, I've written lying in this bed and looking up at those buildings. I don't want to change—change too much." And then she looked at Michael and said, "What's wrong with you?"

"Nothing. Just listening to you."

"Thinking about Blair is what you mean."

"I'm always thinking about Blair. What else is new?"

"If it's any consolation—"

"Don't."

"Don't what?"

"I've heard them all. 'It happens for a reason.' I hate that one the most, but I've also heard, 'Sometimes a child is better with the mom,' 'Sometimes it's better for a child growing up outside New York,' 'He has more family there.' I am up to here," he said, drawing an invisible line across his neck, "with consolation."

"I understand."

"Enough of my drama. What about you?" Michael asked.

"What do you mean? Are you asking, am I ready for what we're going to do today?"

"No. I mean are you over Johnny?"

"Over and done with. Johnny was an addict. And not so much to drugs but to abusing me. He had a rough time as a child, but guess what? Who hasn't? Who has had the perfect childhood? He used that excuse for every-thing, and when they put him in jail for selling that mess for Miss Simmons down the hall, it served him right."

"Unless you get him a good attorney, it's going to be hard to beat—"

"You think for ten seconds I'll give him money to beat a drug charge? That goes against my principles as a black woman." Ani unwrapped a Twix bar and shoved it into her mouth with only two bites. "Please. Serves him right."

"I'm glad to hear you say that."

With her cheeks full of milk chocolate, she said, "I never considered it. God has been *too* good to me. He's answered my prayers, taken that tumor out my body"—heavy breath—"completely, and for me to bring him back into my world would be sinful."

"The tumor's gone? You never told me. The last time we spoke, you said you had three months."

"Well, that's what *they* say. I told the doctor I couldn't pay the bill, so he gave me six more months to live." When Michael did not laugh and looked out the win-dow, Ani sighed, "Oh, well, I guess you heard that one, huh. But seriously, I have no fear of death. And I have some good news and bad news for you."

Michael looked in her direction.

"The good news is you will more than likely not die today." Silence. "The bad news is that one day, you will most definitely die. Let's face it. We're all terminal. So when you look at life that way, do you think I care about what some man in a white coat says?"

"And that's the best medicine."

"And oh, yeah, before I forget. I got some more good news for you."

"Whatchu got this time? A knock-knock joke?"

"Funny man. You are a funny, funny man. Listen, I had a long conversation with the young lady who took over for Pam. What's her name?"

"Rhonda?"

"Yeah. And we talked about you for a while."

"Someone talking about me at Charisma? No," Michael said sarcastically, "please tell me it isn't so."

"First of all, you're not Beelzebub around there, and I know you think you are. Secondly, you did *not* cost Pam her job. Pam's failing up. She is working for an Internet company"—heavy breath—"developing Rocket Books software, so she's fine. But Rhonda is very interested in looking at something by you."

"Looking at what? *Speaking in Tongues?*"

"Ahraa no," Ani said, stretching her eyes. "I don't think they'll consider fiction; but, she is from Plainfield, and she grew up in the neighborhood where Bill Evans is from. As you know he played with Miles, Charles Mingus, George Russell—"

"I know of him well. He played on *Some Kind of Blue,* so what do they want from me?"

"She would like for you to write a book that documents his life. All you need to do is turn in an outline and tell her your research methods, and she'll present it to Vance."

"I don't know, Ani. My name has been trashed in this business."

"To every disadvantage in life . . . there is an advantage. Remember me telling you that years ago? A distinct advantage. I thought about that over and over again. Then I thought about your fiasco, and it occurred to me that you have a magnificent opportunity."

"In what way?"

"I like the Bill Evans angle because there is no way

that could be misconstrued. It's all based on fact backed up with research. But more importantly, look at your life. The things you have been through. You have lived your entire life in the shadows of a name. Look at Martin Luther King IV, look at Paul Robeson Jr., Ron Brown Jr., Jessie Jackson Jr. You guys have had a heavy burden, and in my opinion, other than the little situation you fell into, you all have done a wonderful job. Tell me that's not a book?"

"I don't know," Michael said, and yawned as he rubbed his eyes, which burned dryly from sleepless nights. "The idea of seeing myself going through all of this again is frightening. They say I can get about four nights a week at The Past-Time Paradise, and to be honest, that's what I want to do."

"But I'm sure they'll be willing to give you a decent advance. You still have not given a single interview about everything that happened, and the PR people could have a field day getting your name back out there. In this book you can talk about how the rest of those guys have honored their father's names and how . . . well, how you made a mistake. That's a story people would love to read. A fall-from-grace saga. If you like, I'll write the foreword. You could still play at night, and we could hire a couple of students to assist in the research."

"A friend of mine told me once, and I quote, 'Nothing will own me. Not a man. Not money. And definitely not some *dumb* assed bitch like Pam Wilson,' unquote. When you told me that"—Ani smiled at his words—"I thought you had lost your ever-loving mind. But to be honest, I now understand. Money owned me. It possessed me. And not so much as what it brought, but the money to me was power. The money was a way to keep score. A way to say I'd live up to this name. You have the words, and the money is just a by-product of that. But to be honest, after being *exposed* for lack of a better word, the situation with Joi, after losing Blair, I've rethought a lot of things in life. Listening to them talk about me on talk radio as if I was the worst thing to happen to the publishing industry in the past one hundred years. When you hear those things, you decide what's important in life." Michael's eyebrows rose as if he were amazed, yet he bit his bottom lip so hard he could feel his pulse. "It's not about the money, because I'd give back everything I own tomorrow for Blair and my name."

Ani buried her face in her pillow, closed her eyes and said, "I can only imagine the pain you must be feeling."

"I will have two children down south, whom I can't see. I've brought shame to the only thing of value I've ever owned. In six months I've gone from '60 Minutes' to enjoying my fifteenth minute, and trust me when I say, it's not a fun ride.

"Now I've decided to live each day as if my life depended on me enjoying that day. So to use one of the clichés I hate most," a cold dignity created a stone mask over his face as he said, "everything happens for a reason."

The silence in the room was broken by a knock at the door.

Ani looked at Michael with a foreign look in her eyes. "That has to be them."

"And you're not backing out," Michael said with a smile.

"Why can't we do it tomorrow?" Ani whined. Her freshly made-up face looked like peach-tinted cream, and she had purple bows and ribbons in her hair. "There's too much snow out there now."

"We're doing this today. I told you that I was going to

get you out of this house on your birthday, and guess what," he said as the person knocked again. "Happy Birthday to youuu," he sang out of key.

Michael walked toward the door and opened it for the two male nurses he had hired to assist him in getting Ani out of the apartment, into the elevator and out of the building.

As the men entered the room, Michael realized that of all the rewards he had received from his fifteen minutes, this would be the greatest. "Ani, your chariot has arrived."

After assisting Ani into a specially equipped motorized van with a hydraulic lift, Michael instructed the driver to take them to Times Square. They looked through the window and admired the skaters at Rockefeller Plaza who skated over the ice as if the pull of gravity did not affect them. They rode over to 125th Street, and Michael watched in amazement the look on Ani's face at the sight of Old Navy, The Disney Store, and Bill Clinton's office down the street from the world famous Apollo Theater.

Then their tour of New York took them to Queens, where they looked at the homes of famous celebrities from the past such as Dizzy Gillespie and Billy Holliday as well as the church of Reverend Floyd Flake. Then in the distance Ani saw it. The big white structure she had seen only once.

"Hey, Michael. See that building over there?"

"Yes."

"Remember, I told you I had a daughter?"

"Yes."

"Well, she's—" There was a pause as Ani seemed to

fight for control of her feelings. She looked at Michael, and as the driver pulled into the circular entrance of the facility, she asked in a suffocated whisper, "Why?"

"Happy birthday, dear Annniiiii, happy birthday to youuu."

Michael could see her breath quicken. "But how did you know this was the hospital?"

"You mentioned to me a long time ago that she was not too far from LaGuardia. So after I discovered her name, when I saw it on an envelope in the apartment, it was easy."

"I've talked to her on the phone a few times, but I haven't seen Paula in five years." Ani's fingers grazed the surface of her trembling chin.

"They told me that when I called to set this up."

"Set what up?" The car came to a stop, and one of the nurses went inside. "What did you set up?"

"Ani, they say the end justifies the means, and that's true because what if we never met? How would our lives be different today had I not reached into the garbage and pulled out that manuscript? There has to be a reason for everything in life, and maybe all of what we've gone through . . . was what it took to get us to this point."

The door opened, and Paula, whose hands were held by two men in white coats, saw her mother's face.

Ani opened her mouth to call her name, but nothing came out. The honey-brown-skinned girl stared at her mother as if she had never seen her before. Michael wondered if he had made a dire mistake, but then all it took was a sound.

"Paula?"

The little girl's eyes stretched to twice their normal size, and she started to jump up and down as if she were on an invisible pogo stick. "Momma Ani! Momma Ani! Momma Ani

Momma Ani!" she shouted at the top of her lungs. "Momma Ani!"

As the nurses brought the child to the car, Michael handed Ani a gift to give to Paula wrapped in white with a large golden bow. He looked into Ani's eyes, breathed the words, "Thank you for being a friend," and then kissed her on the lips.

Ani looked at his face as if she saw a part of his soul she had never seen, and her fingers ran through the soft black locks she had never touched. "Next to that little black girl right there, you are the best thing to *ever* happen to me." She shook her head solemnly and continued. Thank you for being my advantage."

A tall, devilishly handsome white man with closely cropped blond hair walked on stage and tapped the microphone with his knuckles. In a deep-timbered voice, he said, "Ladies and gentlemen, we are so glad you could make it to the hottest spot in the Village. We're fortunate enough to have an old friend of The Past-Time Paradise here, and we're pleased to announce that he'll be playing here Thursday through Sunday nights at this time; so make sure you come out and give him some love. So, with no further ado, please give up a big Past-Time Paradise welcome for the piano styling of Mr. Michael Price Brockmier II!"

The bright blue light shined in his face, and Michael rested his fingers on the keys. As the sound of the polite applause sprinkled in his ears, he slid his fingers up and down the smooth surface, and for the first time he felt at home. Michael would usually open his set with "Rocket Love" by Stevie Wonder in keeping with the theme of the club, but decided tonight would be different and he would open by doing something he had rarely done before. He cleared his throat and nodded his head to the waitress to indicate he was thirsty and then tapped the microphone.

"Listen, guys, this will not be easy tonight. I haven't played on stage for a few years, but it seems like a lot longer. I just wanted to say that I am so happy to be back here with you guys. My travels have taken me all over this country and—"

"Nigger, please," someone shouted, "just so we know, will this shit be live or Memorex!"

A few members of the audience laughed; most did not.

"I've traveled all over this country," Michael continued undaunted, "and I must say, there is *no* city like New York City." It's a cocktail, mixed with boom boxes and gunshots. Lost dreams and hip hop." Michael paused as the metaphor settled in his ear.

"Playing here is the pinnacle for me. It's a melody that brings memories of subway trains, Italian crème sodas in the summer and of dimly lit basement parties. When I breathe the air in Harlem I think—"

"What's the difference between you and Millie Vanillie? Bitch, you can't dance!"

A gentleman at the front table turned around and shouted at the heckler, "Yo, give the brother a break!"

"That's all right, man. Let her have her fun," Michael said. "You know there's something very empowering in going through a struggle. No matter how big or small. Because if it does not kill you," he said, and then paused, "it'll make you stronger. It's been a tough six months for me, but no matter how bad it got, there was always music. There was always The Past-Time Paradise, and there was always you." Michael's jaw tightened, his eyes narrowed to slits. "And now I know that—"

"Nigga, is you talking 'cause you can't dance, write *or* play!"

The patrons of the bar started to heckle the woman to the point where a burly bouncer walked over and escorted her out of the bar.

After the clapping subsided, Michael said, "As I was saying, it's very empowering because before I went through that, I had no idea who I was under these dreads." A few people laughed. "I had no idea who I was beyond the name. And so when all of that was shaved away from my life, I found the true Michael, and to be honest, in a way, I've never been happier. Is my life perfect?" He had smiled with his lips, but now his eyes. "But for the first time in my life." His hand dropped from the keys, and his thumbnail dug into the flesh of his thigh. "For the *first* time in my entire life, I've found the one thing I came from my mother's womb to do." Michael lowered his head and whispered into the microphone, "And that's play music for you. I trust you'll enjoy the journey, through the keys of my piano."

Members of the gathering started to clap, followed by a few more, and the man who had previously come to his defense stood. The rest of the crowd followed suit in the intimate nightclub. Michael could hear only the sounds emanating from the piano as he played the first notes of "Rocket Love" and thought of the new meaning the words of the song brought to his heart.

The waitress brought Michael's favorite drink. Jack Daniels with a twist of lime. As she sat it on the veneer of the piano, Michael caught a whiff of her perfume and like a splat of rain fallen from a tree, the oceanic scent brought the sweet remembrance of Joi. The scent, like the drop of rain, brought back the memory of the storm that had past.

He smiled, looked into the bright blue light, swept his fingers over the ivory keys, and just like Ani before him, a hot tear rolled down his cool cheek

CHAPTER

17

Going through his wife's closet, Phillip opened a hope chest given to Joi by her mother and said, "You know, I've never looked in this thing."

"Really?" Joi said, rocking back and forth in an antique rocker as she put tassels on a crocheted purple-and-cream afghan. "I thought you went in there to get one of my blankets before. Are you sure?"

"How could I *ever* forget this picture of you with the four-fingered ring and *JOI* in big gold letters on the belt?"

"Is that where those pictures are? Bring them here."

Joi put down her yarn diversion and rubbed her hands over her fully swollen stomach. It was almost time, and she could feel her love change positions inside of her.

After the election, in which Phillip received a mere three percent of the total vote, Joi researched birthing methods and decided to look into the midwife alternative.

When she had informed Phillip of her decision, he adamantly opposed it. "How can you have a baby at home? You go into panic with a hangnail. You'll never be able to take that much pain. Have you forgotten it was twenty-three hours with Angie?"

After allowing him to vent, Joi explained to him that her research had taught her how the female body was designed to give birth; therefore the requirement of a hospital was not a necessity. She explained that when a woman enters the hospital, surrounded by strange faces, many of whom she does not know, opens a personal part of herself for all the world to see, is told what to eat, how to lie down, how and when to breathe, when and when not to push, it interferes with her own instinctive nature. Joi explained how this dehumanized a woman and treated her less like a thinking, feeling, intelligent adult who would instinctively know the best way to deliver the child.

With Phillip still unconvinced, they attended several workshops and counseling sessions together, and he was eventually able to rid himself of much of his personal fear for his wife's safety.

Outside of the physical reasons for having the child at home, Joi wanted to share the intimate moments with her husband. She wanted him to be more a part of the birth than just there with a pair of shears waiting for the OB to hold the umbilical cord before him and say, "Cut here." She wanted her husband to bring their child into the world.

During the eight weeks of counseling in regard to home delivery, Joi and Phillip rediscovered the love they shared and found ways to mend what had been lost in their union.

Phillip now walked into the family room with the photo album, placed it in Joi's lap and knelt beside her. As he looked for the page, Joi ran her fingers through his hair softly and asked, "Do you remember that video Wilhelmina left for us to watch about home birthing?"

"Yes," he said as he searched for the picture.

"Well, there is a particular scene you might want to see."

Like a little boy just called to the principal's office, he looked into her eyes and asked, "What?"

"Don't get nervous," Joi said, and then kissed him on the forehead. "But I was talking to Wilhelmina, and she said that sometimes when mothers are going through contractions . . ."

"Yes?"

"Well, it's natural to have . . ."

"What?"

"To have sex."

"You're joking, right?"

"No, sweetie. I didn't believe her at first. I thought the people on the video were sick and disturbed, but it's true. When you go into the hospital, they give you a drug called Pitocin to speed up contractions. Well, a woman's body produces the drug naturally, so that's why women sometimes have sex or they may even master—"

"Hey, hey, hey!" Phillip said with his hands over his ears. "You're not suggesting that I—"

"I'm just telling you about everything that *could* happen when we have Ashley."

"I'm not doing that, honey. Call me crazy, but I don't want to be poking Philly-Phil in the head right before he says hello to the world."

"You're crazy," Joi said, laughing, and scratched the stretch mark on her belly. As Phillip flipped to the page the photograph was on, she said, "Just be aware that you've been warned, so if Momma needs her medicine, you better come running!"

"As I was going to say," he said, pointing to the snapshot, "when was this picture taken?"

"Jesus Christ, that's vintage '83. Check out the Sergio Valente jeans with the crease sewn down the leg. Man, that brings back a lot of memories."

"Damn," he said, flipping the page. "In those days I was wearing the Lee jeans, suede Pumas with the *fat* shoelaces and Polo shirts with the matching Polo socks.

"Yes, this picture brings back memories," she said as she turned the page.

"Oh, my goodness, baby," Phillip said, looking at the photo on the next page. "I had no idea you used to wear a scary curl."

"Oh, and you didn't?"

"Naw, my hair wouldn't grow long enough for the curl to take, so I would just have to settle for the waves. "And I also remember my sister with that big rump of hers," Phillip added, "was sooo happy when the Braxtons came out. Remember the big booty Braxton jean? She used to—" Phillip stopped talking mid-sentence as Joi stared into his eyes. He slid the album filled with memories to the floor, and his last words were smothered on her lips.

The past nine months had seen their marriage evolve from the brink of demise to being stronger than the day they said "I do." With the pressure from the political campaign over, Phillip took off a few months to spend time with his wife and to rekindle the lost spark, and with the assistance of a medical aid they also resurrected the romance in other aspects of their marriage as well.

"Just think," he said after their lips mercifully separated, "seven days. Isn't that something?" he said with a smile.

"I know. Joe said he was going to try to get down this weekend. Mom and Dad may make it as well, but let's not hold our breath. As long as you are—"

With his mouth open, Phillip said, "Baby?"

"You felt that one?" Joi asked.

"I did," he replied, and rubbed her tight stomach in a circular motion. "I felt the baby kick. That's the first time I've felt it kick that hard."

"I know. *She's* been kicking up a storm today. In fact, it almost feels like I'm having menstrual cramps as well."

"Can I get you something for the pain?"

"No, dear. It's not really a pain, just an annoyance. Besides, remember I am doing this drug-free. That's unless you're going to give Mommy a little bit of your medicine."

"How did you get so nasty? And don't blame it on the pregnancy either."

"It's not me talking, baby," Joi said. "It's the hormones." And then she pulled him close to her and said, "Just remember, every time I need something for the pain, to whisper and tell me how much you love me. Okay?"

"I love you," Phillip said, and kissed his wife on the lips again. "I love you more than you would ever know."

10:00 A.M.

Choosing to sleep in, Phillip and Joi lay in bed while the television provided background sound. Phillip had on his headphones listening to the sounds of Bob Marley's "Get Up Stand Up," as Joi read *Entertainment Weekly*. Joi felt a pain, but decided to ignore it because Wilhelmina had told her a countless number of times that she could wear herself out worrying about each pain to the point when the actual pain hit, she would be exhausted. But after the throbbing refused to stop, she realized that no matter how much she curled her toes, or how she positioned her body next to Phillip's, her body did not know how to read a calendar and was going to follow its own timetable. With her husband inches away, Joi placed the magazine on the floor beside their bed and relaxed the muscles in her face. And then she allowed her neck to relax as well as her shoulders, stomach muscles, legs and feet, and she noticed the more she relaxed her body, the more she felt relief.

And then she felt it.

Initially she thought she had peed on herself, but then the water started to gush from her body in a flood.

Amazed as he leaped from the bed as if springs were lanced to his back, Phillip said, "What the fuck?"

"Calm down, baby," she said. "It's just my water breaking."

"*Just* your water breaking? What does that mean? *Just your water breaking?*"

"It means, dear, that it's time to call Wilhelmina."

"What happened to seven days? Oh, yeah. That's right. One second, let me get her number."

Joi massaged her stomach as she watched her husband run around the room like Ricky Ricardo when he found out Lucy was about to deliver. She looked down and noticed that the water had run from the bed and made a puddle on the carpet, saturating her magazine.

"Holy shit," she whispered, afraid to show Phillip, who was still trying to deal with the complexities of finding the phone number. "Honey," Joi whispered.

"Yeah, yeah."

"Go to the phone and dial five. Okay? It's on speed dial."

"Damn, that was a good idea. Five," he said as he picked up the phone and repeated it over and over again. As if he would forget it. "Five, five, five."

As Phillip was attempting to do the breathing exercises he had worked with Joi in doing. Joi lay still, closed her eyes and imagined her baby's head moving down, and that gave her an added boost of relief as well. "Damn. I'm actually going to do this," she said to herself. "I'm actually going through with it."

12:30 P.M.

After she arrived, Wilhelmina checked and said, "Today's the day. You just need to be another two centimeters, and we can welcome this angel into the world."

But that was well over an hour ago, and Joi was not fully dilated. She walked on the treadmill, did a squatting exercise and sat in their whirlpool. As she sat amid the jets of pulsating water, she had a fun time calling Phillip, winking at him and saying, "Honey, how 'bout giving Mommy a little something—something for the contractions."

"Stop playing, Joi! Damn."

1:15 P.M.

As Phillip dried Joi's hair, she looked in her mirror and saw her fully nude body sitting between his legs. "Wilhelmina, are you all right out there?" Joi shouted.

"I'm fine, doll face. I'm just watching this fine assed Judge Joe on channel ten. You need me?"

"No, we're fine. If you need something, just yell, okay?"

Joi looked at Phillip and whispered, "Do me a favor?"

"What?"

"Go lock the door."

"Baby, I am not going to——"

"I'm not suggesting that. Just lock the door."

Phillip, with interpretation, stood slowly and locked

their bedroom door. Before he returned to the bed, she said, "Okay, take it off."

"Take what off?"

"Everything. I wanna see you the way God made you."

"Baby, I—"

"Sweetie, I'm going through a lot right now for us. You're going to tell me no? Take it off. Take it *all* off?" she said with a smile.

Knowing it was an argument he could never win, Phillip pulled the tee shirt over his head, kicked off his deck shoes and then pulled down the jeans he wore.

"Yeah, that's the way I like it, baby," she purred with the warmth from her smile echoing in her voice. "Strip for Mommy."

Phillip took off his green silk boxers and allowed his ductile manhood to hang free. Although he had lost the ability to sustain himself, he still looked thick, heavy and erotic to her as she said, "Now come on to bed."

Phillip returned to the bed and positioned himself with his wife between his legs just like before. The feeling of his penis nestled in the pit of her back sent floods of sensations throughout Joi's body. Then he placed his arms around her, and as she opened her eyes to look in the mirror again, the sight of them in bed, naked, yet holding each other made her shiver.

Joi closed her eyes, and Phillip buried his face in her neck. "Remember, baby," she whispered. "Just keep telling me you love me, and I'll be fine, okay? 'Cause, God, I love you so much."

2:00 P.M.

While lying in her husband's arms, Joi timed her contractions by herself by keeping an eye on their digital clock. And then it happened. While Joi was able to breathe through the contractions as instructed, a pain that made her breath freeze in her neck hit her, and her eyes bulged. *What the hell?* Then she heard a noise that sounded more like a cow or a wild boar stuck in a trap, but in actuality, the sound came from her.

"Damn! What was that?" Phillip asked as he scrambled to get out of bed, causing Joi to almost roll off their bed and onto the floor. After she regained her balance and he scrambled to put on his underwear and jeans, Joi felt an amazing pressure she had never felt before, but there was no pain.

Before Phillip ran to the door and pawed at it as if he had forgotten how to unlock it, Wilhelmina knocked on the other side. "You okay?"

"I'm—I'm fine, I think."

"Phillip," Wilhelmina instructed, as he managed to open the door and let her into the room.

"Ma'am?"

"Go fill the tub up with water because she may want to sit in there awhile."

"No! No, I want to have it in our bedroom. In our bed!" she said, and eased back toward the headboard.

"Doll face, as I told you before, lying down is not the best way to have a child because it narrows the pelvis, and you're not allowing gravity to help in the—"

"But I wanna see it," Joi said, breathing faster and every touch of her body speaking in defiance. "I wanna see it—when she comes out."

"Okay, okay. Then, we can use this mirror," she said, pointing to the mirror on their dresser. "Phillip?"

"Ma'am."

"Unscrew the mirror from the dresser and just put it in the corner. What we'll do is have it standing up. Then you can look at the mirror from below."

In a blinding dash, Phillip left the room to find the tools to disassemble the family heirloom.

Sweat poured from her body like water from a sponge as another contraction followed by another and yet another sent jolts of pain throughout Joi's body. Eventually, Wilhelmina acquiesced and allowed Joi to return to bed to deliver the baby in the manner in which her body saw fit.

Tired and cold between contractions, Joi could hear her heart beating as if it were in her throat instead of her chest. And then she closed her eyes, and for a moment she could not feel anything.

She could not feel Phillip's arms around her or his fingers deep massaging the muscles of her neck. She could not feel Wilhelmina checking once to see if she was dilated enough and giving her hot skin an alcohol rubdown. All she felt was freedom, and she could feel her spirit lift from her body, fly close to the ceiling, around the light fixtures, and view everyone in the room.

"Oh, my God, what's happening to me," she said aloud, but no one answered. She felt her body elevate. *Am I dying? Oh, my God, I'm dying?* Joi saw a figure dressed in purple. It was Michael, and he was at the bar where the indiscretion had taken place. She saw him sitting beside Phillip, who was dressed in a black suit carrying a red rose. "Hello," she screamed at the top of her lungs, but neither man moved. "Can you see me," Joi asked, and heard a voice reply, but did not know from where it came. "I said . . . can you see me," she repeated louder. Michael walked across the bar and sat at the piano and started playing. As Phillip watched him, he played in the smoke-filled bar as if his very existence depended on striking the right keys. Then Joi noticed him stop, remove the ring his father had worn when he wrote, place it atop of the piano and resume playing. She looked into his eyes, and there was no sadness. Joi looked for Phillip, but he was gone. The rose was left behind.

Michael continued to play all alone, but appeared content. She wanted to do something she had never done in the past. Joi wanted to throw her arms around him as a friend and comfort him, but before she was able to, she saw a blinding *golden* light. It was so concentrated she could feel its rays bore into the depths of her pores.

She took a deep breath that had no end. It was as if a floodgate of air was opened and rushing into her body, and she could not exhale. Mumbles surrounded her, and she could hear a sound that was distorted and raspy. It reminded her of Phillip's voice, but it was deeper and had a more earthy texture. "What?" Joi asked. "Who is that?"

"I said I love you." And then Joi recognized the voice immediately.

"Is that you?"

"Yes, Mommy," her daughter said, and sounded just as she had before she left the confines of earth. "I love you. I just wanted you to know that. I'm all right. I've been all right, and I am at peace. Don't worry about me, okay?"

"Baby girl, I miss you so much," Joi said, looking for but not seeing her daughter's face. "My heart cries for you every night."

"And when you cry, Mommy"—and then Joi saw Angie's face—"I'm there crying with you. I've seen every tear. I've felt every pain."

Angie wore the last outfit her mother had seen her in, and there was a living moisture on her lips. Her thick black hair hung long and gracefully over the curves of her shoulders, and she looked serene, wise and delicate.

"Mommy, it was my time to leave, and I'm okay with

that now. I was not supposed to stay there a second longer than I did. But I am still with you and Daddy, and I will always be there for all of you. But I need you to dry your eyes, because it's not time for you yet."

"Baby, I love you."

"And I love you, too. I just need you to understand that Daddy needs you and so does the baby. And guess what, Mommy? I've seen the baby, and she looks just like Daddy. Be at peace, Mommy, 'cause God has given you this baby for a reason."

"Angie," Joi screamed. "Angie!" she screeched at the top of her lungs. "Come back, Angie. Please come back!"

But then she was gone. There was no way she was going to allow her daughter to slip away twice, so Joi ran toward the light, determined to turn all of her wrongs into right. The fear of death was secondary to the desire to be with her daughter. "Angie!" she screamed. *Angie, come back!*

Joi heard a voice. It was deeper than her daughter's. "What?" she asked.

"Push a little harder."

"What?"

"I love you, baby. *Push* a little harder!"

Joi crisscrossed her fists over her breast and with all her might let out a guttural sound without a care in the world as to who may have heard her down the block. And then she could feel the baby move a little farther down her birth canal. Again she closed her eyes, and with Phillip bracing her back, she let out another savage shriek and felt the baby drop a little more.

"You're doing great, Joi. Just keep it up, doll face, and we'll have this angel out in no time."

"I need, I need the mirror," Joi panted. "I wanna see it. It's getting ready—It's getting ready to come out!"

After Joi was balanced on the bed, Phillip propped

the mirror in the corner of the room against the wall, giving her the full view of the miracle that was about to transpire. Then he returned to his position behind Joi as she made a fist so tight her palms turned eggshell white. This time she screamed so hard, Phillip subconsciously started to squeeze her shoulders together as if his energy could be transferred into her body and aid in the delivery of the baby.

"Well, Jiminy Crickets. That was a good one there," Wilhelmina said. "It's crowning."

Joi reached down and with her fingertips felt the silky head of her child for the first time. The sensation sent a river of confidence through her body that knocked out any pain she experienced. Joi dug the heels of her palms into her thighs and again squeezed tight to force out the baby and could feel a little more exit her body.

"Do you wanna take a break, doll face?" Wilhelmina asked. "If you want to, you can."

Joi fervidly shook her head no.

"Baby, listen, I know you wanna get this over with, but I don't—"

"Fuck you!" Joi screamed at the top of her lungs and gave another push. This one harder than any she had pushed before.

Unknowingly blocking the mirror, Wilhelmina came around to the front of Joi and said, "Sugar dumpling, you almost cleared the head. Now, if we can just get these shoulders out, we'll—"

"Bitch, if you don't get out the way of that mirror, I'll—" Joi cut off her own sentence to push once again.

"Ugghooogrughhhh!" she bellowed.

Accustomed to such things, Wilhelmina checked again as Joi closed her eyes, to see if the umbilical cord was wrapped around the baby's neck. When it was not, she smiled at Phillip, who was also wet with sweat and held his wife securely in his arms.

Joi opened her eyes, pointed her eyebrows downward, and as Phillip wrapped his strong arms around her torso and whispered, "I love you," in her ear, they both squeezed and squeezed and squeezed again. "O-lee shit" she sighed. She did not feel the baby move an inch, and then from nowhere the word jumped out of her heart, and she screamed with all her might, *Purpose!*

Wilhelmina checked, but this time made sure she did not block the mirror. She looked up at the couple and said, "Doll face, you can stop. It's a girl."

"It's a girl?" Phillip said with a smile. His eyes were fatigued, yet contemplative. "That's right. You did good," Wilhelmina replied. "You have a beautiful baby girl with a head fulla hair!"

"We have a girl, a little girl?" Phillip said with tears running down his cheeks.

While Wilhelmina did her post-birth rituals and Phillip held the child, Joi squeezed the sheets, uncurled her toes, closed her eyes and repeated the word over and over again. "Purpose . . . purpose . . . purpose."

11:30 P.M.

After calling friends and relatives, Joi, Phillip and Phyllis Evans lay in bed for the first time together. There was no television to provide the backdrop of sound. No jazz, reggae or popular music to fill the air. Just two people enjoying the warmth and comfort of their child.

Phillip would occasionally brush his fingertips over the ridge of Joi's eyebrow and whisper so softly she could hardly hear the words. "Purpose." Joi would run the back of her finger over the bridge of Phyllis's nose and reflect on the glorious hours that had brought the child into their lives.

Sleep nestled in her eyes, and Joi thought of the day she lost the role she knew would define her career. How she came home and, since Phillip was not there, sat in her room and cried for hours until her eyes were swollen. When she had awakened that morning and seen the words, "Joi Weston Must Die," flash before her, she had had no idea what it meant. She had put herself in the perfect mindset to give her best performance; but she had heard the word *cut*, and her acting career had faded to black.

It was on that day that Joi Weston had died, and it would take three years for Joi Evans to be born. It was on that day that everything she assumed she wanted had come crashing to an end, and it would take three years for everything she knew she wanted to begin.

"Baby?"

"Yes," Joi softly answered.

"You know, we spent three thousand dollars on decorating this child's room. I'm *not* complaining, but don't you think we should let her sleep in there on her first night?"

Joi remained silent and then whispered, "I know." Joi reminisced on the day she said, "I do," and the years of joy her husband had brought to her. Phillip kissed his wife on her eyelids and covered the infant's torso with his hand and said one last prayer for her safety. Then he said, "I went out and got the more sensitive baby monitor so if she opens her eyes too loudly, you'll hear it."

Joi remained silent. Then again whispered, "I know." As the world went black, Joi closed out the past, inhaled and enjoyed the moment.

Phillip covered his family with a purple afghan, and as he watched them, he said, "You know something? I could not care less about anything outside this house, outside this room," he said, and kissed his wife's hand, "and outside this bed. This is my world. This is all that matters."

Joi remained silent, and then whispered, "I know." She licked her lips, laid her head on her husband's arm, kissed the inside of his bicep, looked into his eyes and smiled. And as silently as a baby's whisper, the three of them fell asleep in each other's arms.

BOOK YOUR PLACE ON OUR WEBSITE
AND MAKE THE
READING CONNECTION!

We've created a customized website just for our very special readers, where you can get the inside scoop on everything that's going on with Zebra, Pinnacle and Kensington books.

When you come online, you'll have the exciting opportunity to:

- View covers of upcoming books
- Read sample chapters
- Learn about our future publishing schedule (listed by publication month *and author*)
- Find out when your favorite authors will be visiting a city near you
- Search for and order backlist books from our online catalog
- Check out author bios and background information
- Send e-mail to your favorite authors
- Meet the Kensington staff online
- Join us in weekly chats with authors, readers and other guests
- Get writing guidelines
- AND MUCH MORE!

Visit our website at
http://www.kensingtonbooks.com

Grab These Other
Dafina Novels
(trade paperback editions)

Grab These Other
Dafina Novels
(mass market editions)

Grab These Other
Thought Provoking Books

Adam by Adam
0-7582-0195-8

by Adam Clayton Powell, Jr.
$15.00US/$21.00CAN

African American Firsts
0-7582-0243-1

by Joan Potter
$15.00US/$21.00CAN

African-American Pride
0-8065-2498-7

by Lakisha Martin
$15.95US/$21.95CAN

The African-American Soldier
0-8065-2049-3

by Michael Lee Lanning
$16.95US/$24.95CAN

African Proverbs and Wisdom
0-7582-0298-9

by Julia Stewart
$12.00US/$17.00CAN

Al on America
0-7582-0351-9

by Rev. Al Sharpton
with Karen Hunter
$16.00US/$23.00CAN

Available Wherever Books Are Sold!

Visit our website at www.kensingtonbooks.com